T0171355

The Fisherman's Wife

The Gospel According to St. Peter's Spouse

KATHLEEN GLAVICH

WestBow
PRESS
A DIVISION OF THOMAS NELSON

WestBow Press books may be ordered through booksellers or by contacting:

WestBow Press
A Division of Thomas Nelson
1663 Liberty Drive
Bloomington, IN 47403
www.westbowpress.com
1-(866) 928-1240

Front cover portrait by Maresa Lilley, S.N.D.

ISBN: 978-1-4497-9058-5 (sc)
ISBN: 978-1-4497-9057-8 (e)

Library of Congress Control Number: 2013906054

Printed in the United States of America.

WestBow Press rev. date: 6/6/2013

$\mathcal{D}$edicated to all Christian women who spread the Good News of Jesus with passion

Prologue

~~~~~~

Fictionalized Bible stories and lives of the saints have always fascinated me. I grew up reading Gladys Malvern's *Behold Your Queen!* (Esther) and *The Foreigner* (Ruth) as well as Louis de Wohl's *The Glorious Folly* (St. Paul), *The Restless Flame* (St. Augustine), and *The Joyful Beggar* (St. Francis of Assisi). Little did I know that someday I would write a book about the wife of St. Peter, the apostle.

I named my heroine Miriam, disregarding the legend that calls her Perpetua, which is a Latin name, not a Jewish one. Miriam in its several forms was a common name for Jewish women. Witness the confusing number of Marys in the Gospels!

The task of writing the story of St. Peter's wife was more challenging than I expected. My familiarity with God's Word and the knowledge I gleaned from writing Scripture-based books for many years served me well. Still, *The Fisherman's Wife* required much research on first-century Jewish women, the town of Capernaum, and the geography of Israel. What did people eat back then? How many miles was it from Capernaum to Jerusalem? What were the steps for making bread and cloth?

3

Also, many assumptions needed to be checked. For example, would Peter eat a raw olive? No, it would be too bitter. Would Peter's children play with dolls and toy animals? Probably not, because images were prohibited. Was Saul thrown from a horse when Jesus spoke to him on the road to Damascus? No, contrary to paintings like Caravaggio's "Conversion on the Way to Damascus," Jewish people didn't ordinarily ride horses. Did the nails of the crucified go through their palms? No, palms could not support the weight of a human body.

Another challenge was avoiding anachronisms. Thanks to reference books and the Internet, I learned a number of things. Jesus didn't wear a yarmulke, the Jewish skullcap, because it wasn't the custom in the first century. Peter's wife would not conjecture that mosquitoes infected her mother with malaria because the source of this disease had not yet been discovered. The term *bombshell* would not be part of Miriam's vocabulary because bombs were invented centuries after she lived. No doubt, some inaccuracies still weaseled their way into this book. My apologies!

One challenge ironically turned out to be an advantage: a great deal about the life and times of Jesus remains a mystery. We don't even know what Jesus looked like. Did he have a beard? It's debatable. On what mountain did Peter witness the transfiguration of Jesus? No one knows for sure. Besides the apostles, who was present at the last supper, which may or may not have been a Passover meal? There is no record. Different theories have been proposed regarding Gospel personages and events, and conflicting traditions and legends abound. At times, the Gospels themselves do not agree. This ambiguity gave me the freedom to make my own decisions in shaping Miriam's story. For instance, one theory is that Peter's wife died before his mother-in-law was cured by Jesus. Adopting that theory would have resulted in a very short book indeed! Instead, I depended on the writings of Clement of Alexandria (150–220 A.D.) for the time of Miriam's death.

My wish is that *The Fisherman's Wife* will enlighten people about the Jewish culture that gave birth to Christianity. I also hope it will lead them to appreciate the faith and courage of those first Christians who gave up everything to follow Jesus. Most of all, after seeing Jesus and his actions through Miriam's eyes, may readers come to view him more personally. And may this new vision awaken in them a deeper love of our Lord and a stronger commitment to him.

I am especially thankful to Maresa Lilley, S.N.D., the artist whose painting of Miriam graces the cover of *The Fisherman's Wife*. I am also indebted to Regina Alfonso, S.N.D., who encouraged me to pursue publishing this book. My gratitude, too, to Mary Anne Harden, who offered invaluable advice, and to Mary Kathleen Ruddy, S.N.D., whose hospitality and moral support sustain me and my writing ministry. Last but not least, I thank Joan LaChance, the teacher who nurtured my talent and love for writing when I was thirteen years old.

You are invited to visit my blog (www.kathleenglavich.org) for spiritual reflections.

Chapter 1

~~~~~~

I am sitting on a grand, gold throne with a red cushion so soft and plump that it almost swallows me whole. On my head a silver crown sparkles, encrusted with jewels of every color in the rainbow. My gown is a shimmering white, like the sun reflecting off the waters of the Sea of Galilee. My gold ring, jangling bracelets, and long earrings match the gold necklace from Egypt that my son, the Messiah, gave me for my birthday. He sits beside me, solemn and dignified, on an even larger throne. With long brown hair, beautiful dark brown eyes, and a straight nose, he looks just like me, except, of course, that he is over six feet tall and has powerful muscles and a trim beard.

Displayed on the marble wall across from us and next to the ceiling-high cedar doors is a map of Israel on a large sheet of parchment. We are now the greatest country on earth, thanks to my victorious son. Along one side wall, ten Roman women seated on purple pillows are strumming lyres, their enchanting songs filling the palace throne room. Along the wall opposite from them, ten husky Roman men in togas stand ready to do my son's bidding. Once they were soldiers; now they are our slaves. My son is kind to them. That's the way I brought him up.

A servant approaches with a tray laden with grapes, dates, and pomegranates. He bows before us as deeply as he can without spilling the fruit. "Your Highnesses," he offers, extending the tray. My son and I each take a bunch of grapes and graciously nod to the servant. Suddenly the doors open, and the general of our army appears. He strides toward us, kneels before my son, and announces, "Good news, Your Highness! We've conquered two more countries!"

My son leans towards me, grasps my hand in his strong one, and looks lovingly into my eyes. In a low, rich voice he says, "Dear Mother, all this is due to you. How can I ever thank you?"

"Miriam, Miriam," my brother Nathan calls, jolting me out of my daydream. I'm not on a throne at all, but perched on a lower branch of an olive tree and leaning against its gnarled trunk. This has been my favorite thinking spot ever since the day I tried to run away from home. Sheltered in the tree and mulling things over, I decided to stay home after all. That was last year, when I was nine. Olive trees are more welcoming than the dark green cypress trees that point to the heavens like spears. While I'm in my olive tree, its silver-green leaves more or less hide me. Yet I can look out over our little village of Capernaum and see fields of wheat ripening in the hot sun and beyond them, the rolling hills cloaked in vineyards and dotted here and there by stone watchtowers. Far in the distance, stands the snow-covered Mount Hermon mountain range, its summits like white knuckles challenging the sky.

Mostly I like to face right and gaze at the Sea of Galilee that our village borders. I'm glad we live in the province of Galilee with its lovely, freshwater sea instead of in the southern province of Judah with the Dead Sea, which is so saturated with salt that nothing living can survive. Today our sea is a sheet of bright blue, mirroring the cloudless azure sky. In the harbor, wooden fishing boats are bobbing, moved by gentle waves, and a few stragglers are looking for a sale at the fish market on the shore. On the opposite side of the sea, the east side, hills sloping down to the shoreline stand guard.

My brother Nathan has waded through the lush green grass and bright red anemones and now stands a few feet from me. He knows I'd be here. "Come on, little sister. Mother says to come home and help her get supper ready," he orders, his arms akimbo, like he's the boss. Nathan is a few years older than I am and is a royal pain sometimes. He seldom gets into trouble like me. What if my dreams come true and I turn out to be the girl chosen to be the mother of the Messiah? How would big brother treat me then?

When I try to scramble down the tree gracefully, Nathan extends a hand to assist me. His skin is burnt brown from the sun like mine. We could almost be twins. We have the same dark brown hair, dreamy brown eyes, and a straight nose like our mother's. We both have a dimple, but Nathan's is on the left and mine is on the right.

As we walk back to the house, Nathan's long-legged stride puts him ahead of me. When we reach the path, Nathan waits for me to catch up. He grins wickedly at me and challenges, "Let's race." I have the reputation of being one of the fastest runners in the village. Gazelle Girl they call me. I've beaten several boys. Nathan and I line up, and then on the count of three we take off running. My arms and legs pump vigorously, and my breaths come short and fast. The air is combing my long hair and making it stream out behind me. My brother and I are even until suddenly I stumble on a rock and land face to face with the dusty ground. For a few long seconds the wind is knocked out of me and I can't breathe at all.

Nathan stops abruptly, jogs backwards, and bends over me, his hands on his knees and concern written all over his face.

"Are you all right?"

"I think so," I say and gingerly rise with Nathan's help. "Stupid rock."

"Uh, oh!" my brother says. "Look at your tunic."

Dark stains streak the cream-colored material, and there is a tear over the right knee. "It can be fixed," I say, shrugging off the damage, although I fear what Mother will say. At least I didn't break any bones or my teeth. The rest of the way home we walk, me limping to favor my aching right leg.

I like our little black house. It's made from chunks of basalt hewn out of our surrounding hills and glued together with mud and pebbles. The dark, volcanic rock of our houses makes our town rather shadowy and drab, but there's something exciting about living inside rock formed from lava. Our house is one of several connected ones built around our courtyard. In Capernaum there are two courtyards close to the sea that feeds our main industry: fishing.

Nathan pushes the wooden door and it creaks open. As we pass through the doorway, he and I touch the mezuzah fastened to it and kiss our fingers. I'm surprised that this little box isn't worn away from people touching it all day long. It holds the Shema, the prayer from our sacred Scriptures that begins "Hear, O Israel, our God is one."

Our Jewish religion makes us different; some would say strange. We pray to one, invisible God who loves us. Other people pray to things God made, like the sun or statues they carved themselves. The Romans, who conquered us and now rule us, pray to men and women gods who have faults just like us human beings. The crazy Romans even declared their emperor a god after he died. It seems to me that if you're going to worship someone, that God should be super good, not like Caesar Augustus. My father says that in the south in Judah, where the Temple is located, most people are Jewish like us. Because they can attend more Temple services and are better at observing the religious laws, they look down their noses at us. Our province is referred to as Galilee of the Gentiles and for good reason.

Here in Capernaum we are right by the Via Maris, or Way of the Sea, the Roman road that runs from Egypt to Damascus. People from distant lands travel this trade route in caravans and stop to restock food at our markets. Some of those foreigners stay awhile. When there's nothing better to do, Sarah, who is my best friend, some others, and I sit and watch the parade going down this road. There are Arabs from faraway lands; camel caravans bearing silks, spices, and dried fruit for trade; people in search of a new home; messengers on horses galloping along and kicking up dust; and Roman soldiers marching, their armor clanking. Sometimes for fun we throw rocks at the mile marker stone post that stands along the Via Maris.

Nathan and I remove our sandals and line them up at the door. Reluctantly I follow him through our one-room house, our bare feet padding softly on the cobblestone floor. Dust motes float in the little stream of light pouring into the dim room from the window in the wall that faces the courtyard. Besides giving us light, this one window airs out our house somewhat when the smoke and smell from our oil lamps become stifling. Right now the mixed aromas of all the suppers cooking in the courtyard reach my nose and make me realize how hungry I am.

Looking through the back doorway, I see Mother among a bevy of other women in the courtyard, all wearing similar veils and tunics. She is easy to spot because she is the largest, a big-boned woman. She has a personality to match. Nathan and I step outside and approach her, disturbing some of the hens pecking at the ground. Mother is busy stirring stew in a clay pot on the flat stone oven, but not too busy to look up and exclaim, "Miriam, what did you do to your tunic? Why must you be such a tomboy?" With one hand she flips her veil back off her shoulders and wipes her forehead with the back of the other hand. "I fell," I mutter. I feel sorry that I made mother angry, especially in weather that is hot enough to melt a rock. I'm also embarrassed because several of the other women preparing supper nearby glance at me and shake their heads. My Aunt Leah, though, who is my friend, casts me a sympathetic look.

"Well, we'll deal with it later," Mother sighs resignedly. "But this time, you're going to be the one to pound out the stains in the stream and sew up the rip, not me. Now go and bring out the mats, the bread, and some grapes and figs. Nathan, fetch your brother. He's probably down the road playing with James and John." Under her breath she says, "Hope they haven't been fighting." She wishes this because one day my seven-year-old brother, Aaron, came home crying, his nose bleeding and his cheek bearing a red blotch, which would turn into an ugly purple and yellow bruise.

"Aaron, what happened?" Mother asked sternly that day. She grabbed for a cloth and dipped it in the pot of water used for our ritual hand washing before meals.

"James punched me. We were playing marbles and he lost, so he said I cheated. But I didn't." Aaron's words came out in starts between ragged sobs. "He's just a poor sport."

After Mother got Aaron cleaned up and quieted, she told me to watch the bread and Aaron. Then she stormed out of the house. I was glad I wasn't James.

Later when Father came home from work, Mother reported the incident to him. That's when I found out how my mother confronted the culprit.

"Jacob, I found James on the road halfway between our houses. As soon as he spied me, he looked as guilty as Cain and as though he was about to run. I grabbed hold of his ear and dragged him to his home, scolding him all the way. When I told Salome what her son had done, you'll never guess what that woman had the nerve to say."

"Knowing Salome, I can imagine," commented my Father, rolling his eyes upward.

"She said that James would never do something like that. And if he did, Aaron probably deserved it!"

"I hope you didn't punch her in the nose, Rebekah."

"I felt like it, but no, I just turned around and left her standing in her doorway, her arms protectively around James. Salome's hopeless when it comes to her precious boys. She thinks they can do no wrong, as if they are angels from heaven. Imagine how those two imps will turn out."

With this incident fresh in my mind, I send up a quick prayer that today James behaved and that Nathan brings Aaron home in one piece. As I hurry back to the house to fetch the mats, our longhaired, black goat looks up and says, "Baa." She too seems to be scolding me for my damaged tunic. I pat her head anyway.

$$\infty\infty\infty$$

I had unrolled the mats and laid them in the shade under the awning. At suppertime we're seated around the pot of stew—my parents, my Aunt Leah and Uncle Joachim, Nathan and Aaron, and I. My aunt and uncle have been married six years but are childless. Aunt Leah is much younger than Mother and lively. Her husband is a serious person with heavy-lidded eyes who seldom smiles. Despite their differences, they get along. The couple lives nearby and often joins us for supper. On some days even more relatives squeeze in. It's a good chance to hear the neighborhood news.

Father says the blessing, and we pass around the bread. I can hardly wait to scoop out a helping of stew with my piece. It seems like my breakfast of barley bread and olives was days ago instead of hours ago. And my mother makes the best stew. It has beans, onions, lentils, cabbage, and leeks with various spices like mustard, dill, and rosemary for a tasty flavor. Thank goodness we're having stew instead of fish. It's tiresome having so much fish: grilled fish, broiled fish, fried fish, minced fish, pickled fish. Soon we might find that our skin has turned into scales! Mother says that I should just be grateful that we live so near the sea.

My father, who is usually good-natured and jovial, is upset this afternoon. I can tell because he isn't smiling and between his eyebrows there are frown lines like deep, twin wrinkles. Besides, when he came home, he called me Miriam instead of Princess.

Although most people in Capernaum are fishermen or farmers, our father works at a shop that trades in stone products like millstones and olive presses. Our town doesn't have an industry that produces these things, but Father takes orders and sees that the goods are shipped in from other towns. Father's father was a fisherman. Before I was born, Grandpa and my uncle were out fishing one night. If you catch fish at night, they are fresh for the morning market. During that night one of the sudden, violent storms the Sea of Galilee is known for blew up. Our sea is like a woman who is beautiful to look at but has a nasty temper. My father's father and brother never made it back to shore, alive that is. After that, my father, with strong input from his mother I'm sure, decided that fishing was not for him.

"All these years I have never been late for work. But this morning I was late," Father informs us. He sets down his metal cup on the mat heavily. A little wine spills on the mat. "Do you know why?"

Since none of us knows why Father was late for work, we all give him blank looks. He explains, as he intended to do all the time. "I was late because as I was walking down the road, there's a Roman soldier at the side of it. At his feet sits a large, bulky backpack. He hails me, 'Hey, you, Jew.' He motions for me to pick up the burden and carry it, but not in the direction I was going. I feel like saying, 'Carry it yourself, pig,' but of course I can't because I want to live. Besides, I don't know much Latin. I hoist the thing on my back like I am a human donkey. It's heavy and cumbersome."

"Poor Jacob," my mother says. She gives his arm a sympathetic squeeze. "What else could you do? It's the law for Jews to carry something a mile for a Roman soldier."

"But I show him, Rebekah," my father says with a wink at me. "After a mile I indicate to the Roman that I will go on farther. And I do, a whole extra mile! No man is going to treat me like a slave. Unfortunately this made me twice as late for work. Isaac understood and won't dock my pay. The same thing happened to him once."

Uncle Joachim's face has grown dark. With eyes narrowed he says, "I'd like to set fire to the Roman garrison in town. They do nothing but bully and humiliate us. Someday, someday we will overthrow these ruffians with their silly laws and taxes. Didn't the prophets tell us that a champion will come and make us a great nation?"

Nathan eyes light up and he adds enthusiastically, "The prophet Isaiah hints that the Messiah might come from Nephtali, which is our region. He says that formerly the land of Zebulun and Naphtali were in contempt, but on them a light will shine."

My brother has learned the Scriptures well. His words bring joy to my heart. If the Messiah is to come from Capernaum, there's a good chance that I might bear him. It's about time that he makes an appearance. We have borne the injustices of the Romans long enough. I haven't shared my ambitious dream with anyone except my friend Sarah. To my chagrin, I learned that she too hopes to be the Messiah's mother. I suppose every Jewish girl does.

I wish I could go to school like Nathan. He knows how to read and write Hebrew and can quote Scripture as though he sees the scrolls before him. My father started teaching him when he was five. Now Nathan goes to the school at the house of Tobiah with other boys. Tobiah is impressed by how smart he is. Girls don't learn to read and write. But I know many Scripture verses by heart from praying them and hearing them read. I wish I could read Hebrew. My father did teach me to write my name one day, tracing the letters in some sand on the shore with a stick. I memorized my written name before the tide's waves washed it away.

"This bread is delicious, Princess," my father states, interrupting my thoughts.

"I'm glad you like it, Father."

Obviously the good food and pleasant company have soothed Father. My mother must have told him how I made the bread this morning. With her guidance I ground the grains on the millstone in the courtyard, rolling the top stone over the bottom one. Then I made the paste with a little olive oil and added a bit of honey and cinnamon to make it special. I shaped the flat, round loaves and carefully watched them as they baked in the dome-shaped bread oven. I didn't tell my father about the painful burn on my arm that I got from being too eager to remove the bread from the oven. Neither did my mother, who treated the burn with aloe.

This house is my school, and my mother is my teacher. I'm learning how to cook, keep house, and make clothes for my future husband and children … and maybe for the Messiah.

"Someday, my daughter, you will make a man very happy," Father comments.

"Maybe a Roman, Sis," Nathan whispers in my ear. I jab him with my elbow, and he yelps. Mother scowls at us and warns, "Children, behave."

I finish my goat's milk, lick the white mustache off my upper lip, and then stand up to help my mother and aunt clear the supper. The two men stay seated and continue their conversation, nibbling on some walnuts. My brothers run off to play with the other boys in the courtyard for as long as they can.

At twilight Father puts the wooden bar down across our door to keep out unwanted visitors. Nathan and I roll up the reed mats and carry them up the stone stairs along the side of our house that lead to our roof. When it's hot, we sleep there, where it's a bit cooler. The roof is thatched: thin branches woven with straw held together with mud. It's a little bumpy under our mats, but it isn't that hard. In fact, the roof is softer than our floor. A little wall along the edges keeps us from rolling off into the courtyard during the night. We grow some grapevines on the roof. After we pick the grapes, we spread some out on the roof to dry and become raisins.

After sunset, still wearing my luckless tunic, I'm lying on the roof with my brothers between my mother and father. I feel secure and happy. I love to lie on my back and look up at the moon and stars. When all our neighbors have extinguished their candles and oil lamps and the town is pitch black, the night sky is amazing. This evening the moon is just a sliver, like the tip of a fingernail. But there must be thousands of stars twinkling in the black bowl curving above me. I tried to count them once, but it was impossible.

The star-studded sky makes me feel very, very small. Still, I know that I am precious in God's eyes. Long ago God told Abraham, the first believer, that he'd have as many descendants as the stars. I am a daughter of Abraham. I'm like a beautiful star.

The night sky makes me realize how awesome our Creator is. It stirs me to pray from one of my favorite psalms: "When I see the heavens, the work of your hands, the moon and the stars you placed there—What are human beings that you should think of them, people that you should care for them?" How good God is to give us something so gorgeous to behold as the moon and the stars. Too bad we spend most of the night with our eyes closed!

My father begins to snore. The sound is gentle and regular like a soft drumbeat. Before long I drift off to sleep.

Chapter 2

Four years have passed since I raced Nathan like a tomboy and fell. During these years I've grown into a young lady who is a credit to Mother, at least most of the time. I have become very practical. I can make stews as tasty as my mother's, bake bread without burning myself, and weave cloth on the loom that a queen would be proud to wear. I know how to select the choicest fruit and vegetables in the market and haggle for the best price. Neighbors trust me to babysit their children. My goal in life is someday to become the kind of valiant wife described in the Book of Proverbs. Mother reminds me of this goal often.

Nathan was married this year to Deborah, who is related to Sarah. Deborah is a good match for Nathan. She is a serious girl and rather plain looking, but she is kind, and I envy her lovely hands. She has long, tapered fingers capped by delicate, oval fingernails, not at all like my blunt, serviceable hands and square nails. The couple has gone off to Jerusalem with Tobiah, our religious leader. I hated to see Nathan leave us. Jerusalem might as well be on the moon. Most sons follow in their father's footsteps. However, Nathan decided that he didn't want to be a businessman but a scribe. This means that someday he'll be an expert in explaining Scripture, a lawyer for God. He'll also copy the Torah and write legal documents. Now, with Tobiah's help, Nathan will find a master scribe to teach him.

When Nathan broke the news to us that he wanted to be a scribe, I expected Father to explode in anger. Instead his chest puffed up, his eyes filled with tears, and he kept saying, "My son, the scribe." Later I overheard my father remark to my mother, "Thank God, Rebekah, that Nathan isn't like Matthew."

Matthew is Sarah's older brother. A while ago Sarah confided, "I'm worried about Matthew. All he thinks about is money. Even as a little kid he would go from neighbor to neighbor, trying to sell them stones he picked up in the street. Remember? Then there was that time Mother caught him sneaking some of her bread out of the storage pot. He said he was going to sell it in the market and make us rich."

One day while Sarah is helping me shell almonds in a secluded corner of the courtyard, she says in a subdued voice, "Matthew is talking about becoming a tax collector." Tears trickle down Sarah's cheeks, and she brushes them away. My heart hurts to see my friend so sad. This job, though, fits Matthew, who is smart when it comes to numbers. He was always good at keeping points for our games.

"My parents are dead set against it, and so am I. Matthew argues that he can earn more money as a tax collector than as a fisherman. So what if he can earn enough to buy a hundred camels? People will despise him for working for the Romans," she wails plaintively. "They'll shun him and probably our whole family. Who will ever want to marry me?"

Tax collection is a big business in Capernaum. We are located in the territory of Herod Antipas and near to his brother Philip's territory. Herod set up a customs house at the edge of our town to collect taxes on imports and exports. Everyone knows how easy it is to cheat travelers or merchants there by overcharging them or helping yourself to some of their wheat or fabric. Matthew would be sorely tempted to fill his own purse with ill-gotten coins.

"Maybe he'll be fired," I say lamely, putting my arm around Sarah's shaking shoulders. "Or maybe he'll be so unhappy that he'll quit." I can think of nothing else to say to console her.

Luckily, Sarah and I don't have to worry about finding a job. We just need to get a good husband. That time is approaching fast. Sarah and I both had our first monthly cramps. Strangely, it was in the same week, although Sarah is a year older. I had mixed emotions about the process that makes us marriageable and at the same time unclean in the eyes of the law. The discomfort and nastiness of it made me mad at Mother Eve for causing this trouble for all her daughters. On the other hand, I was elated that I now had the power to bring a baby into the world. I know how that works. The last time my mother was a midwife for our neighbor Tamara, who has a baby every year, I went with her.

Hearing about a birth and seeing it in person are two different things. When I heard Tamara's ear-piercing screams, I wanted to run away. But then, after it was all over and Mother let me hold the squirming baby boy, who was whimpering, I started to cry right along with him. The whole experience was incredible. Three thoughts ran through my mind: this miracle happens day after day to keep the human race going; I was born the same way; and I will give birth the same way, God willing.

Sometimes Sarah and I speak of our future husbands. Once Sarah said with her contagious giggle, "Somewhere there must be a good man who doesn't mind a woman with a big nose." Her nose is not that large, and she has the most luxurious, curly, black hair. I always say decidedly, "My husband will be handsome, intelligent, and a good provider. But most of all, he will love me and treat me like a princess." In other words, he will be just like Father. I used to think Matthew was a possibility. But that's out of the question now.

This morning I'm going to the market with Aunt Leah. I'm glad. She is not much older than I am, and we always have a good time chattering away like two people who haven't seen each other in years. On our way we might stop to admire a delicate butterfly settled on a purple thistle at the side of the road. Or we might talk baby talk to an infant riding in a sling on its mother's back. With Mother it's different. To her, going to market is serious business and there's no time to waste. You'd think the Day of the Lord was coming tomorrow.

Aunt Leah and I meet in the courtyard as planned, each carrying a large wicker basket for the produce we will buy.

"Shalom, Aunt Leah. Isn't it a beautiful day?" I bend slightly to kiss her ruddy cheek that reminds me of a pomegranate. Aunt Leah is plump and much shorter than I am. I'm almost as tall as Nathan now.

My aunt asks, "What day isn't beautiful here?" and gives her funny tinkling laugh, which I try to imitate sometimes.

My mother is tossing feed to the chickens, whose eggs we enjoyed for breakfast. "Don't forget the olives," she warns me. This must be the third time she's reminded me today.

"I won't forget this time, Mother."

Aunt Leah slips her arm through mine, and locked together we pass through my house onto the cobblestone road that leads to the market on the outskirts of town. A few farmers and their families are already at work in the fields. With rhythmic strokes they slice the golden stalks of wheat with scythes that gleam in the sunlight.

We're at the market in a matter of minutes. One side of the street is lined with the shops offering food. People spread their cucumbers, onions, dates, spices, and other good things on cloth on the ground. More prosperous sellers work under tents, and some have low wooden tables. On the other side of the street are sellers of fine material and artisans hawking wares like pots of clay or stone and assorted jewelry. Aunt Leah and I like to pore over the anklets, bracelets, necklaces, rings, nose rings, and toe rings and decide what we would purchase if we were in the market for such things.

Although it is very early, the market is swarming with people anxious to avoid the hot sun and snatch up the choicest foods at the best prices. As Aunt Leah and I make our way between the two rows of stalls, other shoppers brush up against us. Vendors on both sides hold out samples of their wares to us and cry temptingly, "Fresh dates here. Cheap." "Beans, just picked this morning." "A lovely veil for two lovely ladies."

We are almost finished shopping when a striped, gray cat streaks past me, throwing me off balance. Because of our fishing industry, our town has more than its fair share of well-fed cats. I squeal, my arms fly up, and the contents of my basket spills onto the street. People move back startled. Luckily I don't fall, but cucumbers, dates, peppers, and onions are strewn at my feet. And the olives are rolling every which way, as though they are trying to escape being eaten. Mother's olives!

Just like that, a heavyset young man grabs the basket off my arm as quick as a thief. He darts in and out of tents and under people's feet, capturing the runaway olives. Aunt Leah and I stoop to pick up the other items, although this is awkward for her because her own basket is full. In no time the young man stands before us. He holds my basket out for us so we can deposit in it what we have gathered. I feel that my face is as scarlet as the headband that holds back his black hair. Below thick eyebrows, his dark eyes are laughing. He gives a quick smile that goes straight to my heart, but he doesn't say anything. It's not the custom for men to speak to women in public. I'm too flustered to smile back, but manage to nod a thank-you to him. He helps himself to a date from Aunt Leah's basket, brushes it off on the sleeve of his cloak, pops it in his mouth, winks, and goes off jogging down the street.

"Well!" says Aunt Leah, her eyes fluttering. "Who was that?"

"I don't know. I never laid eyes on him before."

"Not every man would stop to help two women in the market.

They might stop to gawk, but not to help," Aunt Leah notes matter-of-factly.

"Thank goodness, he's different. I can't see you and me crawling around the ground picking up olives."

"And imagine what your mother would say if you came home without them." Aunt Leah laughs at the thought. I do not.

As we walk home, my basket grows heavier with each step and sweat runs down my spine. By this time the sun is so hot that my head with its cover of dark hair feels as though it's cooking like a chicken in a stew pot. I envy Aunt Leah who wears the veil of a married woman. It protects her from the sun's rays as well as from unwelcome male advances. Someday in the not so distant future I'll wear a veil too. The smiling face of the stranger with the red headband flashes across my mind.

Chapter 3

It's the Sabbath, and I'm at Tobiah's house in my usual place, seated on a mat with my mother and Aaron. Father sits with the other elders. Tobiah rises and walks to the front of the room. He is a tall, dignified man respected by everyone in town. All of the men pull their tallits up over their heads, ready for the prayers. It's as if they each have their own tent where they can withdraw from the noise of the world and meet God. In fact, tallit means "little tent." My father still wears the tallit my mother's father gave him when he and Mother were married. It's getting a little worn in places, but Father just jokes, "That's so my holiness can shine through."

When I was little, I used to play with the fringe at the four corners of this long garment while Father was talking to Mother. I remember the day when Father lifted me onto his lap and said gravely, "Princess, those tassels are not just a toy or for decoration."

"Why are they on your robe, Father?"

"The Almighty told us to sew them on the corners of our garments to remind us of our agreement with him. They help me keep the commandments."

"Maybe they'll help me too," I said.

Father kissed the top of my head and asked, "Did you see the blue thread in each tassel?"

"Yes. They're pretty. What do they mean?"

"Blue dye is very expensive. It's the color that wealthy people like kings and princes can afford. That little bit of royal blue in the tassels is a sign that we are kingly people."

"Then I should wear a blue tunic because I'm a princess," I declared emphatically.

"I wish I could buy you a thousand blue tunics. But I can't. Instead, how about whenever you see the blue sky or the blue sea, you think of them as your heavenly Father's ways of reminding you that you are royalty?"

"That would be almost all the time, Father!" I slid down off his lap and ran outside to gaze at the sky, which was a striking blue.

Long ago Capernaum already had a minyan, the ten males required for erecting a synagogue in town. But we just don't have the funds to build one. We did, however, see that we had mikvahs, the pools of running water where men and women purified themselves at the times specified by Jewish law.

As required, Sarah and I went for our first mikvah experience together when our first periods ended. Totally submerged under the cool water, I was alone in the silence. It was like living in my mother's womb again. Then I thought of all the Jewish women down through the centuries who underwent this same ritual cleansing, including my mother and Aunt Leah, and I felt a strong bond with them. I walked the few steps up out of the pool refreshed and like a new person, the water streaming off my body in rivulets.

While Tobiah is intoning a psalm, I glance around to see if I can find Sarah. I spot her sitting near a back wall with her mother and younger sister. And to my surprise, directly behind them is the stranger who rescued Mother's olives! From under his tallit, his black eyes are peering right at me. I whip my head around and feel my face reddening. All during the reading of the passage from the Torah, I struggle to concentrate on the words. But I wonder if the stranger is still looking at me. I wish I had noticed who was sitting with him.

Prayers completed, it is time for open discussion. Sarah's father, Alphaeus, stands up to speak. To me he looks a little older and stooped. Matthew's chosen profession must be weighing heavily on him. However Alphaeus's voice is loud and clear. "We all know that Hannah's husband died suddenly last week. He did not have a good harvest this year, and they were not blessed with children. I'm wondering if we could do something to help Hannah out."

A few quiet moments pass while people reflect. Then I hear footsteps approaching from behind as someone weaves his way to the front, careful not to step on people. Then there is my stranger addressing us, not at all shy for a stranger. He is even taller than I remembered.

With enthusiasm he proposes, "What about throwing a large party? Everyone would be asked to pay an admission fee, which we could donate to Hannah."

"Thank you, Simon bar Jonah, for that suggestion," Tobiah remarks, stroking his beard, "but I don't think it would be practical. What does everyone else think?"

Someone calls out from the back. "That would entail too much work and organizing. Surely we can come up with a simpler plan."

"Any other ideas?" Tobiah asks, looking over our assembly expectantly. Simon strides back to his seat. I would have been embarrassed if my suggestion had been dismissed so promptly, but Simon keeps his head held high. Well, at least now I know that his name is Simon and his father is Jonah.

Other suggestions are offered and discussed. Finally someone proposes that families take turns bringing Hannah food for a week or inviting her to dinner. Everyone agrees and the matter is settled.

When the session is over and everyone stands up to leave, I tell my mother I will walk home with Sarah. I wait outside of the doorway for my friend as the crowd spills out onto the street. As soon as Sarah emerges, I grab her arm and shake it. Trying not to show too much excitement, I say smoothly, "Sarah, that man Simon who spoke first, he's the one I told you about who collected the olives for me in the market."

"Oh my," Sarah replies. "He's as big and handsome as you said." I'm pleased that she agrees with my assessment. I draw her apart from her family so we can talk more privately. We walk on, our arms threaded together.

"I wonder if he's married," I say, as nonchalantly as possible.

Sarah laughs and says, "My mother told me about his family. The other morning at the well she met Judith, Simon's mother, actually his stepmother. His mother died giving birth to his brother, Andrew, and his father remarried quickly. He knew the two young boys needed a mother, and, of course, he needed a wife to cook the meals and wash the clothes." Then, shaking her head, Sarah finally reveals, "No, Simon is not married."

"You can learn a lot at the well," I observe coolly. "Where is the family from?"

"They moved here from Bethsaida two weeks ago. Jonah and his sons are in the fishing business. They got tired of paying the exorbitant taxes required to ship their fish from Bethsaida through Capernaum to Magdala to be salted. They were lucky to find an empty house a few streets from ours.

"I wonder how old Simon is," I muse.

"Eighteen."

"Is there anything your mother didn't find out?"

"Whether he likes you," Sarah teases with a twinkle in her eyes. I guess my thoughts about the stranger haven't been so secret after all.

We reach my house first, and we untwine our arms. I wave goodbye to Sarah. "See you tomorrow." With a quick wave back, she hurries to catch up to her family.

At supper that night we feast on chicken as a special Sabbath treat. Midway though the meal my Father clears his throat and comments solemnly, "That young fellow Simon, who first proposed an idea for helping Hannah, is worth watching. I was impressed with him. It takes courage to address a crowd of your peers most of whom are twice your age."

Looking at me with a twinkle in her eye, Mother chimes in, "I heard that he has a brother. So now there are two new young men in the neighborhood. They are sons of Jonah, who is a fisherman from Bethsaida."

Father wiggles his eyebrows at me and teases, "That widens the pool of possible husbands for our Princess, doesn't it? Maybe I should get to know this Jonah." I pretend to be totally absorbed in gnawing on my drumstick. Meanwhile my heart beats a little faster.

Chapter 4

My afternoon chores in the house are finished. The oil lamps are filled, and the floor is swept with our thistle broom. I'm in my hiding spot in the olive tree, pondering weighty questions. How's Nathan doing in Jerusalem? When will Aunt Leah have a baby and make me an aunt? Will Sarah and I still be friends after we're married? The day is another scorching one. Even breathing takes an effort. It seems that in this heat the birds aren't singing as much as usual. My eyelids grow heavy. Suddenly I find myself waking with a jerk that shakes the limb I'm seated on, and the leaves rustle. Wouldn't you know it? Someone is walking nearby.

"Well, what a surprise! I expected to see a huge bird," Simon says with a chuckle as he gazes up at me through the branches. His eyes are merry, and his broad smile reveals even teeth that gleam bright white against his tanned skin. "Lose any olives lately?"

Flustered, I stutter, "No, have you?" That made no sense, but still half asleep and being addressed by a handsome young man, I am in no condition to speak intelligently. "You're Simon, aren't you?" I quickly talk on to cover my confusion.

"Simon bar Jonah. And who are you?"

"Miriam."

"I knew it. I just wanted to hear you say it."

"How did you know my name?"

"I asked Tobiah after the last Sabbath meeting."

I could feel myself blushing, making my face even warmer. We aren't supposed to be talking, but I don't want to stop. I swivel my head and check the landscape on both sides. Good. No one else is around to see or hear.

"Aren't you supposed to be mending nets or something? What are you doing here?" I notice I'm swinging my leg nervously like a little girl, and I stop.

"We've been working so hard setting up the house and starting the business that my father gave my brother Andrew and me the day off. I thought I'd explore the town." Simon gestures widely toward the houses. He steps closer, and I can see little beads of perspiration glistening on his forehead. A few awkward seconds pass. Suddenly Simon unfastens a leather pouch from his belt. He pulls the cork out and, raising the pouch to me, asks, "Would you like some?"

"No, thank you. I'm fine."

He says, "Excuse me," tilts his head back, and swallows, his Adam's apple moving with each gulp. He is clean-shaven, affording me a view of his chiseled jaw.

"My father thinks you were brave to address the assembly the other day."

"And what do you think? Should I have kept quiet?"

"Well, you *are* young and new in town. But you had an idea, so it was good that you shared it."

"Now why are you in this tree? I don't think you're picking olives."

"I like to come here to get away and think."

"And what do you think about?"

"Oh, my family, my future, sometimes God," I say honestly.

He nods and takes another swig of water. Then he wipes his lips with the back of his hand and hangs the water pouch back on his belt.

"Well, I won't disturb you any longer. Good-bye, Miriam-bird." He turns and goes on his way with long, loping strides, leaving me to my thoughts. Of course, all I can think of now is Simon. He certainly was brash to address me. Definitely he is one of the handsomest eligible men in town, not drop dead gorgeous or pretty, but in a rugged male sort of way. I review our conversation. Did I say the right things? Why did he ask Tobiah what my name was? What does he think of me? Then I wonder when I will see him again. I hope it's soon.

I don't have long to wait to learn what Simon thinks of me. One evening a few days later we are sitting in our house when a strange man appears at our door. "Shalom! I'm Jonah, recently arrived from Bethsaida," he announces briskly. His eyes scan the room and linger on me. My heart skips a beat. "I would like to talk to Jacob, father of Miriam," Jonah states with a serious expression on his face.

"That's me. Come in. Come in," my father invites heartily, leaping to his feet to welcome the unexpected guest.

Jonah climbs the one step into our house and ducks his head to avoid bumping our doorway. He smells of spicy perfume, no doubt intended to mask the odor of his day's labor. It occurs to me that Jonah is a good name for a fisherman since the prophet Jonah was delivered to Nineveh to carry out the Lord's command by a large fish.

Mother shoos me and Aaron into the courtyard far enough away that we are not within earshot of the conversation that will take place. Then she disappears into our house. Aaron is not even curious and does not want to waste time. "I'm going to see if John's home," he says flatly and leaves me to pace back and forth along the far wall.

I avoid the few other people who are still in the courtyard, cleaning up after supper.

My mind is racing madly. Is Jonah here just to introduce himself to Father? Does he want to order a mill press? Maybe he needs Father's help furnishing his house. These thoughts are a rampart I put up to protect me from being disappointed if the real reason for the visit is not what I hope: that Jonah is here to arrange a betrothal for Simon and me. It's time for Simon to find a wife. Any man who is not married by the age of twenty is an oddity. At least I've seen Simon and exchanged a few words with him. Some girls have never even met the man they are paired with for life. I catch myself chewing on a fingernail, a habit my mother has mostly managed to cure me of.

"Miriam!" my father calls from the doorway, and I hasten back to the house. When I reach Father, he puts his arm around me, and we enter the dim room together. Jonah is seated on our low bench. Mother is standing near him, her hands folded across her ample stomach. Her eyes shine with unshed tears in the light of the oil lamp. This startles me because Mother usually conceals her emotions, except for her anger.

"Miriam, as you know, Jonah has two sons," my father begins formally. "He is here because he would like to see his older son, Simon, married. Jonah is proposing that you be Simon's wife. I think this would be a wise arrangement. Simon appears to be a fine, healthy young man, and he has a steady job. He would make a good provider for you. And, Princess, you would live not far from us."

Father really doesn't need to persuade me. I'm giddy with joy. I feel like screaming and prancing around the room like baby goats and lambs jump, but instead, I rein in my emotions and act like a proper young woman. I smile and say in what I hope is a calm, mature voice, "It would be an honor to be Simon's wife." I wonder how much Simon had to do with his father's decision to ask for me.

"Good," Jonah replies firmly. "Then we will go ahead as planned,

Jacob." He turns to me and says, "We will welcome you into our family with open arms—such a lovely young woman." Jonah's eyes are warm and smiling. Simon gets his eyes from him.

I assist my mother in serving wine and small honey cakes. The two fathers have already discussed the details of our betrothal. It will be here at our house next Wednesday. After Jonah leaves, Father informs me that Jonah offered him a sizeable amount of money and two goats for me. This makes up for the loss to my family when I move out and no longer help with the household tasks. As my dowry, Father will provide house furnishings and cookware.

That night it takes me a long time to fall asleep. I try not to toss and turn too much, or I'll wake up the others. I can't turn off my brain, which is spinning like the wooden top I played with as a child. What will it be like to be married to Simon? Will he be satisfied with the meals I prepare for him? According to law, a man can divorce his wife if he doesn't like the way she cooks. Is Andrew as wonderful as his brother? What will he think of me? And their stepmother? Will she accept me and be a support and a friend, or will she be a hovering busybody who criticizes everything I do?

Mostly I think about Simon and imagine being with him day after day and night after night. How blissful it will be to belong to him, to be embraced by him, to bear his children. In my opinion he would make a worthy father of the Messiah. What a lucky girl I am. The only downside to my bright-looking future is leaving my family. I am determined to treasure every day I have left with them before my wedding day and stash it in the storehouse of my memory.

Eventually sleep overtakes me, and I begin to dream about Simon. We are both sitting on a branch in my olive tree, which surprisingly can hold us. He is smiling and feeding me olives, placing them one by one between my lips. Suddenly Simon transforms into a large, white bird, spreads his wings, and flies off. Placing one hand above my eyes to focus better, I watch him soar toward a radiant sun and become smaller and smaller until he is just a speck in the distance. Then Simon is swallowed up by the light.

When I awake, the disquieting feeling that the bizarre dream aroused in me lingers for quite some time.

Chapter 5

Well, my year of betrothal is over. Twelve months ago Simon and I stood and faced each other in this house. Father said a blessing over a cup of wine. Then he handed the metal cup to Simon, and he drank from it. Simon returned the cup to Father, who gave it to me. As I drank from it, I gazed into Simon's beautiful eyes and thought I would drown in them. This is the man who would be my provider, my protector, and my lover. With him I would bring forth children and raise them to follow God's laws and to be faithful members of our people. I shot a quick, fervent prayer to heaven, "Help me, Lord, to be the good wife that this man deserves."

From that day on, Simon and I were regarded as a couple. We were counting the days until we would live together. Whenever I ventured outside, I donned a veil to signal that I was spoken for. During every feast this year—Passover, Tabernacles, Hanukkah, Purim—I was conscious that it would be the last time I celebrated it in my Father's house, and my heart wept a little. I tried to savor each experience.

The year has passed quickly, although on some days the time

crawled by at turtle pace. I've been amassing clothes for my life as a wife—everything from new loincloths to a voluminous mantle so long that it covers my feet. I've also collected cookware and palm leaf mats to prepare to set up housekeeping with Simon.

One morning Mother called me in from the courtyard, where I was removing the seeds from pomegranates for our supper. "I want to give you something special for your wedding," she said. Awash with curiosity, I followed her to the corner where she kept her special chest. She lifted the lid and took out the silver necklace decorated with colored glass that she wore on her wedding day. With a shy smile, Mother proffered the necklace dangling from her fingers to me.

"Oh, Mother, I can't take this," I exclaimed, my eyes filling with tears. I knew how precious this piece of jewelry was to her.

"I can do what I want. Now turn around," she ordered gruffly, giving me a little push. I knew that her rough manner was only to mask the emotions she felt at this poignant moment.

Mother draped the necklace around my neck and hooked it together. It lay heavy on my chest. Then Mother held up our round mirror of polished bronze in front of me. Although the image was not sharp and clear, it still revealed the necklace's exquisite beauty. Throwing my arms around Mother, I hugged her as though I would never let her go. A few weeks later Aunt Leah presented me with silver earrings decorated with three little pomegranates. "You know, Miriam, that pomegranates are a sign of fertility," she teased with a wink. How would I ever be able to leave these two women who have loved and supported me all my life?

With Mother's assistance I designed and sewed my wedding outfit myself. First I spun flax into strands and then wove the strands into cloth. From this I made my tunic. It is yellow and of the softest linen. Carefully I embroidered a red and blue border around the neckline. Then I made a cloak and spent days sewing dozens of beads in colorful patterns on it. The veil that will cover my face until after the wedding is cream-colored and edged in gold ribbon. I purchased a new pair of leather sandals for the occasion. Once in a while I put them on to get used to the stiff thongs between my toes.

My mother and Aunt Leah constantly prepare me for marriage by giving all kinds of womanly advice. Mother will say sternly, "Now Miriam, when Simon comes home from work, don't bore him with all the details of your day. Ask him how his day was." And, "Remember to add honey to wine for special occasions." Aunt Leah will say things like, "Sweetie, before you retire for the night, dab a little perfume on your wrists and behind your ears." And "Tell Simon often that you think he is the strongest, handsomest man in the world. At least once a day let him know that you love him." Aunt Leah also likes reciting to me certain passages from the Song of Songs in Scripture about a young girl's love for her man.

While I've been honing my skills for running a house, Simon has been hard at work building one. It is an addition to his father's house. This has been quite a feat, considering that Simon has to spend most of his time fishing on the Sea of Galilee. Fortunately, his house is only fifty yards from the sea.

Throughout the year Simon has showered me with presents. Weekly he delivered fresh fish for our dinner. Sometimes he left flowers at the door—purple irises, tulips, bougainvillea—whatever was in season. Once, with a smug look on his face, the dear man handed me a clay jar filled with olives. When I took it from him, he placed his hands over mine and said proudly, "Miriam-bird, this is in honor of the day we first met. Remember?" Of course I did. How could I forget?

As customary, Simon and I always had a chaperone, usually my Aunt Leah. Not ever being alone together put a damper on our relationship. Still, I came to know Simon better, and the more I knew him, the more I loved him. Naturally, like any man, Simon has his faults. He sometimes acts without thinking things through. For example, Jonah said that in Simon's eagerness to build our house, he purchased enough rocks and stones to build three houses. And when a bandit was caught stealing some of Simon's fish on the way to market, Simon didn't call the authorities. He just knocked the living daylights out of the thief. Well, I have my share of faults too. No one's perfect. I'm counting on love to help us both overlook a lot.

Last week Nathan and Deborah came home from Jerusalem for my wedding. This adds to my cup of joy. We haven't seen Nathan's face for two years, and my parents are thrilled to have him here again. My brother has grown taller and even more serious. He has spent time during the last days reconnecting with his friends in Capernaum like James and John. These brothers have followed in their father Zebedee's footsteps and are good fishermen, although they still are hot-tempered. Nathan was sorry to hear about Matthew and refused to visit him since tax collectors are considered public sinners. Keeping God's law to the letter means everything to Nathan. Seems to me that sometimes love ought to allow for some exceptions.

So here I sit at home now, a fifteen-year-old bride, decked out in my wedding finery, anxiously waiting for the wedding party to arrive. We don't know exactly when to expect them. It seems as if I've been waiting at least as long as we've waited for the Messiah. Sometime tonight I will be married to Simon and become the wife of a fisherman. Then people will introduce me by saying, "And this is Miriam, Simon's wife." A frisson of delight runs through me at the thought.

Mother, Aunt Leah, Sarah, and some other women friends have been hovering around me all day. Making a bride beautiful is a community project. Yesterday the women accompanied me to the ritual bath before the wedding. I don't think I have ever been so clean and pampered. My skin glows with the scented oil that was rubbed into it. The strong fragrance makes me feel like a walking flower garden. Aunt Leah, who is an expert at makeup, helped me apply mine. My eyes are outlined with kohl, making me look older and mysterious. I'm chewing anise seeds to sweeten my breath. Thankfully my fingernails have grown out and are all the same length. My thick black hair is unbound, flowing freely down my back for this wedding night.

"Esther couldn't have been more ravishing than you when she dared to appear before the king without being summoned, Miriam," Sarah kindly assures me as she removes a speck from my mantle. "I don't think Esther could have been more nervous either," I shoot back.

Sarah was betrothed last month to Eli the tanner. Because producing leather is a smelly job, he works far at the end of town. I think if it weren't for Matthew, Sarah would have made a better catch. But who's to say? Maybe she and Eli will love each other and have a strong marriage blessed by many children.

Ah! Suddenly I hear the faint sound of singing, laughing, and tambourines. The wedding party approaches. My bridegroom is coming to take me to his home. I leap up. "Your veil," Mother reminds me. She helps me adjust my veil so it covers my face and then pats my cheek. I run to the doorway. The night is calm, and I take a deep breath of fresh air to settle my nerves. Hundreds of stars twinkle in the sky as though they are rejoicing with me. In the dark the torches and oil lamps carried by the people in the procession form a brilliant chain, snaking down the road and coming closer.

Then Simon is there in front of me, eyes sparkling and looking down at me with love. Even through the veil I can see how handsome he looks in his white wedding garments, like a prince. And I am his princess. "Come, my Miriam-bird," he whispers sweetly and extends his hand. I place my hand in his big one, calloused by years of rowing, and he gives it a little squeeze. Simon leads me out of the house and into my future. When we reach his house, our house, he will sign the marriage contract with two witnesses. Then we will go to the wedding chamber and be together for the first time that night. While Simon and I enjoy privacy, our guests will celebrate our union for seven days of feasting and dancing. My husband and I will be having our own celebration during those days. Maybe, just maybe, our union will result in the longed-for Messiah.

Chapter 6

After seven years of marriage, you would think that I would be accustomed to Simon and maybe even tired of him. Not so. He continually surprises me—in good ways and bad. Sarah told me that the townspeople comment that they don't know how I can tolerate being married to such an unpredictable man.

We are as well off as any family in Capernaum, for Simon's fishing business is booming. He, Jonah, and Andrew have a partnership with Zebedee and his sons, James and John. This reduces the fee paid to the tax collector to lease the waters for fishing. I think Matthew probably shaves the fee, too, for old times' sake. Andrew, a slightly smaller version of Simon, is a good brother-in-law. He is solid and dependable, more thoughtful and less impulsive than my husband. Simon's stepmother, Judith, has been a boon to me, sharing recipes for Simon's favorite foods and telling me things about him that I didn't know, including some things he probably wouldn't want me to know!

Although I drink camel milk frequently because supposedly it assures many male offspring, our family now includes three girls:

little Leah, and rambunctious three-year-old twins, Rebekah and Sarah. One of my main jobs is keeping them quiet while Simon tries to catch up on sleep lost after a night on the sea. Six-year-old Leah was born first and named after both Simon's biological mother and my aunt. During that first pregnancy, Simon was a doting husband. He couldn't do enough for me. He even snuck down to the well to get water before the village women did, so I wouldn't have to carry the heavy jar on my head or shoulder. And at the end of the day when my feet were swollen, Simon would bathe and massage them and sometimes tickle them.

I love my husband with all my heart. I wondered how I could possibly love a child too. When I shared my concern with Aunt Leah, she laughed merrily and hugged me. "Don't worry," she said reassuringly. "You know how a wineskin stretches as the wine it holds ferments. Your heart can expand too. You will be able to love Simon and as many children as God will send you, even twenty!"

The day I went into labor the sharav was upon us. Hot winds churned up the desert sand and blew it into Capernaum with wild force. Sand was everywhere. We breathed it. We chewed it mixed with our food. We swept it out of our house when it invaded through crevices and coated our furnishings, utensils, and floor. No one went outside into the yellow-gray air unless they had to. I'm surprised that God didn't use a sandstorm as one of the ten plagues.

Simon and I were eating indoors, of course. I had just placed the pot of stew in front of him when the first pain came. I ignored it, thinking it might be just a cramp. But the pain gripped me two more times, and I stopped eating. I waited to tell Simon until he finished his dinner, although I knew this was risky.

"It's time," I said calmly, putting my hand on Simon's arm.

"Now?"

I nodded. Simon leapt up, knocking over his empty cup.

"I'll get your mother and aunt. Stay put," he said nervously, as though I would go anywhere. His face was pale in the flickering light. Wrapping an extra cloth around his head, Simon charged out into the whirlwind of sand, a whirlwind himself.

I got busy preparing for our firstborn while the wind howled outside. I set out olive oil, salt, and warm water for washing our baby and laid out the strips of material for swaddling that would insure that his or her tiny bones would grow straight.

Another paroxysm of pain attacked me just as Simon delivered Mother and Aunt Leah. With a promise of prayers, he left for Zebedee's house, where he would take refuge from the agony of my labor. The women shook as much sand off themselves as they could. Mother said that the sun looked like the moon. My two dear midwives began bustling around. Shortly, all three of us were dripping with sweat from the weather and the stress of bringing new life into the world.

It felt as though I squatted on the ground for hours, willing my baby to come. The herbal sedatives did not seem to help much. During the waves of excruciating pain, I hated Simon, who had done this to me. I decided that I would never let him come near me again.

Suddenly little Leah slipped out of me. I gasped and muttered, "Thank you, God," just as much for relief from the pain as for my child. I heard Mother say, "It's a girl. What a short time of labor. Good thing we came quickly."

"Miriam was made for babies," Aunt Leah commented.

"I don't think so," I said to myself.

Soon little Leah and I were cleaned up and resting. Wrapped in swaddling bands, my exquisite, perfectly formed baby was sound asleep in my arms. That is how Simon found us when he returned from Zebedee's house. This big man tiptoed up to the mat where Leah and I were lying and knelt down. He gazed at his little daughter with awe and gently ran a finger down her cheek. Eyes brimming with tears, he kissed my forehead and whispered tenderly, "She's beautiful. Thank you, Miriam-bird."

The twins were more difficult to bring into this world. They made me so enormous that I felt like a camel clomping around in our house. I worried that Simon would stop loving me. While I was carrying the twins, it seemed as though they were fighting within my womb. Frequently I was starting and crying out because of their jabs. I could identify with the matriarch Rebekah when she was pregnant with her hyperactive twins, Jacob and Esau. How surprised I was to learn that I had two little girls. My dream of being the mother of the Messiah was gradually evaporating.

I don't regret that I have the three girls. Although Leah is only six, she is smart for her age and a big help to me, especially by watching the twins while I'm occupied with cooking or sewing. And the twins are a delight. Their antics and funny statements keep us laughing. And they adore their father. The other day Sarah suggested building a house on the sea so that Simon wouldn't have to leave us to go to work. The twins with their chubby cheeks look like angels, but they often act like little devils.

I wake up early with a feeling of dread camped out in my heart. This is strange because today is the first stomping of grapes in Capernaum. I look forward to this joyful community event each year. I'm taking our girls to watch and be part of the excitement. Thousands of grapes will be poured into the winepress. Then men will tuck up their tunics, thoroughly wash their feet and legs, and climb into the winepress. With a great deal of energy, enthusiasm, and noise they will stomp on the grapes, and the juice will stream through the channel into the waiting containers. Everyone will be laughing and singing as exuberantly as if we had just won a war.

Last year Aaron was one of the stompers. He's gone now, off to see the world. One chance meeting with a persuasive merchant made Aaron decide to strike out on his own and be a merchant of spices. Strange how our lives can be shaped by mere coincidences and spontaneous choices.

Our children are all sleeping peacefully. How innocent our troublesome twins look. Just yesterday they were chasing each other in the house, and Sarah knocked over a clay pot of wheat flour. The pot didn't break, but the flour that was spilt onto our dirt floor was ruined—money and hard work wasted. "How many times have I told you not to run in the house?" I asked crossly, hands on my hips. "You shouldn't have any bread to eat today, maybe for a week!" I sounded just like my mother. Sarah's lip quivered and she burst into tears. "I'm sorry, Mother." "Sorry, Mother," Rebekah echoed. Now as they sleep nestled together like little fledglings, I almost feel guilty for yelling at them—almost.

Simon came home from fishing a few hours ago. Exhausted by the night's labors, he lies wrapped up in his mantle cocoon-like next to little Leah. What a fine husband and father he is despite his glaring flaws. Last week he brought home a little green finch in a wooden cage for Leah. Seeing my raised eyebrows, Simon explained, "Leah's older. She should have something special. Besides, it will be good for her to learn to take care of a pet."

"Well as long as I don't end up feeding it and cleaning the cage. I have enough to do as it is," I grumbled.

"I thought you two would get along, Miriam-bird," Simon said, stressing the *bird* in his pet name for me and coaxing a smile out of me.

Sometime today I will break the news to Simon that I'm pregnant again. I'm praying hard for a boy this time. The child doesn't have to be the Messiah, just a boy for Simon's sake, a son he can take fishing and teach to wrestle. Thinking about the day ahead and the blessings of my family should make me happy, but I can't shake off my apprehension.

The crowing of a rooster and the braying of donkeys let me know it's time to rouse myself and go to the well for water. Moving slowly so as not to wake the others, I stand and stretch. After straightening my clothes and pinning up my hair, I remove the bar from the wooden door. I hoist the water jar to my shoulder, push open the door, and step down. To my surprise, Uncle Joachim is running up the road toward our house, his cloak flapping around him. No dignified Jewish man runs, especially Uncle Joachim, unless there's an emergency.

"Miriam, you must come quickly," he says urgently when he is a few yards away from me. "Your mother needs you. Your father is very ill." Uncle Joachim gasps for breath from the exertion of his run. He is as rotund as Aunt Leah.

My heart stops. I turn around and, with panic in my voice, call into the house, "Simon, wake up." He sits up with a start as though a scorpion stung him, blinks, and looks around. Our daughters are stirring now too.

"What's wrong, Miriam?"

"Father is very sick. I must go home."

I set the empty water jar down inside the house. Out of the corner of my eye I catch Uncle Joachim behind me. He has his hand over his heart and is shaking his head, sending a foreboding signal to Simon.

Simon is standing now and quickly wrapping his leather belt around his tunic. "I'll take the girls to Sarah's and ask her to watch them. Then I'll meet you at your father's house," he says crisply. Our daughters are too much of a challenge to leave in the care of his parents next door.

Then I accompany Uncle Joachim back to my old home, hoping he doesn't mind that I race ahead of him. When I enter the house, Mother is sitting cross-legged on the floor, rocking back and forth and repeating "Jacob" over and over in a pitiful voice that stabs my heart. Aunt Leah sits on her heels beside her, holding her hand. Before them, Father lies on the mat where he always sleeps on the floor. But he is completely motionless. He isn't breathing.

"Miriam," Mother says, extending her free hand to me. Her face is bathed in tears. "Your Father is with Abraham now and with his father and mother."

Time stood still.

"What happened?"

"He wasn't feeling well yesterday and complained of a bad headache last night. I should have called for the physician."

"How would you know he was so sick?" I sink to my knees and embrace my mother, a feeble attempt to lessen her pain.

"He loved you so much," Mother says softly with a sob.

"I know. And I didn't even get to say goodbye!"

Never again will I hear my father call me Princess. Never again will I hear his hearty laugh bubble up from deep inside him. A wave of grief washes over me. Death is so shockingly final. Yet in my heart I feel that my father, who was so full of life, must still exist somewhere. Not just in my memory and not just in Sheol, the land of the dead where people drift around, mere shadows of themselves. I can almost sense Father's presence now. He must be aware of us and our great sorrow. At least this is what I hope.

Quietly Uncle Joachim states, "I'll hire some mourners and send word to the neighbors."

Mother looks at us with red, swollen eyes. "We'll need more spices for the burial. I wasn't expecting this."

"I'll go to the market and get some myrrh and aloes," Aunt Leah volunteers.

My aunt and uncle leave. Mother and I begin the sad duty of washing the body of my father, the body that spent itself in serving us out of love. We will clothe him in his best tunic. When Aunt Leah returns, we will wrap him in wide strips of linen, placing sweet spices in their folds. Because of our hot climate, he needs to be buried before tomorrow morning at the latest.

By the time we finish preparing my father for burial, three women from our village are seated outside the door wailing, singing, and playing a mournful tune on a flute to express our anguish. Simon has arrived. It comforts me just to see him. Simon, Uncle Joachim, Jonah, and Andrew will carry the body of my father on a bier to the caves outside of Capernaum. How sad that Nathan and Aaron will not be present. It will be days before they learn that our father has died. Aunt Leah and I will stay the night with Mother.

The next day Simon and I decide to invite my mother to live with us.

Chapter 7

~~~~~~

My life moves on calmly, and I adapt to its inexorable changes. Father has been gone almost five years now, and I'm quite accustomed to having two more people added to our household: Mother and four-year-old Mark. Today couldn't be more pleasant, now that it's cooler. The sky is a brilliant blue with just a few puffy clouds floating in it like ships, their shadows gliding over our lush Galilean land. The air is filled with birdsong and the humming of wild bees. Small birds are flying in circles, making little dips as though they are riding waves in the air.

Simon and I, along with our brood, are walking home from a trip to the Sea of Galilee. He was eager to show us his new boat, which is larger than his old one, a sign of his growing prosperity. I'm proud of my husband. Simon has grown a trim, black beard, which makes him look older and, in my opinion, more handsome. At the sea we waved to Zebedee, James, and John, who were out in their boat a distance from the shore, stripped to their loincloths and casting nets into the sea. Simon informed us they just hired another man to help haul in the heavy seine net, which usually is loaded with silver, flopping fish.

The next time Simon, Jonah, and Andrew go out fishing, this net will be suspended between Zebedee's boat and Simon's new one.

After chasing some of the large, white egrets scavenging on the shore, the twins are now skipping ahead of us and talking nonstop, probably plotting some mischief. Little Leah, who is not so little anymore, walks sedately beside us, while Mark rides on Simon's broad shoulders. He is the apple of Simon's eye, and the feeling is mutual. God has been good to us in giving us four healthy children. Now if only Mark would stop sucking his thumb. I don't think the Messiah would be sucking his thumb at four.

Sarah too has been blessed with a four-year-old boy, Joel, but only after losing two babies, one in childbirth and one who died in her sleep when she was eighteen months. Those early deaths were devastating for Sarah and Eli. My friend and I often meet at the well in the morning and swap stories about our families. Yesterday Sarah told me she was pregnant again and is hoping for a girl. I'm keeping her tucked in my daily prayers.

As we near our house, I hear the noise of construction, the sharp clank of stone hitting stone and the rumble of men's voices. I can't help smiling.

"Simon, I'm so glad that we're finally going to have our very own synagogue," I remark.

Keeping one hand on Mark, Simon shades his eyes with the other hand and, squinting, peers in the direction of the site. He reports, "The walls are going up fast. They're already waist high."

Tobiah wondered if it was a trick when Antonius, the centurion from the garrison, came and offered whatever money was needed to build a synagogue. Yet, now the Roman soldiers are overseeing the construction too, even helping to cart the black rocks in from the hills. I suppose they're bored. In Capernaum there's not a lot of action that requires soldiering.

"Thank goodness Tobiah trusted that centurion," I say. "Goes to show you that not all Romans are bad ... at least not Antonius."

"Now if we can only get the Romans to build us a bigger house."

"I'll build you one, Father," Mark chirps.

Simon reaches up and tousles Mark's hair. "Thanks, Son."

I turn to my eldest daughter. "Leah, as soon as we get home I have to start getting supper ready. We're having company tonight. Uncle Andrew and James and their wives and John are coming. Your grandmother will help with the food, but would you please see that Mark and your sisters keep out of our way and are happily entertained?"

"All right, Mother. I'll tell them a Scripture story and let them act it out. They like to do that. The last time we performed, the twins pretended to be Abraham and Isaac, Mark was the ram caught in the bushes, and I was the voice of God."

Leah is such a smart and dutiful daughter. Thankfully she has inherited Simon's good looks, but not his spirited personality that makes him bluster and blunder through life. I imagine that when Simon and I are old and gray, our quiet, capable girl will be a comfort to us, just as I hope I am to Mother.

Gathered in the courtyard that evening, my family and our guests are feasting on Mother's delicious grape leaves stuffed with lentils and spices. Andrew's rather shy, pregnant wife, Joanna, brought cheeses flavored with various herbs as she said she would. Seated on the mat beside her three-year-old son, Reuben, she is offering him a fig. I'm between her and Dorcas, the wife of James. Dorcas has a fiery temperament to match his. I wonder just how many clay pots they've shattered during their disagreements. My children and Mother sit opposite me. The men—Simon, Andrew, James, and John—are seated together and as boisterous as usual today.

As Mother refills the wine cups, I think for the hundredth time how fortunate for me that she lives with us. When Mark was a baby, he cried a lot. Mother soothed him to sleep with the same lullabies she sang to Nathan, Aaron, and me when we were little. Being a no-nonsense kind of person, Mother keeps a firm rein on the twins. She also generously helps with the shopping, cooking, and sewing.

"I can hardly wait to take my new boat out on its maiden fishing trip," Simon declares emphatically. "Why wait until tomorrow? We could go tonight."

"Right. We could find out even sooner how many leaks your new boat has," James teases.

"Aw, you're just jealous," counters Simon, giving James a playful punch in the arm. "If you weren't such a miser, you could have a new boat too. Your deathtrap of a boat was probably made of lumber from Noah's ark."

I shoot my husband a warning glance and a mental message, "Careful, Simon. You don't want to anger your fishing partners."

John asks defensively, "If our boat is so unseaworthy, then why did we have one of our best hauls last week?"

Andrew answers, "Because we fished where the warm springs feed into the sea."

"Ha! We could go there again tonight," Simon suggests hopefully.

"Forget it, Simon," James says. "I'm worn out from today's haul. Besides, I want to spend this night with Dorcas, not you!"

"Well, look who's here!" Simon exclaims, his downcast face brightening.

I turn in the direction of his gaze, and there's Aaron standing in the doorway and smiling, his arms folded. With a cry, Mother goes to him as fast as she can and embraces him. I spring up to join her and say with fervor, "Welcome home, stranger!" My brother's strong but pleasant fragrance tickles my nose. "Uncle Aaron," my three girls squeal with glee. They run to him, and he captures all of them in his arms and hugs them. But Mark remains on the mat and watches warily. No wonder. We haven't seen Aaron in almost a year. I think, There's no way that Simon's going fishing tonight.

"Sit. Sit," Mother says, gesturing to a place before the plate of stuffed grape leaves. Everyone shifts over to make room for my brother, who is no longer the skinny fellow he used to be.

"So how is the spice business?" Andrew asks politely.

"Great. I actually went to India myself this year and purchased a large shipment. As I traveled through Judah, it sold out immediately. By the way, Nathan sends all of you his love. I saw him when I was in Jerusalem."

Offering Aaron a piece of garlic bread, Mother asks, "Is he well? I pray for him so often. You too, Aaron, with all those bandits swooping down out of the hills and attacking merchants on the road. I worry about my boys."

"Nathan is Nathan. Although it is unusual for a Galilean to be a scribe, he's still with the revered scribe who took him under his wing, thanks to Tobiah. Nathan will be instructed for many years before he is an official scribe. When I saw him, he was in the Temple courtyard, teaching a group of boys. To support himself he helps vendors sell their goods in the market."

"I have to admire him," James comments, shaking his head. "I love the Torah, but spending my whole life trying to understand it and explaining it to others doesn't appeal to me. I'm happy being a fisherman."

"Me too," the other men chime in.

"By the way, have you heard about the prophet named John who is preaching along the Jordan River?" Aaron looks around at us. He has our undivided attention.

"A prophet?" Simon asks skeptically, his eyebrows raised. "We haven't seen a prophet for five hundred years, ever since Zechariah was killed."

"Well, this John is like the great prophet Elijah. He wears a camel hair outfit and a leather belt just as Elijah did. And his message is the same. He foretells that a Messiah is coming."

"Maybe he really is Elijah," Joanna pipes up. "After all, Elijah is supposed to return to earth someday."

Mark, who has squeezed in next to me, tugs on my sleeve. "Mother, Elijah's the one who was taken up in a fiery chariot, right?"

"Yes, dear." I kiss the top of his head.

Aaron continues with gusto. "John does what all prophets do. He tells people to give up their sinful ways, even fearlessly pointing out the faults of Pharisees and King Herod. He has an innovative twist though. As a sign that people repent, he has them wade to him in the Jordan River and he immerses them."

"Ah, like being purified in a mikvah," says Dorcas.

"Where does this John come from?" our John inquires.

"He hails from Ain Karem near Jerusalem. His father is a priest. Rumor has it that an angel foretold John's birth to his father in the Temple. The odd thing is that his parents never had any children and were quite old before John was born."

"Oh, the poor woman," I can't help remarking sympathetically.

"Sounds like Abraham and Sarah's story," John notes.

"Anyway, from what I hear, John is a charismatic speaker. He attracts crowds like no Pharisee I know of, and several men have become his disciples. They say that even tax collectors are being baptized. And John's a real ascetic, like the holy men of old. We sometimes eat honey and roasted locusts, but that's all John lives on!"

"This bears investigating," John says. He looks at his older brother, James, his eyebrows raised quizzically. "What do you say we go and find this John and hear what he has to say?"

"I'm interested, but where is he?" James is the more practical brother.

"The last I heard, John was on the east shore of the Jordan around Bethany," Aaron says. "That's about a three-day journey for you."

"How will you ever find him if he keeps moving around?" Dorcas asks with a frown, clearly not at all pleased at the prospect of losing her husband for any length of time.

"No problem," Aaron explains. "He's so famous now in Judah that if you travel near the Jordan and ask his whereabouts, you're bound to locate him."

I'm conscious that Simon is listening to this conversation with interest, thoughtfully stroking his short beard. Surely he has more sense than to go along with this harebrained idea.

"I'll go with you," volunteers my husband, his eyes bright.

"Me too," adds Andrew enthusiastically. "Our fathers and the hired men can carry on the fishing without us for a while."

Instantly I react, "Wait a minute. How can you go traipsing off when all of you except John have families to care for?" John, the youngest, isn't married yet.

"Don't worry, Miriam. We won't be away long," John tries to reassure me. "At most three weeks."

"Besides," Peter smugly argues, "in case of emergency, Jonah and Zebedee will still be here."

"And me," adds Mother.

"Whose side are you on?" I ask her with a withering glance.

Later, our guests are gone, the pots and plates are washed, and Aaron has fed his donkey. Only our family is seated in a circle with Aaron in the courtyard. In front of him rests a lopsided leather bag.

"And now," Aaron announces with a broad grin, "it's time for gifts."

Aaron reaches in the bag, draws out three shiny fishing hooks, and gives them to Simon. Then he hands me and Mother small boxes crafted from wood and inlaid with flower designs. When we carefully open them, we find silver necklaces hung with pendants of polished colored stones.

The three girls receive similar boxes. Opening them, they discover jangling silver bracelets and respond with appreciative oohs and ahs. Faces beaming with happiness, they clasp their bracelets on their arms and shake them.

"And for you, Mark, the best gift," Aaron says.

Mark has been clinging to my side like a burr, but the leather ball Aaron draws from the bag works magic. When Aaron rolls it over to Mark, my son's brown eyes grow big. Holding the ball in one hand, he scoots over to Aaron on his knees and hugs him around the neck.

Unlike Mark, I am not mollified so easily by my present. Aaron's unexpected homecoming is wonderful and the source of much joy for all. But his tale about John, the baptizer, has threatened my tranquil life. I have never been separated from Simon for so much as a week. Not only will I miss him enormously, but I'll be a nervous wreck worrying about him day and night.

Who knows what might happen on the journey? Simon could be attacked by bandits, fall off a cliff, or come down with a serious illness. On the other hand, Simon works so hard for us. How can I begrudge him this trip with his good buddies? He clearly has his heart set on it. Secretly I have to admit that I would like to meet John too. These arguments pro and con plague me like mosquitoes buzzing inside my head. I go about my humdrum tasks with a knot in my stomach.

In the end Simon embarks on a journey with the others to investigate the baptizing prophet. Regrettably, I and the new boat lose.

Chapter 8

Three weeks came and went since Simon, Andrew, James, and John left Capernaum in search of the eccentric John. Then weeks four and five passed, and we wives began to wonder if we'd ever see our men again. We also started plotting how we would scold and punish them when they showed up!

Finally one afternoon when I'm relaxing in the house and giving Leah a lesson on ways to put up her hair, I hear footsteps approaching. Leah says, "Someone's coming, Mother." How often during the past weeks I had perked up at such footsteps, hoping they were Simon's—and then trying not to show my disappointment when Aunt Leah, Sarah, Joanna, or Dorcas appeared at the door. But now my husband actually steps up into our house.

"Simon!" "Father!" "Miriam!" our voices ring out simultaneously. I drop the wooden comb, heedless of the hairpins scattering on the floor, and hurry into my husband's widespread arms. Leah is close behind me, her dark hair half up and half cascading down.

"I missed you so much, Miriam-bird," Simon murmurs, crushing my head into his shoulder. He kisses my forehead, both cheeks, and my lips. His clothes are coated with dust from the road, and he smells of sweat. But I don't care. He is safe.

"Missed you too, Leah." He tugs a length of her hair and then wraps her in a hug.

"I missed you very much," I confess. But then I say sharply, "Why were you away so long? 'No more than three weeks,' John said. Do you have any idea what it was like not knowing if you were alive or dead?"

"I'm sorry I caused you distress, sweetheart, but you'll understand when I tell you what happened."

"You better have a good excuse," I say huffily.

Leah asks, "Did you find the prophet, Father? Is he all Uncle Aaron said he was?"

"Yes, we met John and were awed by him, but we met someone else too. I'll give you a full report later. Right now I want to change my clothes."

"And take a bath. Are you hungry?" I ask solicitously. He looks like he lost weight.

"Not very. I'll wait for supper." He removes his sandals, and as they drop to the floor he remarks, "Guess I'll need a new pair. The soles have holes in them now."

I turn to Leah, who is eating up her father with her eyes. "Go outside and tell your sisters, brother, and grandmother that your father's home."

Mark is the first one to arrive. He runs to Simon, who picks him up, kisses him, and then starts tickling him. Soon Mark is rolling on the ground, overcome by gales of laughter, and I have to say to Simon, "Stop or you'll give him the hiccups." Oh, it's good to have us all together again.

That night we are in the courtyard, enjoying supper as a family for the first time in weeks. Only Jonah and Judith, Andrew and

Joanna and their son, Reuben, are with us. We didn't invite others so that we could savor this homecoming alone for a while. Our three daughters can't take their eyes off their father. Mark makes sure he has a seat right next to Simon, even if it means Grandpa Jonah must move over. Joanna's due date is nearing, and Andrew eases her down onto the mat. A pity he wasn't around lately to be of more help to her.

Mother has cooked up the delicious, thick soup that, according to tradition, Esau traded his birthright for one day when he was starved. To our surprise, Simon brings forth the wine to add to the meal. He says, "This is very special," and pours each adult a glass. The wine is remarkably good. As we dine, now and then a few neighbors wave to Simon and Andrew and call out, "Welcome home!"

Both Simon and Andrew are downing their second helping of soup before they are ready to share their adventures with us. Politely they listened to family news first, like how Mark's two new front teeth finally made their appearance. He was chasing Sarah's son, Joel, when Joel stopped abruptly and Mark's head rammed into his. We filled the brothers in on a wedding they missed as well as a funeral. Then I firmly say to them, "All right. Now it's your turn. Don't keep us in suspense any longer. We want a blow-by-blow account of your travels."

"Well," begins Simon, "it was easy to locate John. When we had crossed the Jordan and reached Bethany, we stopped at an inn for supper and overheard two fellows talking about him. We asked them how we could meet John, and they gave us directions to the place at the Jordan where he was preaching every day. After a good night's rest, we walked a couple of miles until we saw a crowd gathered on the banks of the Jordan. As we neared the place, there was John, standing knee-deep in the water. He looked like a visitor from a time long ago."

Andrew elaborates, "He had long, straggly hair and a full beard, as if grooming wasn't high on his priority list. And the rough, ragged tunic that hung on his gaunt frame obviously wasn't made for him by a loving wife."

"If John looks so weird, why then do people flock to him?" Joanna asks, wrinkling her nose. This is precisely what I was wondering myself.

"Because his message resonates with them, and he delivers it in an electrifying way," Simon explains. "When we got there, John was giving a fiery speech. He shouted, 'Don't give up hope, people. Our savior is right around the corner.' Then, pointing his finger and sweeping his arm across the crowd, seeming to fix his piercing eyes on each one, he roared, 'But prepare your heart. Get rid of selfish, greedy ways that displease our God. Be worthy of his loving kindness. Share what you have. Act justly.' After listening to John for an hour or so, like so many others we were stirred to become better persons. All four of us were baptized that day."

"More than that," Andrew added tentatively with a glance at Simon, "we became John's disciples and followed him for four weeks. We watched him baptize many people, even some Pharisees. We heard him refer repeatedly to the wonderful one who is coming. Like John, we fasted a little, something he requires his disciples to do."

I wonder how Simon's fasting will affect my meal plans, how long he will keep it up, and if he will expect the rest of us to fast too. As if to read my mind, Simon says, "Don't worry, Miriam, we don't fast anymore. We are no longer John's disciples."

Somewhat relieved, I say, "Good. Now you won't be off following him around." Simon and Andrew exchange guilty looks, raising my suspicion. "What else happened?" I coax.

Andrew continues cautiously. "One day a man we hadn't seen before approached John, and John called him the Lamb of God who takes away the sins of the world."

"Lamb of God. That's a strange title," Mother remarks. "The only lambs of God I know of are the ones we offer God at Passover. They're sacrificed in memory of the lamb's blood that saved us from death in Egypt. Being referred to as Lamb of God doesn't bode well for that man. Go on, Andrew."

"It seems John had already baptized him and claimed he saw the Spirit come down upon the man. Naturally we wanted to know more about this Spirit-filled person, especially if he can take away sins. Three young men were standing next to us. I asked one of them who this Lamb of God was. He told us the man's name was Jesus. He was a cousin of John's from Nazareth and a carpenter by trade."

"Oh, he is a Galilean then, one of us," I say, recognizing the isolated village in the southern hills of Galilee.

"Yes," my husband confirms with a nod. "He has our accent that the Judeans make fun of. According to John, Jesus is so much greater than he is that John is not worthy to act as his slave and untie his sandal. This Jesus doesn't dress in camel hair like a prophet. His clothes are just like ours. He looks about our age. John does too."

Andrew goes on. "The next afternoon James and I were alone with John the Baptist. As Jesus strode by, John called our attention to him and again identified him as the Lamb of God. Curiosity got the better of us, and we left John and tailed Jesus. Sensing he was being followed, Jesus stopped in his tracks. We almost bumped into him. He turned and asked, 'What are you looking for?' Caught by surprise, I blurted out, 'Where are you staying?' He merely beckoned and said, 'Come and see.' So we ended up spending the rest of the day with him.

"Jesus hasn't had special training in religion. He's not a scribe or a Pharisee, but he spoke to us about God and God's kingdom with great wisdom. And he knows Scripture backwards and forwards. That day we were convinced that he is the Messiah. Of course, we were eager to let the Simon and James know about him too."

"The Messiah? And he comes from Nazareth? I don't think so," Judith says flatly. "You guys have been hoodwinked!"

Simon picks up the story. "Andrew found me as I was exploring the nearby town, and I knew something had happened. I don't think

I've ever seen him so excited. Breathlessly he told me that he and James discovered the Messiah. He had me rush through the narrow streets with him like it was a matter of life or death until we came to the house where Jesus was. He was standing in front of it, as though he expected us. Before Andrew could introduce me, Jesus gazed at my face intently and declared, 'You are Simon son of Jonah.' Then he said a peculiar thing. He said that I am to be called Peter."

"Peter? Why on earth would you be called Peter?" I exclaim irritably, worried about where this story is heading.

"Peter means 'rock' in Greek, you know," Joanna quietly says.

Ah, so my husband is now a rock. That could be bad or good. Maybe it means he is stubborn or as senseless as an inanimate boulder. On the other hand, it may mean that he is strong and reliable, someone who will never leaves me again to run our family by myself. Looking at Simon Peter, I say, "I rather like that name. Since you call me Miriam-bird, I think I will call you Peter from now on."

"That's all right with me, dear. There are worse things you could call me."

"That's for sure," I say, still miffed that he stayed away so long. Everyone laughs.

"Could it be that the Messiah has actually come?" Jonah says half to himself. "Son, could you pour me another cup of wine?" he requests, and Peter refills his cup.

"Well, we've had other would-be Messiahs who got our hopes up in vain," Mother points out frowning. "Don't forget Judas, who was also from Galilee. He led the rebellion against the Roman tax, but then what happened? He perished. Who's to say if this latest Messiah, Jesus, is the promised one?"

"We'll just have to wait and see," I state stiffly and pass the plate of Peter's favorite dessert, balls of honey and nuts, one more time.

Helping himself to three of the sweets, Peter says, "Well, the four of us no longer followed John but began to spend time with Jesus. That's why we were away so long. As Jesus spoke to us, we were more and more convinced that he is a man sent by God. Not only does Jesus offer thought-provoking ideas based on the Scripture, but he exudes confidence and gives the impression that he is on intimate terms with the Almighty.

"We journeyed with Jesus to Cana. Nathaniel, one of the other disciples, was thrilled because that's his hometown. He was able to introduce Jesus and the rest of us to his family and friends. We arrived in Cana in time to attend a wedding on the last day of the celebration. There we met the mother of Jesus, Mary. His father Joseph is deceased. Mary is related to the groom and was one of the women taking care of the refreshments. I could tell immediately she was the mother of Jesus. There is such a striking resemblance that they could have been twins except for the age difference. You would like Mary, Rebekah. She's such a warm, loving person."

"Like me. Right, Peter?" Mother says with a grin.

"Right." My husband plays it safe. "Anyway, a mind-boggling thing happened at the wedding. You tell them about it, Andrew."

"Well, we men had just finished dancing and sat down to catch our breath. Mary walks up to Jesus, bends down, and informs him that the wine ran out."

"Oh, my!" Mother interjects. "How humiliating for the parents of the couple."

"And for the poor bride and groom," adds Joanna. "From now on they'll have a sour memory of their wedding. What a pity!"

"Wait. Listen," Peter orders, holding up his hand. Andrew continues the story.

"Jesus looks at Mary and, as though he is not the least concerned, says, 'Woman, what business is that of ours? It isn't my time yet.' "

"My!" Mother exclaims, scowling. "Is that any way for a good Jewish boy to speak to his mother? Why doesn't he offer to go buy some wine and save the day?"

"Apparently Mary knows her son and trusts that he will act to remedy the situation. She leaves us and walks over to the servers.

They are shrugging, shaking their heads, and turning away a slightly intoxicated man who came for a refill. We hear Mary tell the exasperated servers to do whatever Jesus says. I doubt if these men will take orders from a carpenter from Nazareth just because his mother tells them to. But then Jesus stands and goes over to the servers. He points to the six stone water jars at the door for the ritual washings before meals and commands, 'Fill these the jars with water all the way to the top.' To our amazement the servers actually carry out his order, even though it makes no sense!"

"Water?" Mother hoots and slaps her hand on her thigh. "That's a pretty poor substitute for wine."

"Well, Jesus tells the servers to take a dipperful to the headwaiter to taste. Filled with curiosity, we follow furtively and watch. The headwaiter sips the wine and smacks his lips. He announces that usually the cheaper wine is saved for the end of celebrations when people have already drunk a lot and in their impaired state won't notice the poor quality. Obviously the wine the headwaiter tasted is excellent. Mary, who is hovering in the background, catches her son's eye, smiles, and nods."

"You should have seen the stunned looks on the servers' faces," Peter remarks. He drops his jaw and widens his eyes in imitation. The children giggle. "I thought they might faint. Of course, the servers didn't tell the headwaiter the source of the wine. Otherwise they might lose their jobs for not providing enough wine for the wedding celebration."

"Or for telling him an absurd story," I remark.

"How can it be that water tastes like wine as good as what we're drinking now?" Jonah asks and takes a drink.

"Yes, that's impossible," Judith adds forcefully. "How gullible do you think we are?"

"Well, the wine you are drinking right now happens to be some of the Cana wine," Peter triumphantly proclaims. "There were maybe a hundred and eighty gallons of it, enough for every guest that day to take some home. A servant hurried to the market and purchased leather wineskins for all of us."

"So, we're drinking miraculous water," Joanna concludes, somewhat dazed. "If what you say is true, then this Jesus certainly has extraordinary power. I can see why you think he is the Messiah. I can't understand how water can turn into wine. But then neither do I understand how water makes vineyards grow grapes that yield wine."

"Maybe the servers added wine to the water," suggests Jonah, trying to wrap his mind around the incredible story. "You know how we dilute our wine so that sometimes it is half water."

"No." Peter shakes his head. "We watched carefully, and the water in the jars came to the brim."

"Maybe Jesus is a magician," Joanna suggests.

"He must be," I say with a glint in my eye. "Didn't he make our husbands disappear?"

"Well, Jesus is planning to come to Capernaum soon," Andrew informs us. "You'll be able to judge him for yourself."

"By the way, Miriam-bird, I invited him to stay with us when he comes," glibly says my generous, impetuous husband.

"Maybe he can magically provide all our meals for us while he's here," I say in a surly voice and with a narrowed gaze at Peter. I'm not too happy about playing hostess for the man who was responsible for keeping my husband away from his family and job. I fear what Peter's attraction to him may lead to.

Chapter 9

~~~~~~~~~~~~~~~~~~~~~~~~~~~~~~

A few weeks later Jesus did come to town and is staying at Tobiah's house, not ours. Perhaps Peter communicated to Jesus that I wasn't exactly thrilled to have this supposed prophet at our house, to put it mildly. Or maybe Tobiah invited Jesus, and out of respect for Tobiah's position in our community, Jesus didn't want to refuse.

Today is the Sabbath, and we are in the synagogue that our Roman centurion friend helped to build. We're very proud of it. In the front, next to the ark where the Torah is housed, stands our seat of Moses, designed with ornate figures. Our community has grown, and we now have an assistant synagogue leader, who is younger than Tobiah. His name is Jairus.

There is an air of excitement in the room because Jesus is present, seated with the men on one of the benches carved into the stone wall. He doesn't look extraordinary. You'd think that the Messiah would be very tall and regal-looking and rather aloof. But this Jesus is a typical Jewish man of medium height and build with the usual brown hair and brown eyes. He is comfortably chatting with the men around him.

During our services, any Jewish man is free to read Scripture and then elaborate on it. Jesus has been assuming this role in synagogues throughout Galilee. As expected, today Jesus reads from a scroll. He chooses the passage from the prophet Ezekiel that tells how God will seek out and feed his sheep, meaning us. Then Jesus sits in the seat of Moses and begins his comments by telling a story. This is an engaging teaching device that he uses frequently I heard.

Jesus says that a man has a hundred sheep. One day he discovers that one sheep is missing. It probably wandered off from the flock and perhaps fell on rocks or got caught in brambles. All by itself the stray sheep would be defenseless, easy prey for wolves. The shepherd doesn't hesitate to leave the ninety-nine sheep to go in search of the lost one. When he finds it, he is overjoyed. He carries the sheep back to the fold on his shoulders and calls all his friends and neighbors together to celebrate with him.

Then, for the sake of us women I assume, Jesus tells a similar story. A woman who has ten silver coins loses one. She lights a lamp and sweeps the house. When she finds the coin, she too holds a celebration. A silver coin is equivalent to a whole day's work, and so if the woman was poor, I can understand why she would be ecstatic at finding a missing one. Besides, the coin might have had sentimental value if it was a gift from her father or husband on her wedding day. I still have the clay jar that contained the olives Peter gave me during our betrothal year.

Jesus concludes by teaching that heaven rejoices more over one sinner who repents than over ninety-nine righteous persons. The point of his two stories is easy to grasp. Sinners are like lost sheep or lost coins, and each one is extremely precious in God's eyes. I find it interesting that in the second story Jesus compares God to a woman. What do the Jewish men who are listening think about that?relun

As I listen to Jesus, my attitude toward sinners like Matthew softens. If God cares so much about his wayward people, shouldn't I too? And you never know. Someday I may be guilty of a serious sin. Wouldn't I want God to love me despite my failing? Wouldn't I want people to care about me and not shun me like a leper?

Although I don't want to, I have to agree with Peter. Jesus is a consummate preacher with an uncanny ability to make us think and to change our hearts. I wonder how receptive Pharisees are to his unconventional messages like today's teaching. They pride themselves on adhering to every iota of the law and its multiple interpretations. And for one thing, they scrupulously avoid being corrupted by contact with sinners.

As we file out of the synagogue, everyone is commenting on the superb presentation Jesus gave. A group of men, including Peter and Sarah's husband, Eli, remain inside, clustered around Jesus. No doubt they are questioning him on some of the more complicated passages of Scripture and the law. Sarah and Joel catch up to me and my children. I'm concerned about my friend because lately she's looked tired and sad. Her kind, brown eyes often have dark smudges under them. Today, though, she is fully alive.

"Well, what do you think of the visitor from Nazareth?" she asks as she falls into step with me.

"Pretty impressive. You'd never guess he was from that dinky town and not from Jerusalem and schooled by the most expert scribes."

"Did you hear what he did for Tobiah's wife?"

"No, what?" Esther is not that old, but she has been losing her sight to the point where she can hardly manage their household anymore. She is distressed at being dependent on others to help her shop and prepare meals.

"Tobiah must have told Jesus about Esther's affliction. As soon as Jesus entered their house, he took Esther by the shoulders and murmured, 'May you see clearly.' Just like that, Esther regained her vision. 'Oh! Oh! I see you again, Tobiah, every wrinkle and whisker on your face,' she screamed. They say Esther was so happy that she hugged Jesus. He didn't seem to mind and neither did Tobiah."

"So Jesus is not only a preacher but a healer. He'll find that there's plenty of work for him to do in Capernaum."

"He told Tobiah that he's only staying a few days. Then he'll stop at some other towns on the way back to Nazareth to visit his mother and relatives."

Word about Esther's cure spread like a wind-fanned fire. During the time Jesus was with Tobiah, his visit was repeatedly interrupted by people coming to the house in hopes of a cure for themselves, a family member, or a friend. And they were never disappointed. It was wonderful to have a healer in our town. Sarah's cousin Ruth, who was born with a clubfoot, can now walk without limping. One son in a family who shares our courtyard is eleven years old and never said a word. Jesus loosened his tongue, and now the boy's mother never stops talking about it! The next time Jesus visits Capernaum, he is welcome to stay with us.

∽∽∽

About three weeks later, Peter and his co-workers were fishing a distance away along the shore of the Sea of Galilee. It is midmorning when Peter comes home. Mother, Leah, and I are putting away clothes that had dried quickly in the sun. Peter drops his fishing gear inside the door.

"Welcome home, Peter," I say. He saunters over to me and plants a kiss on my cheek. He smells of sun and fresh air tinged with sweat. Taking me by the hand, he says earnestly, "I need to talk to you, Miriam-bird. Come walk with me." Leaving Mother and Leah to finish folding the laundry, I go outside with Peter, wondering what is so urgent that it can't wait.

"Let's sit under those palm trees," Peter suggests. As we near them, he says, "Jesus is back in town. He's visiting Tobiah right now."

"Oh, I don't mind if he stays with us, Peter. What's one more mouth to feed?"

"Good. I was hoping you'd say that. Jesus will be with us for dinner today." Peter moistens his lips and then says, "It seems he had a terrible experience in his hometown."

"That's not surprising. Nazareth doesn't have the best reputation in the world. What happened?"

We settle ourselves on the soft grass in the shade of the palm trees, frightening off a crested hoopoe that was sunning himself with his wings outspread.

"Yesterday two men from Cana were passing through Capernaum and told Tobiah the story. They had been visiting in Nazareth. There, as Jesus has been doing in other towns, he taught in the synagogue. After he read from Isaiah, he spoke so eloquently that everyone was amazed. His relatives and neighbors couldn't fathom how this carpenter, whose family they knew, could have such a golden tongue. But then Jesus did something that wasn't very smart. He remarked that the townspeople probably wanted him to perform cures the way he has done here in Capernaum. He so much as said that he wouldn't."

"Why not?"

"I don't know, but openly stating that was like throwing a stone into a bees' nest. It enraged the Nazarenes. You'd think that Jesus had cursed God. As one body, the people stood, rushed at him, and drove him out of the synagogue. Yelling, the mob chased him to a cliff and intended to throw him off, but right when Jesus was precariously near the brink, he slipped away."

"How could he vanish when everyone was focused on him?"

"Sounds impossible, doesn't it? But nothing Jesus does surprises me anymore. The bewildered Nazarenes couldn't understand how their prey had eluded them either. They looked at one another utterly stupefied. Unfortunately Mary, the mother of Jesus, was present and observed the whole fiasco."

"Oh, my! She must have been frightened to death. From now on, how can she stand to live side by side with people who tried to kill her son? Imagine what it will be like for her to mingle with the other women at the well or in the market. How can she go to celebrations in town—if she's even invited? She should move here to Capernaum. And, Peter, as far as I'm concerned, Jesus can stay with us as long as he wants. You didn't have to call me away from my work to tell me this latest escapade of Jesus."

Peter doesn't say anything for a while. A little black ant zigzags its way up the sleeve of his robe. Peter flicks it off with his forefinger and thumb.

"There's something else," Peter says slowly. He clears his throat and shifts his position so that he is facing me and looking into my eyes. Suddenly I'm filled with apprehension. "As Andrew and I were casting our net into the sea this morning, we heard our names. We looked up, and there was Jesus standing on the shore. Beckoning to us, he called out, 'Follow me, and I will make you fishers of people.' "

"What's that supposed to mean?"

"I think Jesus wants us to become his disciples and catch other people and bring them to him. Andrew and I pulled up our net, rowed to shore, dropped anchor, and jumped into the water. Then we started walking along the beach with Jesus, his arm around my shoulder. Shortly we came to where James and John were sitting in their boat with Zebedee and the hired men, mending the tears in the strands of their nets. Jesus also called the brothers to follow him. After a few words to Zebedee, James and John joined us, and we walked back here to Capernaum.

"I've heard Jesus and have seen him in action enough to know that he is indeed greater than John the Baptist. There's something about Jesus that draws me to him powerfully. I am certain that I will not be happy unless I follow him."

"Follow him? Do you mean live by what he teaches or literally go where he goes?"

"Both."

This alarming news leaves me totally stunned. I can only stare at Peter in silence for a while. I'm sure my face is as puckered as if I sucked a lemon.

Then I ask tightly, "For how long do you plan to journey with him?"

"I don't know."

"And what about me? While you're gallivanting all over the country with the prophet, I'm here taking care of Mother and our children by myself. Is that fair?" I say acidly and hear my voice rising. "I might as well be a widow."

"Now, dear, I love you more than anything and will miss you every day, but I must do this. Please try to understand," Peter pleads. Apparently his mind is made up. He runs his hand up and down my arm to soothe me. I shake him off.

"It's a funny kind of love that chooses to leave a wife and family and go live with a stranger."

"James and John will be with me."

"That's just fine, "I retort bitterly. "So Joanna will be deserted too, and with a new baby. The hot sun must have made you four men crazy."

I jump up and stomp off in the direction of my old familiar tree, my refuge, tears stinging my eyes. Peter is casting me off as casually as he dispatched the ant.

"Miriam-bird," Peter calls after me hoarsely, "I'm sorry." But he doesn't follow me.

After a while, when I am composed, I return to the house and start preparing the evening meal. Thankfully neither Mother nor Leah comments on my red nose or the vigorous way I attack the vegetables and clatter the pots and plates.

I should feel sorry for Jesus, who has just narrowly escaped being a feast for vultures. Instead, I can only harbor dislike for this man who is stealing my husband from me. Fishing for people! Well, Jesus certainly possesses an irresistible lure. After all, he caught Peter. But it's highly improbable that Peter will be able to attract disciples. He is not exactly known for his charm.

That evening as Jesus sits with our family and the Zebedees around our meal of fish, cheese, and barley bread, I manage to be polite though cool toward him. I pour his wine and offer him second helpings, but withhold my smile from him. And I am uncharacteristically quiet, seldom joining in the conversation swirling around me. Oddly, Jesus looks at me with sympathy, as though he can see right through to my wounded heart. No doubt my bloodshot eyes betray my feelings.

My children, on the other hand, have no reservations about Jesus. Even Mark, who is usually shy around strangers, is bold enough to demonstrate his toy top for our guest. And although some adults would disregard the attention my children are showering on him, Jesus seems to enjoy it. He treats them as little people. For this, I admire him, but I still resent him.

The next morning I'm up early to fetch water from the well. To my surprise, when I step outside, Jesus, who has spent the night on our roof, is seated on the ground outside our door, his arms wrapped around his knees and a peaceful smile lighting his face. He must be watching the spectacular display of our orange-gold sunrise spreading over the Sea of Galilee as if the sky had been torched. "Shalom," he greets me. "Shalom," I return halfheartedly and start to walk on.

"Wait, Miriam." Against my will, I turn to face Jesus. In a soft, firm voice he says, "I have great need of Peter. He is just the man to help me carry out God's plan. I want you to know that I understand the pain and hardship his absence will cause you. I appreciate the sacrifice you will be making. Be assured, it will be worth it in the end. Trust me."

"Well, you just better take good care of him," I snap and quickly pivot to go on my way, balancing the water jar on my head.

Chapter 10

~~~~~~

The following Sabbath, we are gathered in our synagogue. I came reluctantly because Mother has come down with a high fever. Those of us who live by the sea are prone to such illnesses. I was afraid to leave her alone, but she waved me away. "I'll be all right for a few hours. You just go pray for me," she said weakly.

Jesus, who has spent the night at the Zebedee house, is speaking today. Confidently he explains the words of Isaiah in which the prophet foretells a Messiah who will bring good news to the poor, release captives, and cure the blind. Jesus declares, "The kingdom of God has come near. Repent, and believe in the good news." How can a mere carpenter presume to interpret Scripture and be so good at it? What's more, Jesus speaks like a prophet. Well, the prophet Amos was a sheepherder and sycamore tree farmer, so I guess it's not so farfetched that a carpenter would be called to be a prophet. And my husband, the fisherman? What plan does God have in mind for him?

Suddenly a bloodcurdling shriek splits the air and interrupts Jesus. I turn and see Azariah standing and writhing, his face distorted. Who allowed him to come in? Everyone in town knows that Azariah speaks and acts like he is out of his mind. We believe that he is possessed by a demon. Azariah shakes his fist at Jesus. Eyes blazing and with spittle flying, he yells in an unearthly voice, "Let us alone, Jesus of Nazareth! Have you come to destroy us? I know you are the Holy One of God." His bizarre words send chills down my spine. Everyone in the room is frozen with fear. I draw Mark and the twins closer to me in the shelter of my arms. What will happen next?

Jesus looks sternly at Azariah and commands, "Be quiet and come out of him!" Azariah falls heavily to the floor with a thud, and we all gasp. In a minute Azariah sits up dazed. He looks around and whispers, "What happened?"

This is the first time I've witnessed an exorcism. I'm in awe of Jesus who wields such power. No wonder Peter is attracted to him and compelled to follow him. As we exit the synagogue, the whole crowd is at fever pitch, marveling at the astonishing Jesus.

As much as I want to stay to talk with Sarah and others about the remarkable prayer service, because I'm worried about Mother, I go straight home with the children. What if Mother dies? I tend to think the worst. My father has died. I don't want to lose my mother too. She would leave a large hole in my heart and in our home. At the thought of Mother dying, I quicken my pace until the children are running and skipping to keep up with me.

Entering our house, I find Mother stretched out on her mat where I left her. Her face is flushed, and her eyes are closed. When I feel her forehead, it is damp and burning. "Leah, take the water jar and get some cool water," I say. "Hurry." When Leah returns, I soak a cloth in the water and place it on Mother's forehead. Just then Peter walks in the door followed by Jesus, Andrew, James, and John. The last thing I need right now is company. But I suppress my frustration and stand to greet them.

"Miriam's mother is suffering from a high fever," Peter quietly informs the other men.

Kathleen Glavich

Jesus crosses the room, stoops down, and takes Mother by the hand. At once she sits bolt upright, and the wet cloth falls from her forehead. Jesus helps her to stand, an awkward task for her even when she is well. I reach up and place my hand on her forehead. To my great relief, it is normal again, and her eyes have lost their frightening, bright glaze. What amazing power flows through Jesus!

"Sit down. You must be hungry. Let me find you something to eat," Mother directs the men. And she begins energetically foraging for food, as though her sickness had been only a pretense.

"Thank you, Jesus," I say with sincerity. "I don't know how you did that, but thank you." If he is trying to make me more amenable to Peter's leaving me, he is succeeding. The hard resentment in my heart toward Jesus melts a little.

That night as the sun is setting, people begin to congregate in front of our doorway. The news that Jesus, the healer, is here has spread, and people are bringing their family members or friends in hopes of a cure. First our neighbors appear. Then people from the other side of town arrive. Soon there is a constant stream of the healthy accompanying the sick, who are wrapped in bandages, leaning on sticks, or muttering nonsense. One by one Jesus gives relief to the suffering, just as he did to my mother.

I light the oil lamps and send the children to bed although they plead to stay up and watch. Still people come. The whole town must be at our doorstep, begging Jesus for help.

❧

Even though Jesus was up late last night acting as a physician, this morning when I arise at the crack of dawn and glance at the mat where he slept, I find he is already gone. He must have walked off with only starlight to guide him. Peter and Andrew, who has stayed the night, are still sound asleep. By the time I go to the well and bring back the jar of water for the day, Peter is up and moving quietly so as not to wake the children.

"Where is Jesus?" he whispers to me.

"Don't ask me. He left when it was still dark."

A young man leading an elderly man, who has the cloudy, staring eyes of the blind, and a woman leaning on a cane appear at our door. They are all strangers to me. "Is Jesus still here?" the young man inquires hopefully.

"No, he left," Peter says brusquely, disgruntled at this early morning call. The visitors' faces fall, and they walk away slowly.

Peter rouses Andrew by shaking his shoulder. "Jesus is missing, and people are already clamoring to see him. Let's get James and John and go search for him."

Andrew rubs his eyes with his fists, yawns, and says groggily, "Last night Jesus told me that he was needed to be alone for a while. He planned to go a deserted place to pray. But I don't know where he went. Maybe the place of the seven springs."

"We'll find him," Peter says confidently.

"Eat something first," I order and hand the brothers some bread and cheese. They snatch it and dash out the door.

That very day my husband leaves with Jesus and the others to travel to other towns in Galilee. Why did Jesus have to call Peter? He had his pick of all the men in the country. Surely there are others more qualified than Peter to collaborate in the prophet's mission, whatever that is. But for some unknown reason, it seems that I must be resigned to life without a husband. God, give me strength and patience!

Chapter 11

~~~~~~~~~~~~~~~~~~~~~~~~~~~~~~~~~~~~~

Some days later, when Mother and I return from the market with food for the day, to our surprise, Peter, Jesus, and a few other disciples are sitting in the courtyard, talking with our neighbors. Andrew, James, John, and Matthew aren't among them. They've probably gone directly home to their families.

"Quick, Leah," I say, handing her the money pouch. "Run over to Aunt Leah and ask her to go to the market with you. We're going to need more food for all these hungry men. Buy dates, cucumbers, onions, and lentils. Aunt Leah will help you decide what other items we might need."

Turning to Mother, I ask, "Would you please bake more bread. I'm afraid what we made this morning won't be enough."

"Who else has to feed a gang of men like this? Good thing most of the women are finished with the oven by now," Mother grumbles, not appreciating the stress of providing hospitality on short notice. But she heads to the clay jar that holds our precious barley flour. I know that she is secretly pleased to see Jesus again. After all, he cared about her enough to cure her fever without being asked.

I go out to welcome the men with a big smile, a veneer masking my true feelings. For as much as I'm pleased to see Peter again, inside my anger smolders at the certain knowledge that my husband will be running off again sooner or later.

Peter immediately springs up, gallops to me, and enfolds me in a gigantic hug that momentarily makes up for his absence.

"Well, where have you been?" I ask bluntly, struggling to keep my emotions in check.

Peter ticks off several towns in Galilee on his fingers. Nodding toward Jesus, he says, "In each town Jesus spoke in the synagogues and cured people who were possessed, just as he did here."

Hand in hand, my husband and I stroll away from the group, who are engrossed in conversation. We enter our house and sit side by side on the bench. I'd prefer to walk outside with Peter, but I know he must be exhausted from his journey home.

"Miriam-bird, that man Jesus is extraordinary. He's fearless," Peter exclaims. He runs his hand through his thick hair and then turns to look at me. "One day a leper walked right up to him. You know how lepers are not allowed to be near us for fear of contamination. Well, this leper kneels before Jesus and asks to be healed. Jesus merely touches the man and says, 'Be clean,' and the leprosy disappears. The man holds up his hands before his face and gapes as though he can't believe his eyes." Peter looks at his hands, open-mouthed and wide-eyed. "The leper's hands are no longer deformed, and the skin is as unblemished as a newborn babe's."

"Jesus touched him? Doesn't that make Jesus unclean so he can't worship in the Temple?"

"Of course! Not to mention that Jesus could have contracted leprosy himself. Everyone knows how contagious that disease is. But Jesus didn't care. It was more important to him to have personal contact with this poor sufferer. The cured man understandably was overjoyed. He had his life back: his family, his friends, his ability to work. And he can worship in the Temple again."

"Imagine how thrilled his wife was when he walked in the door after being parted from him for so long," I interject pointedly. I can identify with her because I know the pain of not having my husband around day in and day out. Blissfully missing my barb, or else deliberately ignoring it, Peter goes on.

"Jesus ordered the leper who was made clean not to talk about the miracle. Naturally the healed man couldn't keep quiet. It seems that he told everyone he met about his good fortune. As a result, so many people wanted to see Jesus that we had to avoid towns. That didn't stop people. In droves they tracked Jesus down in the countryside."

"Why did Jesus tell the man to keep his healing a secret in the first place?"

"I don't know. Maybe he isn't ready yet to come forth fully as our Messiah." Peter yawns a cavernous yawn and stretches his arms upward.

"Hmm. Maybe Jesus isn't the kind of Messiah we are expecting," I conjecture. "Or maybe he is just humble."

"Could be that Jesus doesn't want to spend all day and all night healing people. He might have other things on his agenda. Besides, it's very draining for him. Still, he doesn't refuse anyone who requests a healing, including Gentiles."

"Gentiles?" I ask, taken aback. "What Gentile would ask a Jew for a favor?"

"Antonius, our centurion. He must have gotten word that Jesus was returning to town. Today as we entered Capernaum, he approached us on the road and we came to a halt. At first I thought we were in trouble. Sword-carrying soldiers are intimidating. But then Antonius walked up to Jesus and with a grim face said that his servant was deathly ill."

"How unusual for an official like him to be so concerned about a servant that he would go out of his way to save him. Either the servant is particularly valuable, or Antonius has an exceptionally tender heart," I comment soberly.

"Tobiah and some elders watching nearby overheard Antonius and pleaded his cause. They informed Jesus that the centurion deserved this favor because he cares about us and even built our synagogue. Jesus said, 'I will come and cure him,' and took a step forward. But Antonius put up his hands to stop him and said, 'I'm not worthy to have you enter my house. Just say the word and my servant will be healed.' "

"Antonius probably knew that Jesus would be made unclean by entering the house of a Gentile."

"Perhaps, but then he compared Jesus to himself as a person of authority, as if to acknowledge that Jesus was greater than himself. Jesus turned to us and praised the man's faith. He said that Antonius had more faith than anyone in Israel."

"Peter, that includes you and me," I point out.

"Then Jesus sent Antonius home and said, 'Let it be done as a result of your faith.' Right before you returned from the market, Miriam-bird, a messenger came from Antonius and announced that the servant was healed."

"What will your Jesus do next? I admit he is a wonder-worker, but I still don't like the fact that you leave us to follow after him. We need you here."

"I know, Miriam-bird," Peter says, looking forlorn. "If only I could be in two places at once."

Once again, my protests are futile.

News travels fast in a small town like ours. Within a few days everyone knew that Jesus was back. A delegation of scribes arrived from Jerusalem, curious to hear this new preacher who has taken our northern province by storm. No doubt they intend to evaluate his orthodoxy. To my delight, my brother Nathan, who is still an apprentice, accompanied them, along with his shy but charming wife, Deborah, and we had a wonderful family reunion. The couple is staying at our house.

Right now our children are in the courtyard, playing with the children of people who have come to listen to Jesus. Their peals of laughter and squeals seep in through the open door and window. Our house is packed with men and women sitting shoulder to shoulder. I smile and wave to Aunt Leah and Uncle Joachim, who are wedged into a corner. The crowd has swelled until people surround our doorway outside, smashed together. Some latecomers in the back of that group stand on tiptoe and crane their necks, attempting to get a glimpse of the popular teacher.

After a few words about how happy he is to be with us in Capernaum again, Jesus bows his head and prays. Then he expounds on the loving care that God our Father has for each one of us. We drink in his words like thirsty camels after a long trek in the desert. At one point Jesus asks with a smile playing about his lips, "Do you know how many hairs are on your head?" There's an outburst of tittering at the comical question as everyone in the audience shakes his or her head—except Obediah, who is almost completely bald. "God knows and loves you so well that he has each hair counted. How he longs for you to love him in return!" Jesus says passionately. My mind wanders, and I start reflecting on the signs of God's love that have blessed my life, first and foremost, my good husband.

All of a sudden there is the sound of footsteps above us on the roof. Bits of dried mud and pieces of straw begin to rain down on Jesus and the folk in the center of the room. They brush off the debris, but more falls. A clod lands on Andrew's shoulder. He yelps and asks indignantly, "What's going on?"

By now everyone is looking up at the ceiling, fascinated. We see four pairs of brown hands busy creating a hole in our roof. I'm shocked. Who has the gall to damage our home like this? Jesus is no longer speaking. The room is abuzz with people speculating on what is occurring. Within minutes the opening is quite large and a brown mat appears.

"Careful. Take it slow," a voice cautions from above. Four pairs of hands lower the mat, and I glimpse a figure lying on it.

"Who is it?" I ask Peter, who has a better view.

"It's a man who used to be a construction worker, but he fell off a building project and became paralyzed from the neck down. Some of his coworkers have stuck by him all these years as though they were family. I suppose they carried him to Jesus, hoping for a cure."

"He's fortunate to have friends who go to such lengths to seek out help for him." Then I can't resist a jab at Peter and say, "I certainly hope you stay home long enough to fix the hole in our roof, dear." He just grins down at me sheepishly.

As the mat swings precariously in the air, people below it reach up to guide it to the ground, and some of the crowd indoors is pushed outside to make room. The man on the mat looks scared to pieces. When the mat and its cargo have safely landed, Jesus looks down at the man and says kindly, "Son, your sins are forgiven."

How odd. I wonder what immoral things this poor man did. At the comforting words of Jesus, he is visibly relieved, but there's a collective gasp in the room. Jesus is in trouble now. Everyone knows that God is the one who forgives sins, the only one. Does Jesus dare to usurp God's power to forgive?

Scribes behind me murmur with disgust: "How can this fellow speak this way? This is blatant blasphemy!"

Jesus turns in their direction, his brow furrowed, and challenges them, "Which is easier to say to a man who is paralyzed, 'Your sins are forgiven' or 'Stand up and take your mat and walk?' "

No one answers him. The scribes look at one another uneasily in surly silence. Then Jesus says, "So you may know that the Son of Man has authority to forgive sins ..." He faces the paralytic again and commands firmly, "I say to you, stand up, pick up your mat, and go home."

The room is as quiet as a tomb. Everyone is mesmerized by the scene before us. Keeping his eyes fixed on Jesus, the paralytic sits up, gets on his knees, and then stands, a little shakily but without any assistance. Jesus nods encouragingly. The man bends down and rolls up the mat. As he carries it out, people move to create an aisle for him. He walks as firmly as anyone else. You'd never guess that a minute ago his limbs were stiff and useless.

Everyone is staggered for a few moments. Then a man behind me cries, "Praised be God," and others take up the prayer. Tobias, shaking his head and clearly awestruck, declares, "I've never seen anything like this."

Apparently Jesus will teach no more today. He dismisses the crowd, and the people gradually disperse. The scribes slink out, talking together and shooting ominous glances back at Jesus as they depart.

I'm glad that Nathan will be staying here with us so he can get to know Jesus better. I'll be interested to hear what he makes of our guest. My brother saunters over to Peter and volunteers, "I'll help you repair the roof." The two of them go out to the courtyard to climb up to the roof and inspect the damage. Jesus goes outside too with the rest of his disciples. And I get to work sweeping up the mud and thatch that is scattered on the floor. It can be used over again.

Chapter 12

Peter hasn't come home for dinner. Earlier today he left with Jesus to go to the sea. "Don't know when we'll be back," he said breezily as he kissed me goodbye. Our life has been anything but normal since Jesus came. I never know when Peter and Jesus will be here or how many apostles will be with them. Tonight again I store the supper leftovers in pots, mostly Peter's and Jesus' uneaten portions, and then take up some sewing to work on while it's still light. My current project is a new tunic for Mark, who is growing as fast as a cucumber plant. I go out to the courtyard and join the circle of women who are sitting and chatting. The topic of our conversation, like everyone else's these days, is Jesus and his exploits.

When the other women go in for the day, I'm just putting in the final stitches. I hear male voices in our house, and Peter and Jesus emerge from the doorway.

"Well, it's about time. Are you hungry?" I ask.

"No, we dined at Matthew's house," Peter replies, smirking and watching my face for my reaction.

"Matthew? Do you mean Sarah's brother, the tax collector?" I am duly shocked.

Peter nods. "Yes, that Matthew."

Jesus strolls over to a group of men still conversing in a corner of the courtyard. Peter sinks down beside me with a grunt.

"All right. How did you ever end up at Matthew's?"

"We are walking along—Jesus, Andrew, James, John, and a number of others. As we near the border, Matthew is sitting there at his tax booth as usual. Jesus goes up to him and says, 'Follow me,' just as he did to the four of us when we were in our boats. Immediately Matthew stands, asks another man to cover the booth, and starts walking with us down the road."

"He must have heard enough about Jesus or experienced his words and deeds firsthand to be moved to follow him on the spot."

"Yes, there are other tax collectors who are with us, scoundrels Matthew knows. Maybe they told him about Jesus. In addition to these tools of Rome, there are public sinners in the group that follows Jesus."

"Why does Jesus associate with such people when everyone knows we're supposed to shun them? He's only fomenting discord."

Peter raises his muscular arms and locks his hands behind his head. He stares up into space, but I know he isn't even conscious of the graceful larks swooping overhead. "Jesus is not like us. He accepts everyone and lives above our petty rules and practices. The scribes today had the same question as you. On the road Matthew was so excited to be called by Jesus that he invited everyone to his house for dinner."

"What a mean thing to do to his wife!" Alphaeus had managed to find Matthew a spouse, a young woman named Abigail, whose family didn't have high standards.

Peter glances at me and chuckles. "Fortunately she had enough food stored up to provide for everyone," he says. "I think she also borrowed food from her neighbors, who helped serve. Well, some scribes knew that we were all dining together at Matthew's house. Afterward, as we left the house, they pulled Andrew and me aside and asked why Jesus ate with tax collectors and sinners. Jesus overheard them. Before we could answer, he explained, 'Those who are healthy do not need a doctor, but those who are sick do. I haven't come for the righteous but for sinners.' The scribes whipped around, their long robes and tassels flying, and scuttled away as though they didn't want to be contaminated by the sinners or by Jesus' wild ideas!"

So Matthew is now a follower of Jesus and gave up his ugly business. God be praised! Sarah will be ecstatic; her prayers have been answered. I can hardly wait to see her at the well tomorrow.

Not long after this, Peter comes home with other gripping news. "I am now officially a disciple of Jesus," he states. Peter can hardly contain his joy. His face is flushed and his eyes sparkle. I haven't seen him this excited since Mark was born.

Breathlessly Peter explains, "Jesus spent the night on a mountain alone, probably praying as usual. At dawn he called some of us by name to come to him: me, Andrew, James, John, Matthew, Nathanael, and a few others. As we climbed up the mountain, we debated what he could want of us. When we reached Jesus, he appointed us apostles. This means he will teach us like a master and then send us out to proclaim his message, cast out demons, and cure the sick. We'll be his agents. There are twelve of us in all."

"Just like the twelve patriarchs of the tribes of Israel," I observe, pleased with myself that I noticed the parallel. "Do you think Jesus chose twelve deliberately, or is it just a coincidence?"

"I'm sure that Jesus intended to set up that comparison. Besides, twelve is a very fitting number because it is three times four. Three stands for heaven, and four stands for earth. So twelve represents the union of heaven and earth. We apostles of earth are somehow bonded to God in heaven through Jesus. Imagine that!"

"Well, apostle of Jesus, you are still husband of Miriam, so go out and find us branches to build our shelter for the feast of Tabernacles. It's only a few days away now."

"Yes, dear, whatever you say," he says humbly, pats me on the cheek, and departs to carry out the mission that I sent him on.

In spite of my light tone, I am shaken to the bone by Peter's promotion. What will being an apostle actually entail? Obviously Peter will be away from home and his family even more often, now that he is charged with teaching others like Jesus. I've seen Jesus cast out a demon, but it's hard to believe that Peter will be able to, although he is a good man. And as for curing diseases, Peter is rather squeamish. When the children are hurt or ill, I have to do all the nursing and cleaning up. Peter can't stand the sight of blood.

As I've heard more than once, Peter thinks that Jesus is the Messiah who will save our nation. But I know the men whom Jesus chose as his leaders. Most of them are fishermen, not warriors. What chance would an army of unarmed, untrained fishermen on donkeys have fighting armor-clad, spear-bearing Roman soldiers astride horses? The picture is utterly ridiculous, and I laugh to myself. I'm afraid that Peter is going to be disappointed, or worse, killed. Now that's a sobering thought.

We've celebrated the feast of Tabernacles by eating and sleeping in our shelter for seven days. Peter constructed our booth with the help of Jesus and despite the help of Mark, who was well intentioned but mostly in the way. Our booth is sturdy and has sides of woven branches and a thatched roof. Last week, as I looked out over Capernaum, it seemed that the population doubled, for our town was crammed with booths. Each year, as God instructed, families build huts in remembrance of our ancestors' forty-year journey out of Egypt. In the desert God's people lived in tents, and God dwelt with them in a tent, or tabernacle, too.

As much trouble as it is, I look forward to Sukkot, as we call this feast. It comes at the end of the harvest season, and safe in our shelter, we praise God for providing for us just as he provided for the Israelites centuries before. I know that God is present with us too, surrounding us with his loving care, even if he is invisible. Every now and then, God gives me a sign that he is near, like the time I wanted to see a rainbow and at the end of the day a bow shimmering with vivid colors appeared arching over our town—a double rainbow at that!

A few days ago Peter, Jesus, and the other apostles left to visit a nearby village. I gave Peter a hard time when he told me they were leaving again.

"How long is this going to go on?" I asked, shoving a loose strand of my hair back under my veil.

"Miriam-bird, I have no idea," Peter said patiently.

"How would you like it if one day I left you here with the children and Mother and I went off to follow … John the Baptist? Huh?" I know my face looked as forbidding as a thundercloud.

Peter only laughed at my preposterous scenario. "I wouldn't like it one bit," he said. "Just as I don't like it when I must leave you to follow Jesus."

I sighed, felt my expression soften, and kissed Peter good-bye.

Now I'm gathering up a load of clothes to wash in the stream before the sun gets too hot. Pounding clothes with a rock is as strenuous as hauling in a net filled with fish. On top of the pile is Peter's old cloak, dingy and stained from weeks of life in the open air. I wonder how often it rained when he slept outside wrapped in it. During the past few days, Mother and I made a new one for Peter, so his old one will be downgraded into new cleaning cloths.

I'm headed for the door when Salome appears there. Bursting with excitement, she says, "Miriam! Rebekah! You'll never guess!" As she speaks, her hands dart here and there, the bangles on her bracelets jingling. "The mother of Jesus, Mary, with a few of his relatives arrived here from Nazareth. They'll be staying at our house. You and the children are invited to come to supper tonight to meet them. Joanna and Dorcas will probably come too. Can you bring some bread and fruit?"

"Sure, Salome. We have plenty because we stocked up for the men."

"What's Mary like?" Mother asks, taking a break from grinding wheat on our millstone. She's as curious as I am.

"Well, she's quiet and calm. Not like me. She is an older, female version of Jesus. She has the sweetest face. I'd say she's about my age, forty-five years old. And Mary's not snooty, even though her son is famous. Immediately she offered to help prepare supper. She's washing the vegetables as we speak."

"I look forward to meeting her," I say sincerely.

"See you later then. So long." And with a quick wave Salome dashes off.

That evening when we arrive at the Zebedee house, Salome ushers us to where Mary is seated in the courtyard. When she introduces us to Mary as Peter's family, the mother of Jesus gracefully stands. She is shorter than I, slender, and has remarkable large, lustrous eyes. As we cheek kiss on both sides, Mary says in a honey-toned voice, "So you are one of the long-suffering wives whose husband follows my son all over creation. I understand that Peter, along with Salome's two sons, is one of his closest friends." Firmly holding me by my shoulders, she looks deeply into my eyes and says, "I'm sure that is not easy for you. May God give you strength." Her love washes over me like a welcome spring rain after a draught. This gentle older woman has touched something in me, and unexpectedly I feel like I am going to cry.

After supper, Zebedee entertains the few male visitors, while we women sit chatting and the children play. We know that Mary is a widow. Her husband, Joseph, died several years ago. Mary sorely misses her son. When we speak of him, her face breaks into the most beautiful smile, but her eyes reflect sadness.

"Jesus lived at home with me for thirty years before he left to be a preacher," Mary reveals. "Now I mostly have to be content with news of him brought by travelers," she says with a little sigh.

"I'm surprised Jesus isn't married. He'd make some woman a fine husband," Salome says.

"And a good father to children," I add, remembering how lovingly Jesus treated my children. "But Jesus is so consumed with doing God's work that I don't think there's room in his life for a family."

"Speaking of children, I had the fright of my life yesterday," Joanna says. "While I was in the market with little Reuben, he wandered off, following a cat. One minute he was at my side, clutching my robe while I spoke with a seller, and the next moment he had vanished. Frantic, I ran through the crowd, calling his name. It seemed like an eternity before I spotted him, hunched down and petting this calico cat that was curled up and purring under a vendor's tent."

"My son was missing once for three days when he was twelve years old," Mary volunteers.

"Three days!" we exclaim.

"How horrible! What happened?" I ask.

"Joseph, Jesus, and I celebrated the Passover in Jerusalem as usual. For the journey home, we joined a large caravan headed for Nazareth. Jesus wasn't with Joseph and me, but we didn't worry. We figured he was with friends or relatives—probably with other children his age—who were traveling with us. At the end of the first day, we started to look for him. We went from group to group, asking, 'Have you seen our son, Jesus?' At each No my panic grew. Eventually we concluded that Jesus was left behind in Jerusalem. So we made the daylong trip back to the city, traveling alone."

"You were fortunate that you weren't attacked," Sarah comments.

"Yes, God was with us," Mary says, nodding slightly.

"I bet you scolded Joseph," Dorcas remarked. That, no doubt, is what she would have done. Only the grace of God keeps her marriage from unraveling.

"How could I scold my husband? I was as much to blame as he was. And I think he felt even worse than I did. He kept muttering, 'Fine protector I am.' Most of the time we walked on in silence, praying. I don't think I ever prayed so hard in my life.

"In Jerusalem, first we returned to the house where we had stayed during the feast, but Jesus wasn't there. Then we inquired at the houses of relatives. No one was able to give us any leads as to our son's whereabouts. We searched for three days in vain."

"Your nights must have been long, sleepless agonies, Mary." I empathize with her. "I'd be imagining the worst—that he was kidnapped and sold as a slave, that a wild beast had attacked him, and so on."

"Yes, I was terrified," Mary admits, wringing her hands at the painful memory. "Then as a last resort, Joseph and I walked to the Temple, and there, to our utter amazement, was Jesus. He was sitting and talking with the teachers. They were gathered around him as though he were Solomon himself."

"I would have wrung his neck," Mother comments.

"I asked Jesus how he could have caused Joseph and me so much distress. But Jesus seemed surprised that we were upset. Looking at us with big, innocent eyes, he said a strange thing. He asked, 'Didn't you know that I must be in my Father's house?' "

"His Father's house?" Joanna asks. "The Temple is God's house, and God is everyone's Father, but why would Jesus expect you to know that he would be there?"

"I have no idea," Mary replies with a shrug. "There are many things about my son that puzzle me. Anyway, once we were back home in Nazareth, Jesus was a good boy and never did anything like that again."

The following afternoon Peter, Jesus, and the men are home again. They show up sporadically, like stray dogs. I never know when to expect them. Peter regaled us with stories of astonishing things that Jesus did. What I found most interesting was their journey through Samaria. We Jews avoid this land between Galilee and Judea because Samaritans are our sworn enemies and are ritually unclean. We go miles out of our way to skirt Samaria.

Jesus, however, boldly led the apostles right through Samaria, as though they were all invisible. While Peter and the other apostles went in search of food, Jesus rested by Jacob's well. When the men returned, they found Jesus conversing with a Samaritan woman, one who had been married five times and now lived with a lover! But as a result of Jesus ignoring taboos and taking time to talk with her, many Samaritans came to believe that he is the Messiah. It's almost as though Jesus planned to meet this woman.

Right now people are crowded into our small house. Most of them are strangers to me. They have traveled from other towns to hear Jesus, the phenomenon who has settled in Capernaum.

Jesus starts telling a parable about sowing, something many people in Capernaum can identify with. Here the barley harvest is followed by the wheat harvest. Until a few weeks ago, every day farmers could be seen bent over in the rolling fields of ripe wheat. They hewed down the stalks of wheat, gathered it up, and took it to be crushed on the threshing floor. On days that were favored by a breeze, the farmers tossed the crushed wheat into the air. The chaff was blown away, leaving the grains that become our daily bread.

Jesus says, "Some seed fell on the path and was trampled on and eaten by birds. Some fell on rock and withered for lack of water.

Some fell among thorns that grew and choked it. But some seed fell on good soil and produced a hundredfold."

No seeds can produce a hundred times as much. Jesus exaggerates, which is characteristic of a good storyteller. Then he says, "Let anyone with ears listen." That, I think, is the key to his parable. God's words are like seeds, and they can bear fruit in our lives or not, depending on the quality of our hearts. When I hear the Torah read, when I hear Tobiah and others explain it, and, yes, when I hear Jesus teach, if I'm not open to the words and don't put them into practice, they are fruitless, sterile. In response to Jesus' parable, I send up a prayer: "O God, make my heart good, fertile ground."

All of a sudden there's a commotion among the listeners closest to the door. A voice rings out, "Jesus, your mother and your brothers are outside. They want to see you." Jesus doesn't stir. His eyes roving over the crowd, he states solemnly, "My mother and brothers are those who hear the word of God and do it."

Mother, who is seated next to me, gasps. Scowling, she quietly says to me, "Those aren't the words of a good son. He's disowning his family and replacing them. What an insult! That sweet mother of Jesus must really be hurt."

"Don't worry, Mother," I reassure her, patting her shoulder. "I'm certain that Mary and the relatives of Jesus hear and obey God, probably even more than we do."

Last night all of the apostles sailed across the lake with Jesus. Surprisingly, they are back already today. Would that all their trips were this short! People who spotted their boat approaching spread the word. Men and women stream past our house on their way to the sea, as though fish were being given away free. I decide to join them, if nothing else, to welcome Peter home.

On the shore a crowd engulfs Jesus and his companions. Everyone is jockeying to get a better view. Now I know how fish must feel squashed together in a net. "Jairus is here. Make way for Jairus." These words travel through the crowd, and people move back to allow our synagogue official through. He is a stocky fellow with a florid face. But today he is as pale as a corpse, and sweat is running in rivulets down the sides of his face. Peering through the spaces between the heads before me, I anxiously watch what unfolds.

When Jairus reaches Jesus, he falls in a heap before him and begs over and over, "My daughter is dying. Come lay your hands on her so that she may live." Jessica, the daughter of Jairus, is a lovely twelve-year-old, almost ready for betrothal. Jairus and his wife, Ruth, must be heartbroken. Jessica is their only girl among five boys.

Jesus stoops and, taking Jairus by the arm, helps him to rise. As the two walk toward us, the crowd parts again like the Red Sea. We all follow Jairus and Jesus up the road. Jairus is well-liked, so people are not only curious but concerned.

A small woman threads her way through the people. Although she is heavily veiled, I know it is Bernice. How dare she come here? The woman has been cursed with a flow of blood for twelve years, which makes her unclean. Anyone who comes in contact with her also becomes unclean. Standing on tiptoe, I keep my eye on her. Bernice manages to get right behind Jesus. Then she dips down out of sight. Suddenly Jesus halts and looks over his shoulder. His eyes survey the mob behind him, and he calls out, "Who touched my cloak?" Guffawing, Peter asks, "With all these people pressing in on you, how can you say, 'Who touched me?' "

Mentally I urge Jesus, "Don't stop now. Jessica is dying. Go. Go." Jairus has to be exasperated and in agony. Every moment of delay brings his daughter closer to death.

I catch sight of Bernice again now. She is trembling. Her veil and robes quiver as though a stiff breeze is blowing them. She must be the culprit. Jairus, who knows of her condition, will probably scold her soundly before everyone. How humiliating. But then Bernice falls to the ground before Jesus. Looking up at him, she admits tremulously,

"I touched your cloak, and I'm healed! I am healed!" Tears pour down her face, but she is radiant with joy. Jesus calls her Daughter, as though she is precious to him, but I doubt that he even knows her. He explains that her faith has cured her. The plucky woman has stolen a cure!

As Jesus is sending Bernice off in peace, a man and a woman who have been hurrying toward the crowd reach Jairus and deliver the cruel news that his daughter is dead.

"Too late!" Jairus cries out in anguish and buries his face in his hands. Everyone falls silent. My heart fills with pity. I know how excruciating it would be if Leah died. Instantly Jesus puts his arm around Jairus's shoulders and says, "Don't be afraid. Just believe."

Jesus wants only Peter, James, and John to come to the house with him and Jairus. I guess Jesus is going to support Jairus as he suffers the shock of seeing the stilled body of his beloved child for the first time and faces his grieving wife. Some onlookers drift away, not expecting any more excitement. After all, the girl is dead. But others of us mill about on the street not far from Jairus's house, talking in hushed tones. Eventually a professional mourner, her clothing ripped as a sign of grief, ambles away from the house and toward us, carrying her flute at her side. "What's going on at Jairus's house?" someone from the crowd shouts out.

"That man Jesus chased us away," the mourner says, clearly disgruntled. "He told us the girl wasn't dead but only sleeping. Can you imagine! As if someone sleeps without breathing and without a heartbeat. What a fool!" She goes on her way cackling and shaking her head.

Eventually the two people who told Jairus that his daughter was dead approach us running, the chunky woman trying to keep up with the man. "Jessica's alive! She's alive!" the man shouts with elation as soon as he is within hearing distance. There is a collective sigh of relief, followed by cheers and exclamations of amazement.

The man draws nearer and explains, "Peter told us that Jesus took her by the hand and said, 'Young lady, get up.' Color came back into her face. Jessica took a deep breath, smiled at Jesus who was smiling at her, and sat up. Still holding onto Jesus' hand and gazing at him, she stood. Then she started walking around the room, and Jairus and his wife rushed to embrace her."

Out of breath, the woman reports in spurts, "Jesus told them … to give Jessica something to eat, … I guess to show everyone … that she isn't a ghost." Or, I speculate, because he realized she must be hungry after her illness.

As far as I know, no one has raised the dead since the prophet Elijah brought a widow's son back to life. Who is this man whose very clothes emanate the power to work miracles? Some people in town are calling him insane. Pharisees and scribes say that he is possessed. But, in my opinion, Jesus is a very holy man—a holy man, however, who is a rival for Peter's affection.

Chapter 13

As Mother and I putter around the house, I notice that an unusual number of people are rushing by outside. Suddenly Sarah, Joanna, and Dorcas come to the door, laughing and talking excitedly. "Miriam, Jesus is speaking about a mile from here. We're going to listen to him. Come with us," Sarah invites, her eyes sparkling. "C'mon." She beckons with her hand.

I glance at Mother, and she waves me off blithely, saying, "Go. Go. I'll keep an eye on the children."

I slip on my sandals and join the women. We hurry toward the hill known for having the most scenic view of our sea. By the time we arrive, people are already listening to Jesus, who is seated on a rock. He is like a teacher with an exceptionally large and varied group of students. Peter and some other apostles I recognize surround Jesus as though they are his bodyguard. I can see my husband's face. He is gazing at the teacher with rapt attention and adulation.

"There's room for us by Bernice," Dorcas says, pointing to a space some yards from where we stand. Trying to disturb as little as possible, we carefully wend our way around a few groups of people as hastily as we can, approaching the woman who surreptitiously got herself a cure. When she turns and sees us, a smile lights her careworn face. She pats the ground beside her, and the four of us sit down.

Leaning towards us, Bernice whispers, "You missed some beautiful words. Jesus told us the secrets to true happiness. He described the kind of people who will make it into God's kingdom, like the gentle, the merciful, and peacemakers."

"We can ask our husbands to fill us in later," I say. I don't want Bernice to continue talking. I'd rather hear Jesus himself.

Although we women are settled on the fringe of the crowd, every word reaches our ears. Sound carries very well in this natural amphitheater.

Jesus looks around intently at all of us and proclaims, "You are the light of the world. A city built on a hill won't be hidden." He points to the town of Safed, which clings to the side of a nearby hill. It is visible even during fog and at night. "Let your light shine so that others may see your good works and glorify your heavenly Father," Jesus exhorts us, lifting his hand to the azure sky.

After a good two hours, Jesus is finished preaching and the crowd is trickling out onto the main cobblestone road. On the way home we discuss the extraordinary new teachings we've just heard.

"I thought it was challenging enough to try to follow the hundreds of laws the Pharisees spelled out, but Jesus is even more demanding," Dorcas remarks, shaking her head.

"Yes, but can you imagine how wonderful life would be if everyone practiced what he said?" Joanna asks. "People wouldn't be angry or mean, and if they were, they would make up quickly. I hope my mother and her sister take his words to heart. They haven't spoken to each other for years."

"I like the idea that men should not lust after women. I hate it when I walk past a group of men and I'm subjected to lewd comments, even from married men," I comment.

"What's even better would be not having to worry that our

husbands will divorce us on a whim," Sarah says. "Of course, Miriam, Peter would never divorce you. He worships the ground you walk on. I wish my husband felt the same way about me," she adds with a sigh. She and Eli have a strained relationship. For one thing, he makes her give a strict accounting of everything she spends. It's not as though they are poor.

"The concept that we should be so honest that we don't need to swear is freeing. It would mean that we could trust everyone—the vendors, our neighbors," Joanna observes.

"Our husbands," Dorcas interjects with a snort, and we all laugh.

The crowd around us on the road is dwindling as people go their separate ways.

"The thing that I find difficult to understand is that Jesus expects us to love our enemies. Our old law proposes we retaliate in kind, an eye for an eye, a tooth for a tooth. That makes sense and sounds just. Besides, our natural reaction when people hurt us is to get back at them and not forgive them," I muse.

"Right," Dorcas says. "And we try to avoid those who hurt us, not love them."

"Well, Jesus did say we are to treat others the way we want to be treated, and I guess that includes enemies too," Joanna points out.

We walk on, each pondering Joanna's conclusion. I think of how Jesus used his power to help Antonius although he was a Roman soldier, one of our oppressors. Jesus modeled what he preached to us. The image of Ebinezar pops into my mind. He is the crotchety old man in our neighborhood who is always complaining that Mark and the twins are too noisy. Hmm. What would happen if some day I would be magnanimous and take him a particularly delicious stew?

Dorcas breaks the silence. "I wonder how the Pharisees in the crowd felt when Jesus told us to give alms, pray, and fast secretly, not like hypocrites. Everyone knows how ostentatious the Pharisees are. The words of Jesus were thinly veiled criticism of them."

"I bet they were grinding their teeth in anger," Sarah remarks.

We arrive at my house first and continue our conversation at the door, reluctant to part.

"By the way, Miriam, what does Nathan think of Jesus?" Joanna asks flatly.

"He was home when Jesus cured the paralytic in our house. I suppose Nathan doesn't know quite what to think yet. He does admire Jesus for his power and kindness, but he is puzzled by his teachings. They aren't always in line with what Nathan is learning in Jerusalem."

Placing her hand over her heart, gentle Joanna comments, "I love the way Jesus talks about God as our loving Father. Isn't it comforting to think of God as someone who will give us what we ask for and who cares for us more than he cares for the birds and the flowers?"

"I wish I could remember the words of the prayer Jesus told us to pray, the one that begins, 'Our Father,' " Sarah says wistfully.

"I'm sure our husbands know it by heart. We can ask them to teach us. Sarah, when I learn it, I'll teach you," I promise.

"Great, Miriam. All I remember is that in the prayer we ask God to forgive us the way we forgive others."

"I'm not sure I want to pray for that," Dorcas says dryly. "I'm not very forgiving sometimes, like when James insults my cooking."

"Speaking of cooking, I need to start preparing dinner," I state, although I hate to withdraw from the discussion. "I'm so glad you invited me to go with you." We say our goodbyes. I wave, touch our mezuzah, and step into the house.

Jesus is staying with James and his family tonight. For once we have Peter all to ourselves at dinner. Looking around at my family, I thank God for them. I wish we could always be together like this. On the other hand, being a close follower of Jesus might turn out to be a privilege for Peter. This new prophet, teacher, and healer has all the earmarks of the Messiah. His teaching today had us all spellbound, and stories of his mighty deeds continue to multiply. One miracle in particular struck me because I fear the sea that is known to drown fathers, brothers, and husbands. I worry every time Peter goes out fishing. A while ago Peter told us that they were in his boat on the Sea of Galilee and Jesus was sound asleep on a cushion when a ferocious storm struck. Their lives were in jeopardy. Jesus was so dead tired that the waves washing overboard and the strong winds didn't disturb his sleep at all. Only when the petrified men shook him did he awake. Jesus simply commanded the storm to be still, and instantly everything was calm. Incredible! Then Jesus scolded his apostles for not trusting him enough. He expected them to know that he wouldn't let any harm come to them.

We are halfway through our meal of pickled fish and wheat bread when Mark begs, "Father, tell us again about how Jesus made the storm stop."

"I have a better story now," Peter says, setting down his hunk of bread. "Actually two stories. One is about fish and bread, like we're eating tonight. It happened right after King Herod had John the Baptist killed."

The prophet's end was outrageous, a tragedy that horrified not only his followers but Jews throughout Israel. King Herod married Herodias, the wife of his brother Philip, who was still living. How Philip can tolerate this, I'll never know. John, like any prophet worth his salt, dared to tell Herod that his adultery was wrong. Herodias resented John for this, and the upshot was that Herod had John imprisoned. Then one day Herod threw a birthday banquet for himself. When he was too drunk to think straight, the king foolishly swore that he would give the daughter of Herodias anything up to half his kingdom just because her dancing pleased him. I suppose her indecent dress and suggestive moves titillated this vulgar man. At Herodias's instigation, the girl asked for John's head on a platter.

Herod was too weak to refuse her gruesome request in front of his high-ranking guests.

This is the kind of man who is in charge of our province under the Roman's rule. He takes after his father, the madman Herod I, who killed three of his sons, his favorite of his ten wives, and other relatives, prompting Caesar Augustus to quip sarcastically, "It's better to be Herod's pig than his son." Because we Jews don't eat the meat of pigs, Herod wouldn't have slaughtered one.

Peter continues, "Jesus was very sad when he heard about John's death. He wanted us to go away with him to be by ourselves. I can understand that. John and Jesus were related, not only biologically but spiritually. Jesus loved John, who was like an advance guard for him. Jesus once said that no one born was greater than John."

"Knowing what happened to John, Jesus must wonder about his own future. After all, he is as bold as John was in exposing people's faults and calling for repentance," Mother remarks.

""His popularity spawns enemies too. I worry about him," Peter admits, stroking his beard and gazing into the distance. After a pause, he takes up his story. "So that Jesus could mourn in peace, we went by boat across the sea to a deserted place. To our dismay, a crowd had gotten wind of our plans and was already there, hoping to hear Jesus. Despite his personal sorrow, he couldn't disappoint them. Jesus began teaching as always. Gradually more people arrived, swelling the crowd to more than five thousand. When it grew late, we urged Jesus to send the people away to eat. We apostles were hungry too. At first, believe it or not, Jesus told us to feed the people."

"You've got to be kidding," Mother cries, her hands flying into the air. "That's ridiculous. How could you feed so many? You're not millionaires."

I added, "And since the place was deserted and it was late, where would you find a market to buy the great quantity of food needed?"

"That's what we wondered. We wanted to please Jesus, but we

were stymied. Then Jesus sent us into the crowd to scrounge for food. We did as he said, even though we knew our quest would be futile."

"Sometimes I have my doubts about Jesus," I say. "He's not normal. I don't know why you insist on keeping him company."

"Just listen," Peter said, looking annoyed. "Andrew discovered a boy named Ignatius who had five loaves and two dried fish in his basket. The lad let us take the food, and we brought it to Jesus. He smiled and directed us to have the people sit on the grass in groups. The twelve of us spread out and managed to arrange the people in pods of hundreds and fifties. Once they were organized, Jesus blessed and broke the bread. Then he divided it and the fish among us to distribute to the people. At first we felt foolish."

"Father," interrupts Leah, "wasn't Jesus asking you to do the impossible?"

"You would think so," Peter replies. "But as we went from group to group, handing out the bread and fish, somehow more always appeared in our baskets. Everyone was flabbergasted, including us, although by now we should be used to miracles. When everyone had filled their stomachs, Jesus told us to collect the leftovers. We actually ended up with our twelve baskets full. I can't explain it."

"Oh, Father!" our Rebekah exclaims, her brown eyes wide with wonder. "Do you think Jesus could fix it so that you don't have to fish and Mother and Grandmother don't have to make bread anymore?"

Peter throws back his head and roars with laughter. "You can ask him, honey. No telling what he will do."

"I wish I could have been at that picnic," Mark says wistfully.

"I wish you could have been there too, Son. Well, Jesus sent us back to Capernaum across the sea, while he remained with the crowd. During the night as we rowed, a strong wind arose. It stirred up waves that crashed against our boat as if they were determined to destroy it. Drenched and driven off course, we struggled just to stay afloat, bailing water and pulling on the oars with all our might. Then in the early morning, we saw the dim shape of a man walking straight toward us on the rough sea as though it were dry land."

"On the water? Was it a ghost, Father?" Leah asks in an awed whisper.

"At first we thought so," Peter says. "We were scared to death and started screaming. But then the figure spoke. He said, 'It is I. Don't be afraid.' The voice sounded like the voice of Jesus. So to prove it, I told him to have me come to him over the water."

"Peter!" I can't help exclaiming. "Whatever possessed you to ask such an idiotic thing?"

"Ah, but here's what happened," he says and stands. "I swung my legs over the side of the boat and carefully lowered myself onto the sea, holding onto the boat with one hand." Peter demonstrates his actions for us. "The water felt solid, as firm as the ground you're sitting on now. I let go of the boat and, with my eyes fixed on Jesus, headed toward him, walking on top of the sea." Peter began walking gingerly across the courtyard. "But then a gust of wind came and whipped my robes so they flapped like a banner in a sharav. Turning my head, I saw the high waves on every side. I panicked, and just like that I began to sink." Peter slumps.

"Oh, Father!" the twins squeal in horror, their hands at their mouths. Mark is as popeyed as a frog.

"It's all right. The story has a happy ending," Peter assures us. "With the water almost waist high, I cried out, 'Lord, save me.' And Jesus caught my arm flailing in the air and pulled me back up. He chided me for not having enough faith. Hand in hand we walked back to the boat and climbed in. Just like that the wind stopped. As you can imagine, I was stunned and awed but also embarrassed. You should have seen the looks on the faces of the other men." Brushing the dust off the bottom of his clothes, Peter rejoins us.

Mother says, "Peter, if I hadn't been cured by Jesus and hadn't seen him cure the paralytic here with my own eyes, I would never believe your outlandish tales."

"And if this walking on water miracle hadn't happened to me, I probably wouldn't have believed it either," Peter adds, shaking his head.

Who is this Jesus who has such power? Is he from another world, perhaps an angel in disguise? He does superhuman things, yet he is as human as we are. He eats my food, sleeps at our house, and laughs at Peter's jokes, even the bad ones. If Jesus truly is the Messiah, as Peter believes, when will he establish his kingdom on earth? And when he does, will he appoint my husband as a governor or maybe prime minister? Now that would truly be a miracle.

Chapter 14

~~~~~~

On the Sabbath, Jesus again is on the seat of Moses teaching. More people than usual pack our synagogue, including some neighbors I haven't seen here in a long time. Mother leans toward me and mutters, "All you have to do to attract people here is fill their stomachs." She is referring to the miracle of the loaves that Jesus performed yesterday.

This recent miracle prompts someone to mention the miraculous manna that came from heaven to feed our ancestors in the desert. Jesus states in a firm voice that the bread God sends from heaven gives life to the world. A voice calls out, "Always give us this bread," and several people echo it. Jesus points to his chest and declares, "I am the bread of life. Whoever comes to me will never be hungry." Now that is an appropriate metaphor for a great teacher. The words of Jesus satisfy our search for truth like bread satisfies our hunger. We especially eat up his teachings in the form of parables about things in our daily lives. For instance, one day as Jesus watched Mother knead dough, he said, "The kingdom of heaven is like yeast that a woman puts into dough. A little bit permeates the whole batch."

Today, after pausing to give us time to digest his words about being the bread of life, Jesus makes an astounding statement. He claims that God sent him from heaven to bring us eternal life, and everyone who believes in him will possess it. Immediately some people, presumably Nazarenes, start mumbling, "How can Jesus be from heaven when we know his parents?" Jesus surely hears the criticism, yet he merely repeats that believing in him leads to eternal life. Then he says, "I am the living bread from heaven. Whoever eats this bread will live forever. The bread I will give for the life of the world is my flesh."

These words are startling and bewildering. Jesus speaks as though we are to consume him not metaphorically but literally! The assembly erupts. People ask one another what in the world Jesus means. I wonder if he will take back what he said, or at least explain it so it is not so offensive. But no. Over the hubbub Jesus shouts stridently, "Unless you eat the Son of Man's flesh and drink his blood, you have no life. Those who eat my flesh and drink my blood have eternal life." My heart sinks. I notice Tobiah is rolling his eyes in disbelief. Jesus goes on to say that if we eat his flesh and drink his blood we will remain in him and he in us.

Unfortunately, it seems that those who consider Jesus insane are correct. He is telling us to eat him. What utter nonsense. We Jews abstain from consuming the blood of animals because it is their life, which belongs to God. How then are we expected to drink a person's blood? That's repulsive. It sounds as though Jesus is telling us to become cannibals.

My four children are looking at me with questioning faces. I just shrug. Mother is shaking her head in dismay.

At our supper that day everyone is as subdued as last Thursday when Leah found her bird's lifeless body on the bottom of its cage. We're all disappointed that Jesus is not proving to be all that we hoped he would be. We are almost finished eating when Peter strides into the courtyard. Jesus isn't with him. He's probably been invited somewhere else, although I wonder who would invite him now.

"What's to eat? I'm famished," Peter announces. He sits down in his usual place and playfully punches Mark in the arm. "Stew," I say, and push the pot in front of him. "It's still warm." Curiously, Peter doesn't seem at all disturbed by the atrocious message of Jesus today.

I broach the subject. "So, Peter, what do you think of what Jesus said at the synagogue?"

"Well, many of his disciples were put off by his words. In fact, they decided to stop following him on the spot."

"I don't blame them," I say. "This talk about eating and drinking him is upsetting, to say the least. Will you be staying at home now?" I ask, hoping with all my heart that Peter will say yes.

"Actually, afterward, when people were walking away, Jesus asked us twelve apostles if we wanted to leave him too. His question hung in the air. Then I spoke up for all of us and asked, 'Lord, to whom can we go?' I declared that he has the words of eternal life and assured him that we believe he is the Holy One of God."

"But, Peter," Mother says, "what about his insisting that we only have eternal life by consuming him? Doesn't that bother you?"

"At this point," Peter states, looking at us with great seriousness, "I'd trust Jesus with my life. I don't always understand what he does or says. This last teaching about food is a total mystery to me. Maybe it will come clear in time. We just have to have faith." With that, he tears off a piece of bread and begins chewing it.

Peter's attitude is a comfort to me. I now know Jesus personally as a kind, gentle man who has extraordinary gifts. Why should I let one concept that is beyond me damage my opinion of him? Why should I let it destroy my hopes that he is our Messiah? I will be patient and see what unfolds. In the meantime, I will just have to put up with

Peter, the head of our household, leaving us to fend for ourselves, not to mention abandoning his marriage bed for long stretches of time.

The next morning Peter and the other apostles are set to leave Capernaum with Jesus to visit other villages. As I'm packing some food for Peter and Jesus, I ask, "How will you survive on the road? None of you are earning money. Do you have time to prepare good meals for all of you?"

"Don't worry," Peter says. "Several women who were healed by Jesus will be traveling along with us. They are so grateful to him that they've become his disciples. They'll support us financially and see that we don't starve. One of them is from Magdala, and another is the wife of Herod's steward Chuza."

"I'm jealous of those women, Peter," I say as I hand him his heavy basket. "If I didn't have four children to take care of, I'd be right with you too."

"I know that," Peter replies, patting my cheek. "I'll be carrying you in my heart every step of the way, Miriam-bird." He suspends the basket from his broad shoulder. "I'll take Jesus his basket. He's saying goodbye to Tobiah and Jairus."

"Children, your father's leaving," I call, and they run in from the courtyard.

"Be good for your mother now," Peter orders them. "I'll miss all of you." He bends to kiss each one.

"Do you really have to go, Father?" Mark asks, looking forlorn, his bottom lip protruding.

"Really, Mark," Peter says.

As I hug my husband goodbye, I can't help sighing. I wonder how long I must wait this time before I feel his soft beard rubbing against my face and hear him call me Miriam-bird again. Peter picks up the basket for Jesus and walks out. Until he returns, no matter how many people show up for supper, our house will seem very empty to me.

Chapter 15

~~~~~~

ccounts of the adventures of Jesus and his apostles trickle into Capernaum over the next several weeks. Each morning while drawing water at the well, we women share what we heard. The wives and mothers of the apostles are especially eager to hear news of the Capernaum men. As far as we know, they have traveled to Tyre, to the Decapolis across the Jordan River, to Bethsaida, to Gennesaret, and to Caesarea Philippi. In addition to teaching, Jesus cured scores of people. Among them was even the daughter of a persistent and quick-witted Gentile mother. It was Dorcas who shared this piece of news with us.

One day as Jesus and the apostles walked along, a Canaanite woman, a Gentile, shouted to Jesus to cure her daughter. When Jesus proceeded on, deaf to her cries, she hounded the group, constantly begging for help like a hungry two-year-old and annoying the apostles. I can just see Peter and the others covering their ears and asking Jesus to put a stop to the racket. Finally the woman ran up to Jesus and knelt before him, blocking his way. Jesus started to go around her, saying, "It isn't fair to throw the children's food to the dogs." The Gentile woman dared to retort, "Even the dogs eat the scraps that fall from the table." Jesus laughed heartily and praised her faith. He granted her wish. This event gave me and the other women great satisfaction. A woman, a Canaanite at that, persuaded Jesus to change his mind! She made him realize that his ministry was not only for Israelites, but for Gentiles too.

That episode reminds me of a parable Jesus told about praying without ceasing. In his story a woman relentlessly pursues a judge, imploring him to hear her case. Finally, to keep her from punching him in the eye, he heeds her desperate plea. In real life Jesus was the one pursued, and the Canaanite woman had her request answered. The only thing that I would ever hound Jesus for is to give me back my husband!

I saved a piece from Peter's old cloak and stashed it with my jewelry in my special chest. On days when I particularly miss him, I just like to hold it. Although it may sound silly, touching this soft, worn material that Peter once wore every day connects me to him and comforts me.

At long last the tired travelers descend on our house again, and Mother and I scurry to find refreshments. We serve some dried figs and diluted wine. The apostles rest on the floor in various positions, as if they were ragdolls just dropped from the sky. Some sit cross-legged, some have their knees drawn up, and others, probably the most fatigued, stick their legs straight out, as if they lack the energy to sit otherwise.

Jesus bluntly asks, "What were you arguing about on the way here?" The apostles look sheepishly at one another. John even blushes. No one answers, and yet Jesus says, "Whoever wants to be first must be last and the servant of all." Either he overheard them talking or read their minds. Then Jesus stands and calls, "Mark, come here a minute." My son, who by now adores Jesus, runs to him, and Jesus lifts him up. Holding Mark in his arms, Jesus says, "Whoever welcomes a child like this in my name welcomes me, and whoever welcomes me, welcomes the one who sent me." He swings Mark around and my son squeals with glee. Then Jesus gently lowers Mark to the ground.

I like how Jesus used Mark to get his point across. No one is of less account than children. They have no rights and are regarded merely as part of the family workforce. But Jesus again challenges our mindset by calling us to treasure children.

From what Jesus just said and did, I surmise that the men had been discussing which of them would have the highest places in the kingdom Jesus will establish. Apparently, according to Jesus, the best leaders are not the ones who are full of themselves and lord it over others, but the humble ones who regard other people as valuable and worthy of their caring service. That certainly doesn't describe Herod or some of the Pharisees I've heard of who love to attract attention and have people kowtow to them. Nathan said that some Pharisees in Jerusalem have phylacteries, prayer boxes, tied to their foreheads so wide that they must get headaches from them. And the tassels on their robes are so long that they almost trip on them. Looking at the hard-working men spread across my floor in their rough, homespun clothes, I scarcely think they will turn into egotistical, overbearing leaders.

Gradually the apostles who have homes and families in Capernaum depart. Peter leaves to check on his boat. Jude, the other James, Judas, Thomas, Nathaniel, Simon, and Jesus stay in the house, where it is somewhat cooler than outside. Mother, Leah, and I begin to prepare supper for everyone.

Before long, Peter comes bounding into the house as if something important happened. He goes to where Jesus is sitting with his back leaning against the wall. Before Peter can say a word, Jesus looks up at him and out of the blue asks, "What do you think? Do kings take tributes from their children or other people?" Peter, looking perplexed, responds, "From others." Then Jesus tells him that in order not to cause offense, he should cast a hook in the sea and open the mouth of the first fish he catches. There he will find a coin to pay the tax for both of them.

My dear, foolish husband actually picks up a line and hook from the corner and leaves again. He doesn't seem to realize that Jesus is teasing him.

"What was that all about?" Judas asks Jesus.

"The collectors of the Temple tax stopped Peter and asked if I paid the tax," he replied. "No problem."

I wonder why Jesus didn't just ask Judas for the tax money. He is the one in charge of the group's finances, although in my opinion Matthew would have been the better choice. Besides, Peter told me once that sometimes money is missing. Judas makes me uneasy. He has shifty eyes.

A short time later Peter returns, carrying the line with a fish dangling on the end. He nods to Jesus and says, "It's taken care of." He removes the fish from the line and hands it me to clean while I stare at it, my mouth agape, looking like a fish myself. The other apostles appear equally amazed. "Let's go outside," Jesus simply says, and all the men get up off the floor sluggishly, as though they were twice their age, and file out to the courtyard.

Mother tugs on my sleeve and whispers, "Did you notice that Jesus told Peter what to do before Peter had a chance to explain that he met the tax collectors?"

"I did. It's as if this carpenter knows everything."

"He also knows the fishing trade. Tilapia carry their young in their mouths until they are grown. Sometimes they carry pebbles and other things. So it's possible that a fish picked up a coin. But how did Jesus know that it would have the exact coin for the tax?"

"And how did he know that Peter would catch that very fish?" I add. "Wouldn't it be nice if Jesus taught Peter his secret for finding money-bearing fish?"

After our meal of lentil soup supplemented by Peter's fish, when the children are presumably asleep with Mother on the roof, and

Jesus and the apostles are in the courtyard, Peter and I are alone in the house talking. I am leaning comfortably against his arm, and our fingers are entwined.

"I know that tonight you can't give me an account of everything that happened on your journey. You can hardly keep your eyes open. So just tell me one thing that stands out in your mind, Peter."

Peter turns to face me. I notice that my husband is aging. Little lines fan out from the corners of his eyes now. "What is most memorable is an event we aren't supposed to talk about, but I know I can trust you to keep it secret." My curiosity is piqued.

"I won't tell a soul, dear, not even Mother. I promise."

"All right, Miriam-bird. One day Jesus asked me and James and John to climb Mount Tabor with him to pray."

"Why does he call the three of you apart? Don't the other apostles feel bad, especially your brother, Andrew?"

"I don't know why Jesus seems to favor us. But I suppose the others respect his right to choose whom he wishes. Everyone is more attracted to certain people than to others. Why is Sarah your best friend and not the other women in town? Who knows?" Peter shrugs and continues the account I'm dying to hear.

"The long path up the mountain was steep and winding, and the sun was beating down on us. I was worn out by the time we reached the flat top and Jesus had us stop. We three sat on the ground, overcome by drowsiness and fighting off sleep. Jesus, however, wasn't fazed by the arduous climb. He walked a short distance away from us and began to pray. As I watched him, he changed. His face shone bright as the sun, and his clothes turned dazzling white. I was almost blinded by the light. I rubbed my fists in my eyes to make sure I wasn't seeing things. The three of us stood and stared. Then Moses and Elijah appeared talking with Jesus. They too were radiant."

"How did you know they were the prophets Moses and Elijah? You've never seen them."

"Because as they spoke, they called one another by name."

"What were they talking about?"

"Something about the exodus, the passing over, that Jesus would undergo in Jerusalem. I was overwhelmed by the unearthly sight and terrified, but I didn't want it to end. I blurted out, 'Lord, it is good that we are here' and offered to set up tents for the three of them, like we build for the feast of Tabernacles. While I spoke, a bright cloud came over all of us. Then I heard a voice proclaim, 'This is my Son, the beloved. I am well pleased with him. Listen to him!' I don't think it was Jesus' father Joseph speaking, but his heavenly Father. At the disembodied sound, the three of us sank to the ground with fright. My heart was beating so fast I thought it was going to burst. When I finally dared to look up again, only Jesus was there, the Jesus we knew."

"Maybe you were dreaming," I suggest helpfully.

"How could all three of us have the same dream? Besides, as we walked down the mountain, Jesus told us not to tell what we saw until after he had risen from the dead."

"Risen from the dead? What on earth does that mean?"

"James, John, and I talked about it, but we can't figure it out. Some days before that odd experience, we were in Caesarea Philippi. Jesus asked us who people were saying he was. We told him John the Baptist and other prophets. Then he gazed at us with his piercing dark eyes and asked, 'Who do you say I am?' Of course, I said spontaneously, 'You are the Messiah, the Son of the living God.' "

"The others think so too, don't they?"

"Yes, but I was the first to say it. Jesus exclaimed that the Father in heaven revealed that truth to me. Then he said some mysterious things. Making a play on words, he said that he will build his church on me, the rock, and hell will not conquer it. He also stated that he will entrust to me the keys to the kingdom of heaven. I don't have a clue what that means, but it sounds like I have a promising future. I felt proud to be singled out and honored by Jesus that way."

Peter frees his hand from mine and drapes his arm around my shoulder. He gives a dry laugh.

"Unfortunately, my pride was short-lived. Jesus then predicted something upsetting. He said that he would suffer a great deal from the religious leaders and even be killed—but would be raised on the third day."

"Oh, my!" I say, my hand flying to my mouth.

"I was shocked too. How could Jesus foretell such awful things about himself? Since I consider myself his friend, I pulled him aside and demanded, 'Stop talking like that. This must never happen to you.' Looking at me with sad eyes, Jesus shook his finger at me and scolded, 'Get behind me, Satan!' He actually called me the devil and a stumbling block. He accused me of setting my mind on human things, not divine things. I was mortified to be reprimanded by Jesus, my hero. Though I meant well, he regarded me not as a friend, but as a tempter. Thankfully, the others didn't hear our exchange."

"Well, Jesus chose you to witness his glory on the mountain afterward. That indicates that he still sees you as special. He must have forgiven you."

"You know, I asked him once how often we should forgive someone. I thought I was being generous in suggesting seven times. But Jesus shook his head and said, 'Not seven times, but seventy-seven times.' "

"In other words, always," I say. Then I warn Peter, "Judging from how scribes and Pharisees react to Jesus, his dire predictions may very well come to pass. He may be killed. As for his rising, no dead person has come back to life except those he raised. How can Jesus claim such a fantastic thing for himself?"

"Who knows?" Peter says, scratching his head. "After admonishing me for balking at his tragic destiny, Jesus called everyone around him and suggested that we might share his fate. He said that we who follow him need to take up our cross, meaning we need to suffer.

But then Jesus posed a paradox. He promised that if we lose our lives for his sake, we will find them."

At my husband's somber words, I shiver although the night is warm. Peter draws me closer. "Whatever happens," he says, "I'm sticking with Jesus."

"And I'm sticking with you," I say fiercely and rest my head on his shoulder. But I'm not so sure how I feel about Peter's hero now. The Messiah should be victorious, triumphant, and surrounded by glory and honor. All this talk about suffering, being killed, and losing your life is disquieting. Besides, I don't like the way Jesus treated my husband.

Chapter 16

Jesus and the apostles did not remain in Capernaum long this time. Early one morning, they packed up and left. To our surprise Salome accompanied them. She decided to follow Jesus and help provide for him, her two sons, and their companions. Zebedee stayed behind to run the family fishing business. I wonder how he feels, being deserted by his wife and sons. Probably the same way I feel without my husband—lonely, hurt, angry, frustrated. I have a name for Dorcas, Joanna, and me, who stay home in Capernaum while our husbands minister: gospel-widows. And I'm only twenty-seven years old!

Week follows week. Without Peter near me, the long days drag on in monotonous repetition. Halfheartedly I fetch water from the well, go to the market, make bread, prepare two meals, and then go to sleep. Only my children keep me from sinking into depression. Leah will soon be of marriageable age. I'm becoming familiar with the eligible young men in Capernaum so I will be able to suggest possible husbands to Peter when he comes home. The twins, Rebekah and Sarah, are at a stage where they are constantly squabbling and sometimes fighting. Yesterday I heard an ear-piercing scream, and the girls came running into the house, both of them bawling.

"Mother, she pulled my hair," Rebekah accused, rubbing her head.

"I was only paying her back," Sarah sniffs. "She called me a fat pig," Sarah sticks out her tongue at her sister.

"Stop it this minute. Why can't you two get along?" I ask, exasperated. "I can't be with you every minute. When you are grown up, you'll be sorry you acted like this. Now dry your tears and ask Grandma if she can use your help getting supper ready."

At times like that I really miss Peter. He could be a support to me. He could also be there for Mark, who needs a father. Jonah and Uncle Zebedee do their best to cover for Peter, but it's not the same. We're like a ship without a captain, and some days I feel lost at sea. While I'm mulling over our family situation, Tobiah appears at the door. He clasps a small scroll in his hand.

"Shalom," he greets me with a smile. "I have something to brighten your day."

"Shalom, Tobiah. What is it?"

"A traveler from Jerusalem brought this letter for you from Peter. Would you like me to read it to you?"

A letter? I'm thrilled. Why hadn't Peter ever done this before? "Oh, yes, please. Would you like some wine and cheese?"

"No, Miriam. Esther just served a big meal. Let's go outside. My old eyes don't work so well in this dim room."

We leave the house and walk to where a fig tree grows. Its leaves shaped like little hands seem to be clapping with delight for me. We settle on two large rocks that are conveniently under the tree, and Tobiah proceeds to unroll the scroll. He clears his voice and begins to read, and I hang on every word:

"My dear Miriam, peace to you, our children, and our parents. My heart longs to be with you, but I know I must stay with Jesus. We have been traveling through Judea and on the other side of the Jordan River. Jesus

continues to captivate people with his stories. The other day to teach love of neighbor, he told of a man who was on his way to Jericho and was beaten by robbers, who stole everything from him. As he lay at the side of the road, two religious leaders walked by and ignored him. But then a Samaritan stopped, treated his wounds, and took him to an inn, where he cared for him. The next day the Samaritan paid the innkeeper and offered to pay more on his way back if it was required. What a stroke of genius to make a Samaritan, our enemy, the hero of the story and a model for us. Jesus is a teacher unlike any other. I'll have other parables to tell you when I see you.

"I hope Mark helped Uncle Joachim build your tent for the feast of Tabernacles this year. We were at the Temple for that feast. Jesus spoke there so powerfully that everyone is debating whether or not he is the Messiah. The Pharisees are disturbed by his behavior. They sent Temple police to arrest him, but the police were so impressed by Jesus that they disobeyed orders! At the festival the priest pours water on the altar. Jesus picked up on that symbol of water and invited everyone who thirsts to come to him. Also, giant candelabras are lit each night at the Temple. It's a glorious sight. With those candles as his backdrop, Jesus claimed, 'I am the light of the world.' These are the kinds of statements he makes that simply infuriate the Pharisees. Once when Jesus said, 'Before Abraham I am,' people construed this as blasphemy and tried to stone him."

Tobiah stops and explains, "By saying 'I am' Jesus is using for himself the name of God that was revealed to Moses. It's little wonder that the Pharisees think he is blaspheming. There is only one God." Then he lifts the scroll and continues reading.

"Then too the religious leaders find fault with the marvelous things Jesus does. Recently he cured a young man blind from birth. Instead of being awed, the Pharisees criticized Jesus for healing on the Sabbath! They didn't believe the man was blind from birth, so they questioned his parents. The mother and father, however, were afraid to testify to the cure and risk being banned from the synagogue. The Pharisees have decreed that any person who calls Jesus the Messiah will be put out of the synagogue.

"I could go on and on about Jesus, which I would love to do. But I'm

mainly writing because I have a request, Miriam. More than anything I would like you to come to Jerusalem this year for the Passover."

"Drop everything and come to Jerusalem?" I cry. "I've never been out of Capernaum, except for a wedding in Bethsaida. Is Peter forgetting that we have four children? Even though my husband has grown in years, he hasn't grown in common sense."

"Wait, Miriam," Tobiah says, holding up a hand. "Peter has written more about the trip."

"I'm sure your mother and aunt and uncle wouldn't mind watching the younger children. You could bring little Leah with you. I know that Tobiah and Esther are planning to come to the Holy City. You could travel with them. Don't hesitate to go through Samaria. That way you can cut off thirty miles from your journey. We are staying at the house of John Mark's mother. He and she are both disciples."

At this, Tobiah looks up and says, "It would be a pleasure to have you go with us. I have kind relatives in Jerusalem who would provide accommodations for all of us."

"I'll think about it," I say. Who knows? Maybe Peter's outrageous proposal is possible after all. "What else does Peter write?"

"The other day something occurred that confirmed that following Jesus is the right thing for me. A wealthy young man asked Jesus how he could have eternal life. Jesus told him to keep the commandments, to sell all he had, give the money the poor, and follow him. The man walked away sadly, and Jesus remarked that it is difficult for a rich person to enter the kingdom of God. Boldly I said, 'We have left everything and followed you. What will we have?' Jesus replied that when he is seated on the throne of glory, we will sit on twelve thrones. We will receive a hundredfold and inherit eternal life.

"So, my dear wife, I look forward to rich blessings in the future. And my greatest wish is that you too will enjoy them. Please tell the children I love them and give them a hug for me. You are all in my thoughts and prayers every day. I hope to see you in a few weeks. Your loving husband, Peter"

Tobiah rolls up the scroll and hands it to me. "I'll let you know our arrangements, Miriam. I do hope you decide to go with us."

My heart has already made up its mind. I will be reunited with my husband. What's more, for the first time I will see the Holy City, the hub of our religion and our worship. My head, though, is whirling with questions and arguments against the long journey. I thank Tobiah and walk back to the house lost in thought.

Two weeks later I return from the market to find my brother Nathan and Deborah in the house talking with Mother and Leah. "Well, what brings our scribe home?" I ask as I deposit my basket on the ground. Nathan and I meet in the middle of the room and hug.

"I just wanted to see your faces again," Nathan says, cupping my face in his hands. I go over to embrace my sister-in-law, who grants me one of her rare smiles. "It's so good to see you, Deborah."

"Tell me, Nathan, do you ever see Peter in Jerusalem?" I inquire, hoping to learn how my love is faring.

"Now and then. He belongs to the group that follows Jesus as their teacher, and Jesus has been in Jerusalem quite a bit lately, where he is a major attraction. Everyone, myself included, goes out to listen to Jesus, which makes the Jewish leaders as nervous as dogs during a storm. They fear that the Romans will suspect that Jesus is inciting the crowds against them like other rebels did. You never know when Rome will clamp down on all of us again. Also, I'm afraid Jesus is getting deeper and deeper into trouble with the authorities."

"What do you mean?" Mother asks, looking worried.

"You might find this hard to believe, but Jesus brought back to life a man who was dead for four days."

"You're right, Nathan. I'm skeptical," I say, wrinkling my nose. Three days is how long we wait before we check a tomb to make sure someone is really dead. By then in our hot climate a corpse would be decomposing and smelling really bad.

Nathan ignores me. "Peter told me that the man, Lazarus, and his two sisters are good friends of Jesus. Their house in Bethany, two miles east of Jerusalem, is a favorite place for Jesus to visit. When Lazarus became sick, his sisters sent for Jesus, but by the time he arrived, Lazarus was entombed. Peter said that Jesus loved Lazarus so much that he cried right along with the sisters."

"Wait, didn't Jesus know he had power to raise Lazarus? Why was he crying?" Mother asks perceptively.

Deborah says, "I think Jesus felt sorry that Lazarus had to undergo death. He probably also was moved at the sight of the sisters and friends of Lazarus, who were grieving keenly."

"In any case," Nathan continues, "at the tomb, Jesus simply prayed and commanded, 'Lazarus, come forth,' and the dead man staggered out of the tomb with his wrappings partly hanging off him."

"Can you imagine how his sisters felt?" Leah asks, all agog.

"Can you imagine how Lazarus felt?" I add.

Nathan says, "The Pharisees hate Jesus for that stupendous feat because it makes him even more popular. Now the authorities are determined not only to get rid of Jesus, but Lazarus as well."

"That makes no sense," Mother states flatly. "Seems to me that everyone would want to be a friend of Jesus after that miracle, even thickheaded Pharisees."

Peter's letter mentioned people attempting to stone Jesus and police trying to arrest him. Nathan's news about the mounting danger that Jesus is in only increases my apprehension. If the religious authorities are bent on killing Jesus and Lazarus, won't they want to do away with the chief followers of Jesus, the apostles, too? I feel as though an icy hand is squeezing my heart.

"I've made up my mind," I abruptly announce. "I'm going to Jerusalem for the Passover this year. And, Leah, you're coming with me."

Chapter 17

Our caravan to Jerusalem comprises twelve adults, far fewer than if we had chosen to take the longer route across the Jordan River to avoid Samaria. Providentially we are traveling in the spring when it doesn't rain.

During the first part of our trip through beautiful southern Galilee, I am fresh and eager to travel. How delightful to see new views of our sea and hilly vistas I had only heard about. Some fields are a riot of colorful wildflowers. We pass the twin mountains on either side of a volcano crater near the town of Hittin. People call them horns, but from the east I think they more closely resemble the perky breasts of a young girl. Supposedly Moses' wife, Zipporah, and his father-in-law, Jethro, are buried at the foot of one peak. We travel past Tiberius, the town Herod founded as Galilee's new capital. When a cemetery was discovered in it, we Jews regarded the city as unclean and refused to live there.

To break the monotony of most our journey, I devise games for Leah. "See that rock in the distance," I say. "How many steps do you think it will take to reach it?" Leah suggests a number and so do I. Whoever is closer to the right answer wins. Sometimes we vie to see who will be the first to see a certain thing like a house, a butterfly, or a bird on the ground.

As we journey south into Judea, the terrain becomes rockier and browner. It takes longer to navigate the paths between hills and crags. I envy our donkey who plods on with ease despite being burdened with our bundles of clothes and food supplies. How many battles were fought on this land. Perhaps King David once trod on the very road where we now walk. These cave-pocked hills may have sheltered him when he fled from mad King Saul's jealousy-driven wrath. According to prophecies, the Messiah will be one of David's descendants. I wonder if Jesus is from the house of David.

One afternoon, as we trudge along, I spot a herd of strange, white animals in the distance, drinking from a stream. "Look over there, Leah," I say, not wanting her to miss this sight. "We don't see those in Capernaum."

Leah peers in the direction I am pointing and then stands still in amazement, her mouth wide-open. "There must be at least ten of them!" she says with glee. "What are they?"

Tobiah overheard us and explains, "Those are oryxes. See how their long horns shoot straight up into the sky? If you view the animal from the side, the two horns look like one. The Greeks believe there is a one-horned horse somewhere called a unicorn. The oryx resembles it."

Those unusual beasts give me another idea for passing the time. "Leah, why don't we praise God for the different creatures he put on this earth? Let's take turns naming one, and then after each we can say, 'Blessed be God.' " She nods, so I begin, "For oryxes," and we both respond, "Blessed be God." Soon Tobiah and Esther join in our litany.

After four days and countless steps, Leah and I reach Jericho, the city of palms. Only two more days and we will be in Jerusalem.

Because it is near Passover, many people are en route to Jerusalem. Only males within a twenty-five mile radius are obliged to celebrate the feast in the Holy City, but many people, like us, make the pilgrimage anyway. For that reason Tobiah has a difficult time finding a place for us at an inn in Jericho. The third one he tries is near the center of town. Thankfully the innkeeper welcomes us and leads us to a shelter in the courtyard where Tobiah, Esther, Leah, and I will spend the night.

The innkeeper's wife, a plump woman with a large brown mole marring her cheek, is high-strung and garrulous. I certainly wouldn't want to be married to her. Not blessed with children, she hovers over her guests as though she were personally responsible for them. Like a mother hen, she goes from shelter to shelter, giving directions and bestowing advice. She seems to take a liking to Leah, for she parks at our shelter and chatters on, while I want nothing more than to rest a bit. Maybe she'll notice my eyes glazing over.

Suddenly I hear the name Jesus, and my ears perk up. "Yes, indeed, he was here a few days ago," says the innkeeper's wife. "He and his motley crew. As they strolled down the street, you would think Emperor Tiberius himself was paying us a visit. People dropped everything and ran to see him. Naturally I did too. The funniest thing happened. One of our tax collectors, Zacchaeus by name, is so short that when he sits at his tollbooth, about all you can see is his head. Anyway, as we were crushed together on the road waiting for Jesus to pass by, Zacchaeus was jumping up and down like a grasshopper, trying to get a glimpse of Jesus. The people in front of the poor man towered over him and blocked his view. But Zacchaeus was clever. He scurried down the road as fast as his short legs could carry him. There, where the crowd was thinner, he scrambled up a sycamore tree and lay in wait. Imagine that! Our pompous dignitary acting like a kid." The woman slaps her thigh and giggles.

I can't help laughing at the picture that her description evokes in my mind. Leah, Tobiah, and Esther are chuckling too.

"Zacchaeus probably thought he was as invisible as a chameleon among the leaves. Not so. When Jesus and his entourage reached the tree, he looked up with a big grin on his face, ordered Zacchaeus to come down, and invited himself to dinner at Zacchaeus's house. Naturally we were shocked. Didn't Jesus know what a crooked, unscrupulous man Zacchaeus was? But Zacchaeus fooled us all. He said he would give half of his possessions to the poor and repay anything he stole fourfold!"

"We're from Capernaum," Tobiah says, "and Jesus has done many wonderful things in our town too."

Before Tobiah can elaborate, the innkeeper's wife gushes on. "Right before that, outside of town Jesus cured a blind beggar. Bartimaeus sat in his customary spot at the side of a road. Hearing the hubbub of a crowd, he asked what was happening. When he learned that Jesus was coming, he raised a ruckus calling out, 'Jesus, Son of David, have mercy on me.' Embarrassed bystanders tried to make Bartimaeus shut up, but he was as determined as a trapped quail struggling to get free. He only shouted even louder. Jesus stopped in his tracks and had the blind man walk over to him. Then Jesus asked Bartimaeus what he wanted him to do for him. Now wasn't that a silly question? When Bartimaeus implored, 'I want to see,' Jesus cured him and said it was because of his faith.

"Bartimaeus follows Jesus now. You might say it was love at first sight. Someone pointed Bartimaeus out to me when we were waiting for Jesus to come by. The beggar was the only man not wearing a cloak. He had cast it off in his eagerness to get to Jesus. People said it wasn't worth saving anyhow because it was so threadbare. Well, I better see to our other guests. Enjoy your night here." And she waddles off to the next shelter.

Well, that answered my question about the lineage of Jesus. He is a son of David. That fact sparks in me a glimmer of hope that he is the Messiah. Now if only Jesus weren't born in Nazareth. Scripture names not Nazareth but Bethlehem in Judea as the birthplace of the ruler we hope for. That town is known as the city of David, for it was where the great King David was born and lived his early life.

The next morning I am ascending to Jerusalem, lumbering up a slope on very sore and dirty feet, my eyes fixed on the dry, rocky ground. How the Israelites survived forty years trekking through the desert I'll never know. Come to think of it, all but two of them died before they reached the promised land! I start reflecting how I could be home right now doing nothing, seated on a cushion of lush Galilee grass beneath an almond tree bejeweled with beautiful white blossoms.

Leah's voice rings out jubilantly, shattering my daydream, "I see it! I see the Temple!"

I shift my focus from the dirt path before me to the horizon. There, miles away, I can barely see a shining structure surmounting a peak. The Temple is still under construction, one of Herod's many grandiose projects to ingratiate himself with us and inflate his reputation as a builder. I have to give him credit though. He actually managed to shave off the top of Mount Moriah and extend its surface by adding a retaining wall and landfill.

As we draw closer, I can tell that even from a distance the Temple is magnificent. It is a vision of pure, white marble and gold, gleaming in the sunlight. Nathan told me that the Temple has an enormous marble-paved courtyard, gigantic doors, and numerous marble pillars thirty-feet tall. Some of the massive stones in the wall around the Temple weigh more than four hundred tons. This place must please our God who dwells in its Holy of Holies room. I wish I could go into that dark room and be in God's presence if only for a minute. But the high priest alone dares to enter and just once a year on the Day of Atonement to burn incense and sprinkle blood from a sacrificed animal.

Near the end of the day, the whole city of Jerusalem lies glowing before us like a lovely vision of heaven. The setting sun is painting its limestone buildings a rosy-golden hue.

"Isn't that an awesome sight, Mother?" Leah says, her face rapt and radiant. "I'm so glad you let me come with you."

"And the best part is that your father is there somewhere waiting for us," I say with a sigh.

The leader of our caravan, who has been this way numerous times, begins to sing Psalm 122, one of the fifteen pilgrim psalms. His bushy beard may be grizzled, but his voice is strong and vibrant as he sings, "I was happy when they said to me, 'Let us go to the house of the Lord!' " We all join in as we approach the Holy City. Our road leads through a dense grove of olive trees on the appropriately named Mount of Olives.

We pass the Jewish cemetery on the Mount, where hundreds of tombstones are painted white to help us avoid touching them and becoming unclean. I ask why the deceased there weren't buried in caves. Tobiah explains, "Those who follow the teachings of the Pharisees, and not the Sadducees, believe in an afterlife. They think that when the Messiah comes, the resurrection of the dead will begin on the Mount of Olives. One of their goals in life is to buried here, but the cost can be prohibitive."

A little later we merge with the throng pouring through the Damascus Gate in the city wall. Then we are standing in Jerusalem. Hordes of pilgrims have come days earlier because before celebrating Passover, everyone needs to be purified in one of the thousand mikvahs around the Temple. Many of these pilgrims are staying in tents pitched on a plain like an army camp.

Tobiah leads us through the maze of streets toward the home where we will stay. With people jostling us on both sides, it is sometimes a challenge to keep him and Esther in sight. I grasp Leah's hand firmly, as though she were a three-year-old. It's a relief when Tobiah stops before a door in a gate and says, "Whew! This is it." He sounds as relieved as I am that our journey is ended.

Tobiah's relatives, Seth and his wife, Lydia, couldn't be more gracious in welcoming Leah and me, who are strangers to them. Their two little boys with large brown eyes greet us politely, as though they are used to having guests. From the looks house with several rooms, the family is well-to-do. The centerpiece of the main room is a large, and, I presume, expensive, decorated vase, overflowing with an array of fresh, variegated flowers. My twins would have that vase reduced to shards in no time. Although I've only been away from my young ones a few days, I miss them already.

I definitely want to make myself presentable before I encounter my husband for the first time in months. While Leah and I are freshening up, splashing our faces with the water that was considerately placed in the guest room and combing our hair, Tobiah and Seth are out in the city, trying to locate the house of John Mark's mother. Jacob has a pretty good idea where it is. Leah, Esther, and I are relaxing and getting acquainted with Lydia, our charming hostess, when the men return.

"We're in luck," Tobiah nods to me. "Jesus, your husband, and the other apostles are not far from here. If you're ready, we can go to them now."

"Let's go," I swiftly say. Tobiah, Leah, and I step out into the dusk. The streets are narrow, more like alleys, and clogged with people and cats. Occasionally we must walk up or down stone stairs. We pass vendors seated on rugs next to their wares or standing next to carts loaded with bread and fruit. The evening is as busy as a day back in Capernaum.

At a door right on the street, Tobiah stops and knocks. A young man, clean-shaven and handsome, opens it and says jovially, "Ah, Tobiah, we've been expecting you. Welcome!" Tobiah introduces us to John Mark, who escorts us into a long narrow room with earthen walls. A woman swathed in black is bent over an oven, stirring a pot of something tantalizingly spicy and steaming. John Mark says, "This is my mother, Mary. She has her hands full providing for Jesus and his friends, but she loves to do it." Mary, looks up, her full, pleasant face wreathed in smiles, and nods to us. "Mother, this is Peter's wife, Miriam, and his daughter, Leah." "Welcome," she says. "Rhoda there helps me." Mary gestures toward a tall woman placing dates on a plate. The servant looks up and gives a quick smile. "Peter's been counting the minutes to your arrival," she says.

Beyond Mary I immediately see Peter seated with Jesus and the other apostles, and my heart leaps. He rises and strides toward us. Once more I am engulfed in the familiar arms of my husband. "I'm so glad you came, Miriam-bird," he says fervently. Then Peter releases me, all too soon, and hugs Leah. Over her head he says to Tobiah, "You are so good to bring my girls with you from Capernaum."

We walk past Mary to where the others are. I notice that Jesus looks tired and rather distracted, but his face lights up when he greets Leah and me. After acknowledging the other apostles, I move to a corner of the room with Peter and Leah, where we settle down apart from the rest. Peter inquires about our journey, and we tell him that thankfully it was uneventful. Leah delights in describing the innkeeper's wife in Jericho. Our daughter must be as fatigued as I am, but now that she is with her father, she is wound up and as bubbly as a little brook.

Leah says, "We heard about what Jesus did for Bartimaeus and Zacchaeus."

"And Lazarus," I add. "I guess it pays to be a friend of Jesus. If that fantastic miracle doesn't convince people that Jesus is the Messiah, I don't know what will."

Peter says wistfully, "I wish you could have been here a few days ago when we first entered Jerusalem. Jesus had us bring him a young donkey. Somehow he knew exactly where we'd find it."

"I'm not surprised," I comment. "But why a donkey? It would have been more fitting if he had you bring him the white steed of a conquering hero to ride into the city."

"That's not his way. Several of us laid our cloaks on the donkey's back to make it more comfortable, and Jesus mounted the animal and headed toward Jerusalem. People spread their cloaks and branches on the road before him. They hailed him, shouting, 'Hosanna. Blessed is the one who comes in the name of the Lord.' We processed down the Mount of Olives. Oddly, instead of smiling and waving to the crowds, Jesus looked grim. At one point he halted and stared at the city beyond the Kidron Valley. I was startled to see tears trickling down his face. Then Jesus made an ominous prediction. He said that Jerusalem would be totally destroyed by enemies because it didn't recognize what God was doing on earth."

"Let's hope he's wrong," I say earnestly. "It's hard to imagine our immense Temple being demolished. Besides, how could God allow his house to be destroyed?"

"Well, the Babylonians destroyed the previous one," Peter reminds me. "Anyway, the crowd swelled and accompanied us through the city entrance known as the Beautiful Gate. All the time they were cheering as though Jesus were Caesar."

"Or the Messiah," I proposed quickly. "*Hosanna* does mean 'save us.' It sounds as though Jesus is going to establish his kingdom any day now. Nathan told me that the authorities are determined to kill Jesus. How did they react to the crowd's enthusiastic reception?"

"I bet they were jealous," my astute daughter says, pinpointing what I think is the main source of the leaders' animosity toward Jesus. Because his popularity is eclipsing theirs, they consider him not only a threat and a nuisance, but their rival.

Peter says, "Some Pharisees told Jesus to order his followers to stop their acclamations, but Jesus wasn't fazed in the least. He said that if we were silent, the stones would shout out!"

"That comment surely didn't make the Pharisees happy," Leah notes wryly.

"They were even angrier the next day. We went to the Temple. The Court of Gentiles is the large plaza where the animals for sacrifice are sold and the coins acceptable for the Temple donation are exchanged for foreign ones. When we entered it, Jesus went berserk. He started chasing everyone out, the buyers and the sellers, and he overturned tables. Coins were rolling noisily on the marble floor, and doves were squawking and flapping their wings. It was chaos."

"Meek and mild Jesus did that? I thought he preaches against anger," I say, rather mystified.

"He does," Peter confirmed. "But his rage was justified. When everything calmed down, Jesus started teaching. He quoted Scripture, saying, 'My house shall be called a house of prayer for all peoples.' Then he accused, 'You have turned it into a lair of thieves.' Evidently the vendors were gouging people from afar who needed to purchase animals, and the moneychangers were cheating them."

Shaking my head, I say, "I'm sure that the Pharisees are furious. I can just hear them asking, 'What right does that man have to create such a scene in the sacred Temple? That's our domain.' "

"It was the apostle Jude who recalled the line in Psalm 69 about being consumed with zeal for God's house. Those words certainly applied to Jesus on the day he purged the Temple. Too bad that our Jewish leaders don't appreciate his zeal," Peter states.

"I fear for Jesus' life and for your life too," I say tremulously.

"You and me both," Peter admits, his dear face full of concern.

Chapter 18

~~~~~~~~~~~~~~~~~~~~~~~~~~~~~~~~~~~~~~

Peter asked me to assist with the Passover meal for Jesus and his disciples. The mother of Jesus, Mary of Magdala, and Salome will also help. Peter and John were charged by Jesus to do most of the preparation. They found a room, purchased lambs, and had them sacrificed in the Temple. They bought herbs, wine, desserts, and other foods needed for the meal. But we women are needed to cook, serve, and clean up. I have a premonition that this will be no ordinary meal, but a prelude to events that will greatly impact our lives. The upsurge in the acts of Jesus that provoke the establishment seem to be barreling toward some climax.

When we arrive at the large upstairs room reserved for the meal, I am pleased to see that Mary, the mother of Jesus, is already there. She greets me warmly with the customary cheek kisses, as though I were a beloved relative. In the cooking area Salome enthusiastically greets me and then introduces me to the lovely Mary of Magdala, a follower of Jesus who was healed by him. I start arranging the bread on a large plate.

A few hours later, Jesus and the twelve are reclining together around a low table. John and Judas, not Peter, are in the privileged places on either side of the master. We servers carry the first course of food out to the table. As I walk back to the cooking area, Mary of Magdala grabs my arm and says, "Jesus would like a basin, a pitcher of water, and a towel." I locate a basin and a long towel easily. Mary dips a pitcher into the large water jar in the corner of the room and brings it up dripping with water. She briskly wipes off the pitcher with a cloth, and I hand her the towel. Then she drapes it over her arm and carries the pitcher and basin to Jesus.

Curious, we pause in our work to see what will happen. Jesus stands and removes his long, outer garment. All eyes are on him. Clad only in his short tunic, Jesus ties the towel around his waist, pours the water into the basin, and stoops before Thomas. He washes Thomas's dusty feet with his hands and dries them with the towel. Jesus moves from one apostle to the other, while everyone watches in complete silence, stunned. Until he comes to my husband, that is.

Peter impulsively protests, "You will never wash my feet!" Foot washing is a servant's job. I can understand why Peter would object. He adores Jesus. But Jesus says, "Unless I wash you, you cannot be my disciple." Peter declares with typical exuberance, "Not just my feet but my hands and head too!" And he plunges his feet into the basin, splashing water onto the floor. As Jesus washes Peter's feet, he says, "A person who has bathed only needs to wash the feet. You are clean, but not everyone." He looks about at his friends and his eyes rest on Judas, whose face is inscrutable. Then Jesus puts his outer garment back on and returns to his place.

We resume our tasks. As I circle the table, checking to see where food needs to be replenished, I catch snatches of the conversation. Jesus says in a somber voice, "You are to do as I did. You are to wash one another's feet." I know he doesn't mean this literally. He is instructing the apostles that they are to serve one another. Ha! We women are servants day in and day out.

I'm busy every minute, but I freeze in place like a statue when a shadow seems to cross the face of Jesus and he hurls a thunderbolt. He announces, "One of you will betray me." The apostles look helplessly at one another. John is reclining next to Jesus with his head against Jesus' chest. Peter raises his eyebrows and turns up his hand, signaling to John to ask who the betrayer will be. John asks, and Jesus states that it is the one to whom he gives bread. Then he dips a piece of bread into the olive oil and hands it to Judas. I hear him say in a low voice, "Do quickly what you are planning to do." Judas blanches, snatches the bread, and bolts from the room.

I don't know what to make of what just transpired, but I go about filling wine cups, removing empty bowls, and setting out the other traditional foods. My husband's voice reaches my ears, perhaps because I am so attuned to it. He asks Jesus, "Where are you going?" I sidle up to their table to eavesdrop. Jesus tells Peter that he can't follow him now, but he will later. Peter asks, "Lord, why can't I follow you now? I will go to death with you." Jesus says, "I have prayed that your faith may be strong and that you might strengthen the others." He smiles thinly. "Before the cock crows, you will deny knowing me three times." Bewildered, Peter insists, "Even if everyone else deserts you, I never will." The other apostles assert, "Neither will I."

Peter is ready to die for Jesus. Would he die for me too, I wonder. I'm embarrassed for my husband. He makes a courageous declaration of love only to be slapped down. Doesn't Jesus believe him? Is he mocking Peter? But what if Jesus really can see the future and Peter does deny him? Maybe that will destroy their relationship, and Peter will come home for good. In my heart I hope this won't occur. All my misgivings about Jesus have evaporated like dew under the hot sun. I've come to respect Jesus, yes, to be in awe of him. I want Peter to remain his friend. Without Jesus, Peter will be a broken man.

The rest of the evening is a blur for me. Jesus speaks at length to the apostles, while I and the other three women collect the leftovers and wash the dishes. Drying a plate, Salome asks me, "Did you hear

Jesus say the bread was his body?" "No," I reply. "Well, I was nearby when he did so. It was right before he passed the bread around. Then he said the cup of wine was his blood of the covenant poured out for many. He passed the cup around to his disciples too. Weren't those strange words?"

"Yes, but remember, once when Jesus was preaching in Capernaum, he talked about bread being his body and wine being his blood. He said that eating and drinking them would bring eternal life. His words tonight echo that teaching. I'll ask Peter later if he can interpret just what Jesus means."

At long last Jesus stands, shakes out his garments, and leaves the table. The apostles rise to their feet and follow him down the stairs and out of the house. Strains of the psalm of praise they are singing waft back to us. I can easily discern Peter's rich baritone. Now we servants can enjoy our own meal in peace.

❧❧❧

The next morning Esther and I help Lydia to clear breakfast. Tobiah and Seth are out for a walk. Then seated on pillows with the two women and Leah, I give them a more detailed account of last night's unusual meal. Suddenly I'm interrupted when the two men enter the house out of breath. Tobiah says frantically with a stricken face, "They're going to crucify Jesus. Pilate condemned him to death. They have him carrying a cross out to Golgotha right now."

My heart stops. "Why are they doing this?"

Tobiah said, "They accused Jesus of treason, saying that he claimed to be king. He was arrested last night, betrayed by one of his apostles, Judas."

"Judas!" I fairly spit out the name.

"All night Roman soldiers tortured Jesus and tormented him. They shoved a crown of thorns onto his head to mock him. They whipped Jesus so fiercely that people don't think he will live to be crucified."

I'm horrified. Possessing a vivid imagination, I picture the violence Jesus endured and what he must look like now and I shudder.

"People throng the streets, jeering at Jesus," Seth says.

"Let's go to support him," I say. Turning to my daughter, I order, "Leah, you stay here and watch the children." A crucifixion is gruesome, nothing a young girl should be subjected to. Crucifixion is the cruelest, most humiliating form of execution human beings have ever devised. It's so abominable that Roman citizens can't be crucified, only slaves and rebels.

The two women and I leave the house in haste with the two men. As much as I dread witnessing the suffering of Jesus, a man who would never make anyone suffer, I know I must be there.

It isn't hard to find where Jesus is. We follow the roar of voices. Drops of blood splattered on the street show where Jesus passed. The route is through the busy narrow streets lined with vendors' stalls so that as many people as possible can see him and be deterred from actions that threaten mighty Rome. We run through back streets and emerge on the road to Golgotha ahead of the mob. Among a group of sobbing women, I spot familiar faces—Mary of Magdala, John Mark's mother, and Salome. Esther, Lydia, and I join them. Between the heads of people standing before me, I glimpse Jesus, struggling to carry a rough wooden cross. His gentle, regal face is swollen and bloody, his white garment streaked with blood. How painful it was when I cut my hand slightly on a broken clay jar recently. The slashes inflicted by the lash of the Roman whips must be excruciating. Deeply moved at the pitiful sight, I feel hot tears coursing down my cheeks.

Jesus stumbles and falls on the rocky road, the heavy looking cross bounces brutally against his back, and onlookers gasp. A Roman soldier prods Jesus with a whip until he lurches up again and moves on, barely able to take a step. Another soldier grabs a dark-skinned man from the crowd and, pushing him toward Jesus, forces him to take the cross from Jesus and carry it. I doubt that the soldier is acting out of compassion; he is only determined to keep Jesus alive. If Jesus dies on the road, the populace will be deprived of the spectacle of the crucifixion.

Slowly we move toward the city gates with the crowd, an ugly tide of human beings. Oh, no! Across the road from us, Mary, the mother of Jesus, walks along, her lovely face contorted with anguish. The apostle John is at her side with his arm around her. Good. He will catch her if she collapses. The poor lady. How can this be happening? Perhaps I'm trapped in a nightmare.

On Golgotha I huddle with the other women at a distance from where Roman soldiers are affixing three men to crosses. We are not so far away that I can't hear the nails being pounded into the hands and feet of Mary's son. I flinch at the sound of each dull clank. Then one by one the crosses are hoisted up and dropped into the holes prepared in the ground, jarring the bodies of the condemned men. Mary and John move to stand directly beneath the cross. How can Mary bear this? She must be a very strong woman. If Jesus were my son, I would have fainted at the first sight of him on the road.

Where is Peter? I scan the groups of people watching on the hill, some sobbing, some gawking, and some gloating. I'm surprised to see Nathan and Deborah, whom I haven't visited yet. Deborah is nestled against Nathan's side, seeking comfort from him as they witness the horror displayed before us. But I don't see my husband. Nor do I see any other apostle besides John. Was Peter arrested too? Is he in prison? We stand there transfixed, watching the dreadful scene play out. Four soldiers are tossing dice next to a pile of clothes. I suppose they are dividing up the garments of Jesus that Mary lovingly sewed for him.

A few hours pass. Then Jesus gives a loud cry that wrenches my heart, and his head drops down to his chest. I think he is dead. With a mallet Roman soldiers strike and break the legs of the men on either side of him. That way the criminals can't push themselves up to get a breath, and so they die. The soldiers go to the foot of the cross where Jesus hangs and confer. Suddenly one of them thrusts a spear into the side of Jesus, and I give an involuntary cry. What an ignominious end for such a noble human being. A little while later Tobiah walks over to the three of us. Taking Esther by the elbow, he says, "It's all over. Let's go."

I'm absolutely numb and move woodenly, oblivious to the people around me. No one speaks all the way back to the house. Although it's afternoon, an eerie darkness cloaks the city, as though the sun is dying. My heart is pounding inside me, chanting, "Where is Peter? Where is Peter?" like a mantra.

That night a full moon shines through the window of the back guestroom, where I am trying to sleep next to Leah. The bright light doesn't bother me, though, because my mind is in turmoil, replaying the day's appalling events. And I am filled with anxiety, not knowing whether or not Peter is safe. Furthermore, my crying has brought on a dull headache.

As the hours pass, the noise from the streets dies down and there's only the monotonous chirping of crickets. Suddenly I hear, "Psst, Miriam," and Lydia stands in the doorway. "You have a visitor," she whispers. Quietly I rise, wrap my mantle around me, and walk into the main room. As I tiptoe past Lydia, she gives me a quick squeeze, and I know it is Peter who waits. "Outside," Lydia says in my ear. I slip out the door into the moonlit night, and there on the deserted street stands a large figure with cloth shrouding most of his face.

"Miriam," Peter says in a choked voice. He clutches my hand and leads me a few yards away from the house and into a shadowed area. "Miriam, I had to see you."

"Oh, Peter. I was so worried about you!" I place my hands on either side of his face to caress it, and I feel that it is wet. "I know what happened. I was there. It was horrible. I'm so sorry you lost your friend and so tragically."

"My friend?" Peter scoffs. "Do you know what I did? After Jesus was arrested, I followed him to the high priest's house. In the courtyard I joined people who were standing and warming themselves by a charcoal fire. Three times I was asked if I was a disciple of Jesus."

"Why would they suspect you?" I ask.

"Because of my Galilean accent or because they recognized me as being with Jesus in the garden. All three times I denied knowing Jesus. I even cursed." His voice cracks on the word, and he pauses, trying to regain control. "And then I heard a cock crow just as Jesus was being led by. He turned and looked at me, not with anger but with pity that pierced me to the heart. Then I remembered how Jesus foretold that I would deny him." Peter gives a loud sob. I embrace him tightly, wishing my love would penetrate him and act as a soothing balm. "I haven't stopped crying since," he says, his shoulders heaving. "I'm so ashamed."

After a while Peter continues. "I failed Jesus earlier too. In the garden of Gethsemane after supper, Jesus became another person, very jittery. He told us that he was extremely sad and asked James, John, and me to stay with him while he prayed. Then he fell to the ground and began praying desperately. Even though Jesus, my good master, was obviously in distress, I fell asleep. He shook my shoulder to wake me and chided, 'Couldn't you keep awake one hour? Pray that you may not be tested.' His face was a mask of sorrow and disappointment. Believe it or not, Jesus found me sleeping two more times."

"But, Peter, you just had a big meal and four cups of wine. In the dark and still of the garden, of course you fell asleep."

"That's no excuse. I should have been so concerned about Jesus that I would find it impossible to sleep." Peter gulps. "And then I didn't have the courage to stay with him when he needed me most. I was too scared for my own life. I'll never forgive myself."

"I'm sure Jesus understood," I say, attempting to assuage my husband's guilt.

"When the soldiers came to arrest Jesus, I did strike out with my sword. But I only cut a piece off a servant's ear. Jesus healed it. That's just like him, doing good to those who hate him."

"Where are the other apostles?" I question.

"We are all back in the upper room in hiding. We fear that the authorities will be after us next. Remember how they intend to kill Lazarus?"

"You're risking your life coming here," I warn. "Go now quickly. And God be with you." I release Peter and give him a little push.

"As soon as we can, we should return to Galilee," he says, looking back at me. "Right after Passover."

"Yes, back to a normal life."

"Will you be able to live with me, knowing I'm a disloyal coward?"

"Oh, Peter," I cry, "you are my life and my joy. I would live with you forever if I could."

He kisses me, a long, hard kiss, and then the night swallows him up.

I ache for my husband. He is a good man. Who wouldn't have reacted as he did? We never know how we will behave during a crisis. We might do something noble or something despicable. In addition to his remorse, Peter will be dealing with the cold reality that we've all been disillusioned. Jesus has not proved to be our Messiah after all.

Back on my mat next to Leah, I pray long and fervently that Peter's keen anguish will dissolve with time. Finally sleep overtakes me. But I sleep restlessly and a nightmare terrifies me. I dream of a bloodied man carrying a cross and stumbling. When the face turns toward me and looks up, it is Peter's. I awake with a start, my heart hammering as though it will burst out of my chest.

Chapter 19

~~~~~~~~~~~~~~~~~~~~~~~~~~~~

My great joy on entering Jerusalem has been supplanted by a dull sorrow and a gnawing apprehension. Yesterday, the Sabbath, was spent in deep shock. Leah and I, Tobiah and Esther, and our host family went through the motions of eating and praying the Sabbath prayers. We spoke only when it was necessary. Each of us was grieving privately for the wise and gentle man we had pinned our hopes on. Our Messiah was locked in a tomb, lifeless. He was laid there hastily already on Friday so as not to desecrate the Sabbath. Our future looks bleak.

I feel terrible; but Mary, Peter, and the other apostles must be devastated. Time and again my thoughts turn to Peter. He had been positive that Jesus was the Messiah. He had sacrificed his family and his business to devote himself to our future king. And all in vain. But Jesus was surely a man of God. Otherwise, how could he teach so beautifully and wisely? And how could he perform such tremendous deeds, even calling the dead to life? Why would God let Jesus be killed and in such an awful manner, even if he weren't the promised Messiah? True, God's prophets were murdered, but as far as I know, none of them was subjected to the extreme brutality that Jesus suffered. What was Peter thinking now? He must be tortured by the same questions that are plaguing me. How is he coping with his suffocating guilt? Most of all, is Peter safe?

Finally I can no longer stand not knowing how my husband is faring. This morning I approach Tobiah and venture, "I must find out how my husband is. Would you please go with me to John Mark to see if he can tell me." Tobiah, his eyes soft with sympathy, kindly says, "I would be happy to go with you. I'm wondering myself how the followers of Jesus are bearing up."

When we arrive at John Mark's house, Rhoda, smiling brightly, answers the door, greets us merrily, and ushers us in. Her cheery demeanor is disturbingly incongruous when we are all mourning. Has the woman no heart? John Mark and his mother Mary rise to greet us. "Have you heard?" John Mark says excitedly. "Jesus is alive!" Mary nods her head vigorously like a hoopoe as it walks.

"What? How can this be?" Tobiah asks, stupefied.

Astounded, I stammer, "But, but, we were there. He died right before our eyes, an awful death. He can't still be alive."

"It's incredible, I know," John Mark says. "But people have seen him—his mother, Peter, Mary of Magdala, and others."

Tobiah inquires, "Where? What did he look like?" At the same time I ask, "What did he say?"

John Mark begins to explain. "Early this morning some women went with spices to anoint his body."

Mary comments, bubbling with laughter, "They were so eager, they never stopped to think how they would move the large stone away from the entrance."

John Mark speaks rapidly. "But when they got there, the rock was already rolled away. The women walked into the tomb, but the body of Jesus wasn't there. A radiant young man sitting in the tomb told them that Jesus was raised. The man, no doubt, was an angel in disguise. He sent the women to tell the apostles to go to Galilee where Jesus would meet them."

Then Mary's words too come tumbling out. "The way Salome told it, Mary of Magdala was the first to see the empty tomb. She ran and told Peter and John that the body of Jesus was missing. The two apostles sped to the tomb. John got there first, but respectfully he let Peter enter before him. They saw the linens that wrapped the body, but the body of Jesus was gone. The two apostles left, but Mary, bless her heart, stayed behind, weeping. That is when she encountered the risen Jesus.

"Viewing him through her tears, at first she thought he was the gardener." Mary chuckles. "She asked where he had laid the body and said she would take it away. Can you picture that—petite Mary Magdalen carrying off the body of a full-grown man in her arms? But as soon as Jesus said her name, just as he had so many times before, Mary recognized him. Then she went to the disciples and told them she had seen Jesus. They had to be jealous."

"If I had seen Jesus, I would have been delirious with joy but frightened to death," I frankly admit.

"I imagine that is exactly how the women felt," John Mark says. "I suggest you go home and start packing for Galilee. I don't know where Peter is right now, but when he returns, I will let him know that you are looking for him."

With light hearts and renewed hope, Tobiah and I hurry back to tell the others the good news and dispel their sorrow. Esther, Leah, Seth and Lydia are gathered in the main room, waiting for our return. When we break the news to them, their elation knows no bounds. Leah weeps for joy.

"I knew that Jesus brought others back to life: the daughter of Jairus, the son of a widow, and Lazarus, who, incredibly, was dead for four whole days. But who would ever think that Jesus himself could come back to life, especially after enduring those atrocious torments?" Tobiah says. I cringe at the memory of Jesus' death.

"Obviously Jesus has superhuman power. It seems that we prayed for a Messiah, and we got a real son of God," Esther says solemnly.

"I'm just glad that Jesus is alive again. He's such a good person, and I love him so much," Leah says giddily, hugging herself. "Imagine how happy Father is now."

Rubbing his forehead, Seth comments, "I wonder when and how Jesus will free Israel from the yoke of Rome and make us a mighty nation."

Then it hit me like a bolt of lightning. I say pensively, "Peter told me that Jesus foretold that he would rise from the dead. Just think, if Jesus could rise from the dead, that means that his promise of eternal life for us must be true!" Everyone is momentarily silenced, pondering the implications of this. I think how someday I will be reunited with my father; Peter will see Leah, his birth mother, once more; and Sarah will meet her babies who died. I can hardly wait to see Peter and talk to him about the risen Jesus. What will my husband do now?

Our trip back home after the days of Passover goes much faster than our journey to Jerusalem, partly because Peter arranged to return with Leah and me, Tobiah, Esther, and Salome. Spending these days on the road with him is heavenly. As we walk along the wide path carved out by other pilgrims and merchants, I hear from Peter's own lips the account of his discovering the empty tomb with John. He also describes for me and Leah a marvelous thing that happened on the night that Jesus rose from the dead.

"The eleven of us apostles were in hiding, discussing the amazing things that were occurring. Thomas courageously volunteered to go out to purchase some food for us. Because we were afraid that the authorities were hunting us, we made doubly sure that the doors of the house were locked. Despite our tight security, as we were speaking about Jesus, lo and behold, he somehow appeared in the room."

"Do you mean he came through the locked doors?" I ask, dumbfounded.

"Yes. Evidently, rising from the dead changed Jesus and gave him new powers. He's different, yet he is himself. He verified it by showing us his pierced hands and side. I could barely look at him. I felt lower than a worm and wished the ground would swallow me up. After what I did and didn't do, I expected Jesus to scold me severely or tell me how disappointed he was in me. In fact, all of us except John deserved a tongue-lashing. But instead, Jesus greeted us kindly, wishing us peace, which made me feel even worse. Then he said, 'As the Father sent me, I send you.' He breathed on us and said, 'Receive the Holy Spirit. Sins you forgive are forgiven.' "

"Jesus was always forgiving people's sins. Remember the paralyzed man who came through our ceiling? It sounds as though Jesus passed on the authority to forgive sins to you. But who is this Holy Spirit?" I ask, puzzled by the unfamiliar name.

"On the night before Jesus died, he talked at length about the Holy Spirit. Supposedly this Spirit will come as our counselor and help us understand things that are a mystery to us now."

"Like why Jesus died such a dreadful death, and why you see him alive now?"

"Right. After Jesus left us, Thomas returned, carrying provisions. The ten of us swarmed around him like bees around a hive and told him with great excitement and repetition that Jesus had visited. But Thomas stubbornly refused to believe us. Granted, we scarcely could believe the event ourselves. Thomas accused us of playing a trick on him. Then he insisted that we were just seeing things that we wanted to see. Finally he angrily declared he wouldn't believe until he touched the nail wounds and the wound in the side of Jesus."

"Personally I think Thomas just felt bad that Jesus chose to appear when he wasn't there. I know I would," I say sympathetically. I always liked Thomas. He was quiet and calm, unlike the Zebedee brothers.

"You may be right, Miriam-bird. Thomas thought the world of Jesus. In fact, when Jesus wanted to go to Judea after he heard that Lazarus was ill, all of us tried to dissuade him. He had just almost been stoned to death there. It was Thomas who bravely said, 'Let's also go, that we may die with him.' Well, that certainly didn't happen," Peter says ruefully.

"Anyway, a week after his first visit, the risen Jesus came to us again. And again, mysteriously, locked doors were no obstacle for him. Fortunately, this time Thomas was present. Jesus invited Thomas to touch his wounds. Thomas turned as white as the snow on top of Mount Hermon. He sank to his knees and declared, "My Lord and my God!" Jesus looked around at us and said, 'Blessed are those who haven't seen and yet believe.' "

"Ha! That includes me, Peter. Jesus hasn't visited me, but I believe what you are saying. I believe that Jesus lives. He must be the Messiah after all!"

When we are finally back home in Capernaum, I eagerly tell Mother and the children the amazing things that happened in Jerusalem. Of course I abridge the story of Jesus' death quite a bit, omitting the gory details. Like the rest of us, my family is ecstatic to know that Jesus is still alive. They have grown to love him.

I can tell that Peter is still troubled by what he calls his dastardly behavior at the time of Jesus' arrest and execution. Sometimes I catch him staring off into space with a hangdog expression on his face, and I can guess what he is thinking. I've pointed out that if Jesus held a grudge, he wouldn't have greeted them all with "Peace be with you." Still, Peter broods.

One evening Thomas, Nathanael, James, John, and two other apostles are idly lounging in our courtyard. Obviously they are bored. They are like lost little boys now that Jesus is not with them. Peter is absentmindedly tossing a coin up in the air over and over.

Abruptly he heaves himself up and states, "I'm going fishing." John perks up and says, "I'll go with you." In unison the others say, "Me too." They all tramp out of the house, and I wish them luck. At last they'll be doing something useful.

Late the next morning Peter comes home whistling the way he used to do. I thank God that he's finally in a good mood. He enters the house with a shy, goofy smile on his face. His haunted look is gone. Having just finished scrubbing the oven outside, I must look a sight. But Peter takes three big steps toward me, grabs me by the waist, lifts me high, and twirls me around, no easy feat for anyone but a strong man like him. "Peter, what's gotten into you?" I exclaim, flustered but pleased. Peter ordinarily isn't so demonstrative, especially lately.

"Miriam-bird, I'm a new man," he crows, setting me down. I almost lose my balance. He holds me firmly by the shoulders and says, "Jesus made everything all right between us."

"You saw the risen Lord again? Here?" I ask, awed. This would be the first time Jesus has appeared in Galilee.

"Yes. We fished all night but didn't catch one measly fish. We were frustrated and depressed. After the sun rose, a man on the beach called out to us to cast our net on the right side of the boat. I figured the water was so clear that possibly he could see a school of fish swimming near us. We did as the stranger said, and we pulled up such a large catch that even with all of us straining, we couldn't lift the net on board. As the fish flopped around in the net, there wasn't one small one among them. John nudged me and said, 'It is the Lord!' I was so happy and eager to see Jesus that I threw on my tunic and cloak, dove into the sea, and swam about a hundred yards to him."

"I'm surprised you had the energy to do that after working all night," I say.

"I wanted to get to Jesus as quickly as possible."

"Obviously."

"I joked with Jesus, telling him he should have been a fisherman instead of a carpenter. Near where we stood, I saw fish roasting over a charcoal fire and some bread. I told Jesus I was glad to see he was making breakfast because I was starving. Truthfully though, I felt a little ill because the sight of the charcoal fire evoked the memory of the one in the courtyard where I denied Jesus."

Changing the subject, I ask, "What about your soaking wet clothes?"

"We sat down near the fire. Between its heat and the blazing morning sun, my clothes and I were drying quickly. When the others landed on the beach, dragging the net behind the boat, Jesus told us to bring him some of the fish we caught. I ran to the boat, waded into the water, and, with much grunting, managed to haul in the net. I felt as though I were lugging one of the huge stones in the Temple wall."

"Why didn't the other men help you?"

"They were too spellbound, being in the presence of the risen Lord. I didn't mind. I had my private time with him. We caught one hundred and fifty-three large fish. One hundred and fifty-three," Peter repeats the total, pausing after each word for emphasis. "I counted them myself. Oddly there were no tears in the net. I grabbed a few flapping fish, knocked them out with a rock, and took them to Jesus. He tossed them on the fire."

"How thoughtful of Jesus to include your fresh fish in the breakfast," I observe.

"After we finished eating, Jesus invited me to walk along the beach with him. As we leisurely strolled over the stones rubbed smooth by the wind and waves, I couldn't help noticing the wounds in Jesus' feet and felt uneasy. Then Jesus startled me. He asked if I loved him. I answered, 'Yes, you know that I love you,' and he told me to feed his lambs. He asked me a second time, and I answered the same. He told me to feed his sheep. When he questioned me a third time, I was baffled and hurt. I thought maybe Jesus didn't believe me. I swallowed hard and then huffed, 'Lord you know everything. You know that I love you.' Jesus told me again to feed his sheep. Later on it dawned on me that Jesus was doing me a kindness by giving me the chance to declare my love for him three times." Peter's voice is quivering with emotion. "You see. He let me cancel out my three denials."

"Oh, Peter!" was all I could say. My husband was healed, at least partially.

"Then Jesus made a puzzling prediction. He said that when I am old I will stretch out my hands and someone will fasten a belt around me and take me where I do not wish to go."

"God forbid," I utter, and I shiver as though from the blast of a cold wind.

"I noticed that John was following us, so I asked about him. Jesus as much as said I shouldn't worry about John. Then Jesus commanded, 'Follow me,' just as he said when he first called me from fishing with Andrew."

"I suppose this means you will devote the rest of your life to carrying on the work of Jesus." I make no effort to suppress a long, deep sigh.

"How can I resist, Miriam-bird?" He takes my hands, dirty as they are, lifts them to his lips and kisses them gently. "Please understand," he says looking at me with loving eyes. This time I say with conviction, "I do understand, dear, I do."

"Good," Peter says emphatically. "Because Jesus wants us apostles to return to Jerusalem."

Chapter 20

~~~~~~

Two months have passed since Peter and the other Capernaum apostles departed for Jerusalem. Before Peter left, he saw to it that Leah was betrothed to a nice young man here named Amos, who also happens to be a fisherman. Amos is one of the assistants Zebedee hired to replace his sons in the business. Unfortunately, two weeks after Peter left, Judith, his stepmother, took sick and died suddenly. Peter did not return to town. I didn't expect him to. I doubt that he would have arrived in time for any of the seven-day mourning period.

Travelers bring us news from Jerusalem now and then. Otherwise I wouldn't know if Peter is alive or dead. My husband and the other apostles are causing quite a stir preaching that Jesus rose from the dead and saved us from sin. There's talk of Peter giving such a powerful sermon during the harvest feast of Pentecost that three thousand people decided to follow Jesus on one day. That I find hard to believe. Peter was never known for speaking in our synagogue here. But you can never tell what gifts lie dormant in a person. I'm so very proud of my husband.

The Jewish authorities are incensed by the way the man they thought they got rid of is still causing trouble. They're clamping down on the followers of Jesus. I heard that Peter was arrested and even flogged. It's distressing to think of Peter's beautiful body that expressed such love for me and my children beaten and bruised like a common criminal's. I wish I were there to alleviate his soreness with soothing balm and my caresses.

As I sit on my heels in the courtyard, grinding the day's wheat with a stone mortar and pestle, lost in reverie, the twins come running out. "Mother! Mother! Uncle Nathan and Aunt Deborah are here!" Sure enough, Nathan and Deborah step into the courtyard, and I spring up to greet them. I send the girls to let Aunt Leah and Uncle Joachim know about our company.

Soon my brother and his wife are resting under the goat-hair awning in the courtyard, entertaining all of us with tales from Jerusalem. Nathan says, "As you know, for quite some time I've been pondering who Jesus was. I was leery about him and his unorthodox teachings. I couldn't reconcile his wondrous deeds with his flagrant disregard for some of our laws and customs. But after Peter's great sermon on Pentecost, both Deborah and I were baptized."

"Oh, so you were two of the three thousand," I say. "Tell us. How did that drastic change in the apostles come about? Peter and the other apostles were in hiding, fearing for their lives. And suddenly Peter is out in the open preaching?"

"It's true," Nathan says. "For forty days after he rose from the dead, Jesus instructed the apostles. Then he returned to heaven. On the day Jesus said goodbye, he assured the apostles that he would always be with them. He told them to wait in Jerusalem for the Holy Spirit. So Peter and the others went back to the upper room. They prayed there in suspense, not knowing exactly what they were waiting for."

"Mary, the mother of Jesus, was there too," Deborah interjects, "and some other women disciples, who cooked the meals for the large group. Altogether there were about one hundred and twenty people."

Nathan goes on, "Peter has undoubtedly emerged as the leader of the apostles. His first act was to call for a replacement for Judas while they were in the upper room. Perhaps you heard that Judas died."

"No, but I don't feel one bit sorry for that traitor," I say sharply. "Peter told me that Judas accepted thirty pieces of silver for turning Jesus over. How contemptible!"

"I agree," Nathan says. "Matthias, who had been a follower of Jesus from the start, was chosen as the new twelfth apostle. Then on the ninth day of prayer, early in the morning during the harvest festival of Pentecost, the sound of a strong wind blowing filled the house. Tongues of fire rested over the heads of the apostles."

"Did the fire hurt them?" Mark asks with consternation.

"No, no." Nathan reassures him. "It was not a normal fire. The wind and flames were signs that the Holy Spirit filled the apostles. Marveling at the events, the apostles began talking about them to one another and discovered they were speaking Parthian, Medic, Greek, Arabic, Latin, you name it. Then boldly the apostles went outside for the first time in nine days, and taught about God. They immediately attracted a crowd.

"Deborah and I happened to be nearby and heard the commotion, so we joined the rest and witnessed the event. The amazing thing was that although the people in town for the feast were from different nations and spoke various languages, they all understood what the apostles were saying."

"How could that be?" Rebekah asks, as flummoxed as I am.

"The Holy Spirit, the Spirit of Jesus, who had come upon them bestowed that gift," Nathan says simply.

"But some onlookers attributed the phenomenon to drinking new wine," Deborah adds. "Peter pointed out that it was only nine o'clock in the morning. They were not drunk on wine, but drunk on the Holy Spirit."

Nathan looks me in the eye and says, "But then, Miriam, your husband addressed the crowd in a masterful way, referring to several prophets and David. He convinced many people that Jesus is the Messiah—including us." Nathan and Deborah exchange glances, and Nathan takes her hand and squeezes it.

"Peter once told me that Jesus promised to make him and the other apostles fishers of people. Three thousand is quite a large catch for a single day," I say.

"Yes, indeed. Those of us who were baptized meet together in the Temple," Nathan explains. "We listen to the apostles talk about Jesus, his mission to save us, and what he taught. We break bread together as Jesus did on the night before he died. And everything we owned, we hold in common now. No one has need of anything."

"Dear, tell them about the miracles," Deborah prompts.

"Just as Jesus worked wonders, so do the apostles now."

"Can Father really heal people?" Sarah asks, her eyes as wide as clay plates.

"Oh, yes. Many people. Let me give you an example. One afternoon Peter and John went to pray at the Temple. We still are good Jews, you know. A crippled man was lying at the Beautiful Gate. People carry him there every day so he can beg. I've seen him myself. When the beggar asked Peter and John for alms, Peter replied, 'I don't have silver or gold, but what I have I give you. In the name of Jesus Christ of Nazareth, stand up and walk.' Peter helped the man up, and the lame man was healed. He entered the Temple, not just walking but actually leaping for joy and praising God."

"The man got more than he asked for, didn't he?" Rebekah observes, tilting her head.

"That's for sure," Nathan says. "On the Temple plaza, the cured man stood with Peter and John as proud and straight as a palm tree. People who recognized the beggar ran to them. Others were attracted by all the fuss, and the group swelled. Of course, Peter seized the opportunity to talk to the crowd about Jesus and his resurrection. People were enthralled. As a result of the healing miracle and Peter's convincing words, an astounding five thousand more people believed."

Deborah says, "Unfortunately, the Temple authorities, influenced by the Sadducees, who don't believe in the resurrection of the dead, arrested Peter and John. The next day the two prisoners had to appear before the rulers, including the high priest. The cured man stood beside them. Peter boldly declared that the man was cured through the name of Jesus. The rulers marveled at the courage of these plain fisherman. Seeing the cured man with their own eyes, they merely warned the apostles to stop preaching. Peter wisely retorted, "We must obey God rather than you.""

"The authorities' hands are tied because they know if they harm the miracle-workers, the people will rebel," Nathan explains. "God is working so powerfully through Peter now that people carry the sick into the streets on cots and mats in hopes that his shadow might fall on them as he passes by."

"Oh, my!" I exclaim. "Peter was always someone special to me. Now he is special to the whole world."

"Except to the Jewish leaders who resent that Peter's popularity eclipses theirs," Nathan amends. "Another time when the apostles were arrested, an angel freed them from prison."

"Like the time an angel saved the prophet Daniel when he was locked in the lions' den," Leah says.

"You're right, Leah." Nathan says, smiling at her. "Like Daniel, your father and the other apostles are good men who are just trying to do God's work. So guess what they did? They went right back to preaching in the Temple and were immediately arrested again. This time the council members were so enraged at their persistent disobedience that they wanted to kill the apostles. But a Pharisee named Gamaliel persuaded the others to bide their time. He pointed out that if the Jesus movement was not God's work, it would fizzle.

If it was God's work, however, no matter how hard they tried, they would never be able to destroy it."

"At least someone there has common sense," Mother comments dryly, her fists on her hips.

"Yes. Nevertheless the leaders couldn't resist one last attempt to halt the spread of the gospel. They had the apostles beaten and ordered them once more to stop preaching."

"But of course they didn't," Deborah remarks.

Chapter 21

~~~~~~

Today my oldest daughter is getting married. Our house is full of women, all aflutter and busy decking out the bride. How fast the years have flown! Leah is fourteen. Wasn't it only a short while ago that I gave birth to her during a violent sandstorm? My memory of that ordeal is still vivid. As I help slip the soft, linen, wedding tunic over Leah's head, I think of the night I first beheld her, the living symbol of the love between Peter and me. She was so tiny and helpless, her puffy eyes tight shut in her little pink face.

Leah has blossomed into a lovely young woman, blessed with Peter's straight nose and his dark, penetrating eyes. Last week I handed on to her the precious silver necklace that Mother gave me before my marriage. Now I place it around my daughter's swanlike neck, and she fingers it lovingly.

"Perfect!" Aunt Leah proclaims.

During the past months, I schooled Leah in the art of being a wife, sharing with her the numerous tips that Mother and Aunt Leah had offered me. I'm confident that Leah, a quick learner, is ready to manage her own home. My role as her mother while under the same roof has come to an end. It's as though the umbilical cord is being severed again.

Leah is remarkably calm for a bride, preparing for her wedding in a matter-of-fact way. But then, Leah always has been mature for her age. She was my mainstay as I raised the three younger children. I will miss her sorely.

The day is bittersweet. I'm losing Leah, but Peter is home, at least briefly. It's been almost a year since I've seen him. He tore himself away from his ministry in Jerusalem and arrived in record time last night, thoroughly exhausted.

After Nathan's account of the miracles Peter works, I was anxious about meeting my husband again. I'm in awe at his new supernatural powers that make him godlike. How will this new Peter regard me, plain old Miriam, whose greatest power is cooking a good meal? I needn't have worried. As soon as Peter entered our house and said, "Miriam-bird, my love," and swept me off my feet, I knew our relationship was as strong as ever.

Now he is out of our way at the house of Amos, helping the parents of Leah's betrothed with last minute arrangements for the celebration.

Finally, Leah is arrayed in her wedding garments to everyone's satisfaction. Rebekah and Sarah, who have been hovering on the sidelines during the dressing, gaze in awe at their big sister. In three years' time they too will be leaving. Mother gives Leah's veil one last tug so that it drapes gracefully over her shoulder. Then Leah begins her vigil, awaiting Amos and the procession that will escort her to her new life, just as I once anticipated my first night as Simon Peter's wife.

At the wedding feast Peter and I are at the main table with the parents of Amos. Zebedee, who is Amos's boss, and Salome are also there. Jairus prays the blessing before the meal. Then we are ready to partake of the sumptuous banquet spread in front of us.

Rubbing his hands together, the father of Amos says with enthusiasm, "Peter, I speak for my whole family when I say that we are delighted that you are able to join us for this occasion."

"Believe me, I am too," I say fervently. "Leah would have been heartbroken if her father hadn't come."

"Well, how could I miss the wedding of my firstborn?" Peter asks, shrugging his broad shoulders. "Besides, I left the church in good hands."

"How is your mission progressing?" I ask. With the whole focus on the wedding, this is this is my first opportunity to hear from Peter about the disciples' progress.

"The church is growing rapidly," Peter says, setting down his cup of wine. "The number of believers increases at such an extraordinary rate that it must be the work of the Holy Spirit."

"And the hard work of you, our two sons, and the other apostles," Zebedee adds, shaking his finger. Peter grins at him, acknowledging his tribute.

"The church is thriving so well," Peter says, "that the twelve of us couldn't handle preaching along with distributing food every day. The Greek disciples complained that their widows were being overlooked by us Jewish apostles."

"That's Greeks for you—always watching after their own interests," Salome comments, as she helps herself to a large hunk of meat. Zebedee glares at his outspoken wife.

"The charge was most likely true," Peter admits. "So the twelve of us got together and came up with a solution. We gathered all of the disciples together and directed them to choose seven wise men of integrity to oversee the food distribution. They did so. Then we apostles prayed over the seven chosen men and laid our hands on them to appoint them to their new role in the church. We created a new title for these Spirit-filled men: deacons, from the Greek word for servants."

"Ah! That frees you to devote yourselves to your main work of prayer and preaching," I say.

"And probably saves you from having a nervous breakdown," the petite mother of Amos adds.

"That's the truth!" Peter exclaims. "I was losing sleep trying to figure out how to juggle all of my responsibilities. Luckily the Greeks spoke up." He winks at Salome.

Peter says nothing of his miracles, but then Zebedee asks, "I hear that you are curing people like Jesus did."

Peter clears his throat and asserts, "Many people have been cured, but it's not my doing. I heal in the name of Jesus. He works through me. I'm only an instrument, like a fishing net. When you fish, Zebedee, it's you who are doing the work, not the net."

"Clearly the miracles are netting many more disciples for Jesus," I remark.

"Peter, we know that the Jewish authorities have not only eluded your nets, but treat you like criminals," the father of Amos says. "Do you think they will obliterate the church someday?"

"Of course, not!" Peter says, slamming the table with his hand. "Where's your faith? Jesus predicted that we would suffer, just as he did. But he said that no evil would conquer the church. Furthermore, our Lord promised that he would always be with us." Peter's voice has crescendoed with each statement.

After that outburst, hoping to steer the conversation in another direction, I ask, "Don't Leah and Amos make a beautiful couple?"

The rest of the meal proceeds peacefully and without incident.

Peter was pleased to learn that people who follow Jesus meet in our house for prayer each week. While Peter is here, we celebrate the breaking of the bread. He draws a larger crowd that usual. How providential that our house is a large one. When it is time for a teaching, Peter stands to address the assembly. He is an imposing figure, and the townspeople esteem him. Immediately his has their full attention.

Peter's eyes sweep over the group, and then he begins to speak. "You all know how Jesus often talked about his Father in heaven. One story he told illustrates the great love God has for us, especially for sinners. It's a very moving parable.

"A son has the gall to demand his share of the inheritance before his father dies. The doting father hands it over to him. The insolent son goes to a Gentile land and foolishly squanders all the money on immoral activities. Then a famine comes. To survive, the son finds a despised job feeding pigs, those unclean animals. Still, the son is so hungry that he longs to eat the pigs' food. One day he decides to return to his father, admit his sin, and ask to be hired.

"Now the loving father has been looking for his son every day. So he spots him while he is still a long way off and runs to meet him. He embraces and kisses the boy. The son begins his rehearsed speech, but before he can ask to be hired, the father cuts him off. The father tells his servants to bring his son the best robe, a ring, and sandals. What's more, he orders a calf killed and throws a party to celebrate the return.

"An older son, who has always faithfully worked for his father, can't understand the father's easy forgiveness and joy. He is resentful and angry. But the father insists that they must celebrate, for his lost son is back home."

Peter told this parable with the expression, dramatic pauses, and gestures of a born storyteller. I'm so very proud of him.

He concludes, "Wouldn't you say that the love the father shows is extraordinary, prodigal, far beyond what was called for? You might even think the father was a fool. Through this parable Jesus is telling us, 'Look. This is the kind of tremendous love that the father has for you.'

"No one is without sin except our Lord. How comforting it is to know that no matter how great our sin, our heavenly Father welcomes us back. He shows as much love and mercy toward us as the father in the story. The proof of this is that the Father cancelled the sins of the world by sacrificing his only Son, Jesus. Now we forgiven sinners can be with him and enjoy a banquet in his kingdom as his very own children."

The parable Peter told was new to me. Now I think it is my favorite one. I wonder what other things Peter could teach me about Jesus. How I wish I could hear every one of his sermons!

Right after Leah's wedding week is over, my husband returns to Jerusalem.

Chapter 22

$\sim\sim\sim\sim\sim\sim\sim\sim\sim\sim\sim\sim\sim\sim\sim\sim\sim\sim\sim$

A year later my family and I are dining at Sarah's house one evening. Her brother, Matthew, arrived from Jerusalem yesterday with his wife, Abigail, who travels with him. They have not been blessed with a child yet. My fellow gospel-widows, Dorcas and Joanna, and their children have also been invited to the meal to welcome Matthew home.

I am anxious to learn how my husband is. I'm looking forward to hearing a firsthand account of how Peter's life as an apostle is unfolding.

Tonight we are feasting on goat meat, a rarity, served in honor of Matthew. The thought occurs to me that Matthew, the tax collector-turned-apostle, is like the wayward son who had a change of heart in the parable Jesus told. And here we are celebrating with him.

Once pleasantries have been exchanged, Alphaeus fixes his eyes on Matthew and says, "Son, give us a report on the state of the church in Jerusalem." Good. This is what we gospel-widows in particular are longing to hear.

Matthew finishes chewing a mouthful, washes it down with a

swig of wine, clears his throat, and begins, "More and more people are coming to believe in Jesus as our Lord and Messiah. Even a number of priests have joined our community. The seven deacons have proven to be an immense help to us."

"That's good news, Matthew," Sarah says.

"Well, unfortunately, I have some bad news. One deacon named Stephen did not only distribute food. He performed miracles and was a fabulous speaker. I say 'was' because right before I left, Stephen was killed. He is the first one to lose his life because of believing in Jesus. All of us were devastated, especially Peter."

A chill runs down my spine. Everyone has stopped eating. "How did it happen?" Joanna asks.

"At the synagogue, Stephen got into an argument with several men from different countries. Because he was so intelligent, he easily bested them. This made them furious, and they persuaded some men to falsely accuse Stephen of blasphemy. Stephen was arrested and brought before the council. He gave a masterful speech, outlining the history of our people. But then he ended by bluntly blaming the religious leaders for the death of the promised one."

"Well, that was inviting trouble," Dorcas comments.

"To make matters worse, Stephen suddenly looked up and declared that he could see Jesus standing at God's right hand. The council members ganged up on Stephen and dragged him outside the city. There they stoned him to death. As the rocks were flying, Stephen asked Jesus to receive his spirit. Then he fell to his knees and asked God not to hold the murderers' sin against them."

"That's what Jesus prayed when he was dying on the cross," I say quietly.

Matthew nods his head and says, "That's what I heard. Anyway, after Stephen died, some disciples buried his body."

"Killing someone because he doesn't believe what you believe! How awful and unjust!" Sarah exclaims. "I don't understand how people can do such dastardly things and think that they are doing them to please God."

"You can imagine how everyone was overwhelmed with grief and outrage," Matthew says. "Peter tried to lift everyone's spirits by reminding us that Stephen is now with Jesus. One of the Greek disciples informed us that the name Stephen comes from the Greek word for crown. Stephen now wears a crown of glory in heaven, the crown of a faithful witness for Jesus."

"I fear for the other disciples," I say. Of course, my primary concern is Peter. What if he is killed in Jerusalem and I never see him again?

"Your fears are well grounded, Miriam," Matthew says, to my dismay. "I hate to alarm you, but on the very day of Stephen's death, a Pharisee named Saul began going from house to house in Jerusalem and dragging disciples to prison. You see, we view ourselves as a Jewish sect, but the religious authorities regard us as heretics, a malignancy that must be eliminated. This man Saul is our chief adversary."

"The families of believers in the Holy City must be scared to death," Joanna comments.

"You're right," Matthew says. "Everyone is fleeing the city and taking refuge in the country, except for the apostles. I will be going back to Jerusalem straight from here and staying there too. Abigail will come with me." He trades glances with Abigail, and she gives him a wan smile. I detect fear in her eyes.

Dorcas says, "Thanks for spoiling our appetites, Matthew."

He says, "I'm sorry to be the bearer of such grim news. But this is the current state of the church. I recommend that we storm heaven for the safety of our brothers and sisters in Jerusalem."

Right then and there I renew my resolve to join Peter as soon as possible. But this won't happen until the twins and Mark are on their own. And who knows when that will be?

On the way home after the dinner, my children are abnormally subdued. I wish Matthew hadn't spoken of the persecution while they were present. He may be an apostle, but he certainly wasn't prudent.

Sure enough, halfway home Mark asks, "Mother, will Father be killed?" He and the two girls are gazing at me with worry etched on their faces. We all come to a halt.

"I hardly think so, Mark," I carefully reply. "Listen. Your father is too important. Jesus needs him to guide the church in these first years. Our Lord wouldn't harm his church by taking your father to heaven."

Not just yet, I say to myself.

The children are visibly relieved. Dark gray storm clouds are rolling in from the east and there's a rumble of thunder in the distance. "We better hurry home and beat the storm," I say, and we walk on.

Just as we reach our house, I hear loud cries and see hundreds of gray cranes approaching in the sky, migrating south. I give them a message to deliver in Jerusalem. "Take Peter my love," I mentally tell them. "Let him know that he's in my heart and in my prayers."

Chapter 23

~~~~~~

A whole year and a half goes by before I see Peter again. He is making his rounds of towns in Galilee to connect with communities of disciples. Because Capernaum is one of his stops, he pays us a visit. As soon as Peter walks through the door, conflicting emotions well up within me. I'm overwhelmed with joy, but at the same time I'm angry that Peter's mission keeps him away from me. Joy prevails, and I greet my husband with a radiant smile and a sincere, "Welcome home, my love."

Immediately I notice that Peter's grueling work and the opposition he encounters are taking a toll on him. There are gray flecks in his hair and beard and creases in his forehead. One thing that hasn't changed is his love for me. He might look different, but that night as we made love after such a long draught, he was as tender and sweet as always, in fact, more so. While Peter was gone, the thought never crossed my mind that he might be unfaithful. I know that our long periods apart are just as difficult for him as they are for me.

On the day after Peter arrived, the house is a beehive of activity. To celebrate his homecoming, we invite Jonah; Leah and her husband,

Amos; Dorcas and Joanna; Zebedee and Salome; as well as Aunt Leah and Uncle Joachim to supper. While we womenfolk prepare the meal, Peter is out visiting Tobiah and some other old friends, and, no doubt, corralling people to hear more about Jesus.

That evening as soon as we start passing the bread, Zebedee asks jovially, "So, Peter, what are my two sons up to these days? Are they living up to their nickname, sons of thunder?"

"Well, James is like a firebrand in the Jerusalem community. He is zealous in guiding believers, teaching them about the Lord, and encouraging them to spread the word. He is highly respected and doing a splendid job."

"James always has been a take charge person," Zebedee says.

"Bossy is more like it," Dorcas says, making us laugh. "But I'm not surprised that he is a successful leader."

"And you would be proud of John," Peter continues, smiling at Zebedee and Salome. "Your younger son cares for Mary with solicitude and tenderness. It's touching to see. And Mary always makes sure John is eating enough. You don't have to worry, Salome."

"Sounds as though Salome's boys have turned out all right after all," I whisper in Mother's ear.

"Recently John and I were in Samaria together," Peter says. "The deacon Philip had laid the groundwork in Samaria, telling the people about the Messiah and curing them. Because he baptized so many Samaritans, the other apostles decided to send John and me to them."

"Did Mary go with you?" Aunt Leah asks.

"No, John arranged for her to stay at John Mark's house." My thoughts often turn to the gentle mother of Jesus. The sight of her standing beneath the cross is burned into my memory. Sure, she knows that Jesus is alive, but he is in heaven now. I wonder if she longs for death so that she will be reunited with her son face-to-face. In the meantime, what a treasure she is for us. I suppose the apostles and others pump her for information about the early life of Jesus.

Peter continues, "After we arrived in the area of Samaria where Philip had been ministering, one day he assembled all the baptized Christians. John and I prayed and laid our hands on them so that they received the Holy Spirit too. One wicked man there—unfortunately he was named Simon like me—actually thought he could buy the power to confer the Holy Spirit. I set him straight about God's gift and urged him to repent. In the end Simon begged me to pray for him."

"Then for sure he will mend his ways," Jonah says with conviction, slapping his son on the back. Jonah is as proud of Peter as I am. He never misses an opportunity to slip a mention of Peter and his achievements into a conversation. Tonight Jonah is in good spirits since at least one of his sons is home. I intend to encourage Peter to spend as much time as possible with his father while he's here. Jonah is still grieving for Judith.

Peter recounts, "On the way back to Jerusalem, we preached the good news about Jesus to many villages in Samaria. We visited the village where a woman who had five husbands and then a lover encountered Jesus and became instrumental in turning all of the townspeople into believers. Their faith is still strong and vibrant."

"Isn't it strange that the despised Samaritans are now our brothers and sisters in Jesus? It's like the prophecy about the lion lying down in peace with the lamb," Joachim says thoughtfully. "I guess we haven't given our enemies enough credit," Peter says. "I remember one day Jesus cured ten lepers and sent them to the priest to verify that they were no longer unclean. As the lepers walked on, they realized they were healed. But only one came back to thank Jesus. Guess who? It was the Samaritan."

"Speaking of enemies," Zebedee says, "I heard that Saul, our chief persecutor, has made a complete turnabout and is now preaching that Jesus is the Messiah."

"You heard correctly," Peter confirms. "The disciple Barnabas brought Saul to us in Jerusalem and explained how the risen Jesus converted him."

"So it took Jesus himself to make that bloodthirsty Pharisee see the light!" Uncle Joachim exclaims.

"Evidently," Peter says. "The story is bizarre. Saul was traveling to Damascus, bent on arresting those who follow the Way. We've dubbed our movement the Way. John came up with that name. He remembered that Jesus once called himself the way, the truth, and the life."

"I like that name," our Sarah comments, nodding approval. "It's simple, and it conveys that following Jesus leads somewhere. And we know that it leads to happiness. Right, Mother?" She looks up at me for confirmation.

"Yes, dear, happiness in heaven with the Father. Go on, Peter."

"Saul was almost at Damascus when a brilliant light flashed around him. Stunned, he fell to the ground. A voice asked, 'Saul, Saul, why do you persecute me?' Saul's companions heard the voice but couldn't see anyone. They were dumbfounded."

"I would have fainted dead away," Aunt Leah remarks, fanning her face.

"When Saul asked who it was, Jesus identified himself and instructed him to enter the city, where he would be told what to do. The event left Saul blind."

"Say, during the supper in the upper room, I overheard Jesus talking about being united with him like a vine and its branches," I comment. "That's why he says he is being persecuted. He identifies with any follower who is being persecuted."

"Yes," Peter says. "And at that same meal Jesus foretold that we would be persecuted. But then he said that we should take heart because he conquered the world."

"So what happened to poor, blind Saul, Father?" Mark asks, his little face screwed up.

"The men led Saul by the hand into Damascus. For three whole days Saul didn't eat or drink anything while he pondered his encounter with the risen Jesus. Then, while Saul was praying, he had a vision that a man named Ananias came and healed him. At the same time, the Lord appeared to the disciple Ananias in a vision and sent him to lay his hands on Saul to cure his blindness."

"Ananias must have been terrified. Everyone knows that Saul is obsessed with hunting Christians." Joanna says what we are all probably thinking.

"He was frightened indeed," Peter says, nodding. "But the Lord assured Ananias that he had chosen Saul to speak in his name to Gentiles and Jews. So Ananias trusted God and, despite his fear, located the persecutor. He cured Saul and then baptized him. Saul joined the disciples in Damascus and right away began preaching in the synagogues that Jesus is the Son of God."

"Imagine that!" Jonah says, his face laced with amazement.

Peter continues his account. "Saul was so successful that the religious leaders in Damascus thought they better kill him. Luckily, Saul was able to escape one night, but it wasn't easy. Now that the danger was over, the disciple Barnabas described the escape with much good-natured laughter at Saul's expense. Some disciples knew of a hole in the city walls. They found a sturdy basket, tied a strong rope to it, and dangled it out the hole. Saul eased himself feet first through the hole and stepped into the basket. The disciples quietly lowered him to the ground like a large load of bread. Saul came to Jerusalem, but the disciples there feared and distrusted him. They couldn't fathom that the monster had truly been transformed into a believer."

"I can understand how they felt," Dorcas says. "Look at Judas. He turned out to be a vile traitor." Peter winces. Not noticing, Dorcas continues, "If you can't trust an apostle, how can you trust a persecutor?"

Peter says, "Well, after listening to Barnabas, we did give Saul our blessing to preach in Jerusalem. By the way, Saul now goes by his Roman name, Paul. Now while I finish my dinner, why don't you give me a progress report on the church in Capernaum. Are there many new believers?"

"Your house is packed for the prayer services, Peter. People love to reminisce about the marvels Jesus did when he lived with us," Uncle Joachim states, starting out on a positive note. "But to tell you the truth, many people in town refuse to accept Jesus as the Messiah. They say the story of his rising from the dead is just that, a story concocted by his apostles. Sorry, Peter."

"They say that if Jesus really were the Messiah, we wouldn't still be paying taxes to Rome," Joanna adds with a shrug.

"What's more, you know how often Jesus preached that we are to turn away from sin. Well, his message hasn't made a dent in the lives of many people here.

Some of our neighbors are confirmed thieves, bullies, prostitutes, and adulterers," Leah says frowning. "Amos and I are thinking about moving to Magdala, especially for the sake of our children." She pats her stomach, which I know is swollen under her robes. In a couple more months she will make Peter and me grandparents, God willing.

"I'm not surprised that so many sinners roam the streets here," Peter says. "Jesus once said that Capernaum's lack of repentance made it worse than Sodom, which, if you recall, was destroyed by fire for its depravity. He predicted that our town would end in disaster."

A long, uncomfortable silence settles over us as we contemplate this bitter information.

"Time for dessert," Mother announces with forced heartiness.

Peter stays in Capernaum long enough to clinch betrothals for the twins. Will he be here for their weddings? God only knows.

Chapter 24

My prayers are answered, and a year later Peter is home for the twins' weddings. Out of consideration for him, Rebekah and Sarah have planned to hold them within a week of each other. To determine whose wedding would be first, they had me hold two sticks of unequal length behind my back. Sarah chose the hand with the longer stick, so she will be married first. Thankfully, Mother and Aunt Leah are around to help me with all the preparations. On Peter's first day home, the girls delight in showing him their wedding garments and other clothes they made under my supervision.

Peter is an appreciative audience and admires our daughters' handiwork, praising the intricate designs painstakingly embroidered onto the cloth. Holding Sarah's new cloak in his hand, he says, "I know a good woman, a widow named Tabitha, who makes beautiful clothing like yours. Much of it she gives to the poor, for she is devoted to them.

"I met Tabitha under strange circumstances. I was in Joppa for quite some time. That's a lovely city on the shore of the Mediterranean Sea. One day two men came to see me from Lydda, a town about nine miles from Joppa. They said that Tabitha, a beloved disciple, had died, and they asked me to go with them to her house. So I did."

"Father," Rebekah says, "why did they want you to go?"

"To pray or speak at her funeral, silly," Sarah speaks for Peter. Although they are about to be brides, the twins occasionally act like the young girls they are.

"I wasn't sure what they wanted, dear," Peter replies. "All the way to Lydda, I prayed, asking the Holy Spirit to help me know what to do. When we went upstairs to Tabitha's room, many other widows were there grieving. With tears running down their cheeks, they opened a chest and took out tunics, mantles, and other things Tabitha had sewn. As they showed the items to me, the women spoke about how the community would sorely miss Tabitha, not only for her sewing talent but for her kindness and loving support.

"I sent everyone out of the room and knelt and prayed. Then I said to the lifeless body, 'Tabitha, get up,' and she opened her eyes and sat up. I said, 'Shalom, Tabitha! I'm Peter, and I'm very pleased to meet you.' I helped her up off her pallet and called all her friends back. Momentarily they stood there stunned to see Tabitha alive. Then they almost smothered her with hugs and kisses."

"Peter, that is what Jesus did for the daughter of Jairus, brought her back to life," Mother recalls.

"Yes, I remember," Peter says, carefully handing the cloak back to Sarah. "Now Jesus works through us with the same amazing power. Because Tabitha came back to life, many more people came to believe in our Lord."

I wonder at the man I married. This worker of miracles is the same person who makes love with me and whose children I bore. Zebedee tells me that Peter has emerged as the one at the helm of the fledgling church. Others defer to him and seek his counsel. Peter would never tell me that himself. God has certainly favored me more than any woman in Capernaum. Only the mother of Jesus herself has been more blessed. Mary must live in continual awe at what God has done through her. I hope that someday I might meet her again. Maybe I'll see her when I'm finally free to go to Jerusalem and join Peter in spreading the good news of God's great love for us.

In the meantime I try to be a good mother. I also work at being a good disciple. I corner every newcomer in Capernaum and make known what Jesus did here. Like Peter, I proclaim the great mystery I witnessed in Jerusalem, the death of Jesus, and the glorious outcome.

I'm happy that Peter is in town so he can celebrate the breaking of the bread with the followers of the Way who meet regularly in our house. This evening more people than usual are seated on our floor. Jonah is positioned near his son, waiting to be taught by him. Peter begins by referring to Jonah the prophet. I love that short story in Scripture. The prophet Jonah is so very human. First when God sends him to convert the Ninevites, he is a coward and sails in the opposite direction. Then when Jonah does convert these enemies of his country, he wants to see them annihilated. Besides, the story illustrates the boundless mercy of God in forgiving the repentant Ninevites, who he says don't know their right hand from their left.

Peter compares Jesus to Jonah. When the prophet tried to avoid his mission, he ended up in the belly of a great fish for three days. Likewise Jesus was trapped in the maw of death for three days. Peter says that at one time Jesus prophesied that he would be like Jonah, who survived his ordeal. Then Peter speaks eloquently about the death and resurrection of Jesus, stressing the mercy of God who offers us eternal life in return for repentance.

This fisherman hasn't been taught the skills of an orator, but he has a natural gift. His voice is low and pleasing, and he punctuates his speech with strong, wide gestures. I think he is such a dynamic speaker for two reasons: his sincerity and his deep love for Jesus. I only wish some of the inveterate sinners in town were here in the crowd so they could be touched by Peter's words.

When Peter is finished speaking, Noah, stands. He is a wizened man with a scrawny beard and a thin, pointed nose, who meticulously follows Jewish rules. Leaning on his cane, Noah states in a thin, wavering voice, "Peter, my relative from Joppa was visiting last week. He told me that you baptized Gentiles and even ate with them. I'm hoping that isn't true."

Everyone gasps and starts murmuring. To be honest, I immediately think, Who is spreading such vicious rumors about my husband?

But then Peter smiles broadly and says, "Noah, my friend, let me tell you the wonderful revelation God made to us. In Joppa, I was praying on the roof of a house by the seaside. It was about noon. While my hosts were fixing something for me to eat, I fell into a trance. I saw what looked like a large sheet descending from the sky. It was filled with all kinds of creatures. A voice told me to kill and eat. I objected, explaining that I've never eaten unclean food. Like you, Noah, I only eat animals that chew their cud and have cloven hoofs and only seafood that have fins and scales. But the voice replied, 'What God made clean, you must not call profane.' This happened two more times."

"So what?" Noah sneers. "You must have been dreaming, or maybe the hot sun crazed you." I cannot believe the audacity of that man. But surprisingly Peter replies calmly.

"To tell you the truth, I was wondering the same things myself at first, Noah. But then, while I was trying to make sense out of the apparition, the Holy Spirit spoke. I heard him as clearly as I hear you. He told me that three men were looking for me. I was to go with them immediately because he had sent them.

"When I went downstairs, I saw a Roman soldier and two other men who turned out to be slaves. They told me that an angel had directed a centurion named Cornelius to send for me and listen to my words. They assured me that Cornelius was a good man respected by our people.

"The next day I, along with some disciples from Joppa, went with the three men to Caesarea. As soon as Cornelius saw me, he fell at my feet as though I were a god. I assured him I was a mere mortal. In the house many people were gathered. I reminded them that we Jews were not allowed to associate with Gentiles. But then I told them that God saw things differently and taught me that no one was profane or unclean. Cornelius invited me to speak, and I told the story of Jesus and the need for repentance. Even before I finished, the Holy Spirit came upon the Gentiles and they spoke in tongues. Then we baptized them."

"Amazing!" someone hollers. "Our great God extends his loving kindness not only to us, but to Gentiles!" Individuals in the crowd burst forth with "Praise God!" Everyone stands and claps—even Noah, I notice with satisfaction.

"Why don't we sing Psalm 150?" Peter suggests. And we do, with such vigor that I expect our house to explode.

Chapter 25

I wake up with a start from a pleasant dream in which Peter and I were sitting together in his boat, floating on the sea. We were totally alone under a brilliant sun, whose rays were sprinkling shining diamonds across the surface of the water. Peter was not fishing, but holding me close and tantalizing me by blowing on my neck. Reluctantly I relinquish that dream. It takes a few seconds for me to realize where I am: lying on the roof of our house, sandwiched between Mother and Mark. Mother's gentle snoring is sending puffs of air directly onto my neck.

As I emerge from the cozy oblivion of sleep, harsh reality sets in. Peter is gone. The thought shocks me like a splash of cold water. For the past several days I've had the pleasure of awakening curled up beside my husband, his chin resting on the top of my head and his strong arm flung protectively and possessively around my waist. What joy it was to have him with me once more—to hear his stories from his own lips, to watch him rekindle his relationship with our children, and to be locked in his familiar tight embrace. But now Peter is somewhere between our house and Jerusalem, on a journey back to carry on the Lord's work. Only God knows when I will see his dear face again.

The soft, orange glow that heralds the sun's appearance over the Sea of Galilee is just beginning to edge out the inky night sky. I indulge in a little daydreaming and imagine what Peter is doing at this moment. Maybe he is just getting up from a night sleeping out in the open, shaking out his mantle that served as a blanket and draping it over his shoulders. Or perhaps he found shelter in a cave and is having a quick breakfast, sitting cross-legged in front of the cave and sinking his teeth into a slab of barley bread. Could be that Peter and his traveling companions were fortunate enough to spend the night in a roadside inn. I picture him fending off the prostitutes who hang around inns, like leeches looking for prey. Undoubtedly Peter would attract them. Considering the long trip that's ahead of the caravan, most likely Peter is already trudging along the road in the ghostly predawn, moving farther and farther away from me.

Yesterday when Peter was getting ready to leave, lacing on his sandals and filling his goatskin bag with water, I concentrated on packing his other provisions for the road, woodenly going through the motions. I so wanted to put on a brave front, to be the supportive wife he deserves. I tried to blink back my tears. Nevertheless, they escaped and rolled down my cheeks. I dashed them away with the back of my hand. Peter's departures never get any easier.

As usual, Peter resorted to teasing to ease the sad situation. As we embraced for a final time, he gently rubbed a lingering tear from my face with his thumb and said, "Now, Miriam-bird, don't run off with Eli while I'm gone." I had to smile, for Sarah's obnoxious husband would be a mighty poor substitute for Peter.

Mark, a youth who has not yet adjusted to his growing body, stood awkwardly at Mother's side, shifting from foot to foot. Peter took him by the shoulders, looked him in the eye, and said, "Mark, you're the man of the house now. Take care of my two women." He enveloped our son in a bear hug, thumping him on the back.

Turning next to Mother, Peter declared, "Rebekah, I will miss your cooking almost as much as I'll miss you." As he hugged Mother, her face beamed.

I handed Peter the basket filled with bread and fruit. Then he stepped out the door into the bright sunlight, followed by the three of us. We waved him off as he headed to the Via Maris, where a caravan going south was assembling. I watched Peter, my husband and best friend, until he came to a corner, turned back, and waved. Then he vanished from our sight and our lives.

This morning, replaying yesterday's farewells before I stir is a mistake, for it puts me a forlorn mood. This is no way to start a new day. I stretch and yawn. Then quietly I arise and go down the steps without waking the rest of the family—all two of them. It was hard enough getting used to life without little Leah, but now with Sarah and Rebekah married and Peter away, our house will seem empty and far too silent. As exasperating as the twins were sometimes, I will miss them sorely. Combing my long hair with brisk strokes, I catch myself sighing. Cooking and sewing for only three people will mean more spare time. What will I do?

After I pray, praising God for all his blessings, my spirits are lifted. I take myself in hand. All right, Miriam, wallowing in grief won't change a thing. In a few years you will join Peter. Until then, you still have your life to live here. Let's make the most of it.

I lift the wooden bar off the door, hoist the water jar to my shoulder, and go outside. There, loud tweets, calls, and chirps of hundreds of birds greet me. Nature's music. The carefree birds make me think of how God loves me, Miriam-bird, even more than he loves them. Didn't Jesus teach that? So what if I don't understand why certain things happen: why I married an itinerant apostle—the chief one at that, why Father died so young, or why I find weevils in my wheat. In his wisdom and goodness, God must have a grand design for everything, and somehow my life fits into it.

Walking pensively down the path to the well, I start to plan my strategy for a useful and fulfilling future. First of all, I'm a grandmother. I find that hard to believe, because I still feel like a young girl. I do enjoy my new role as a matriarch. Leah's boy, who is almost two years old, is a sheer delight—except when his chin puckers and quivers and he bursts into a tantrum. Leah is expecting another child in a few months. I see myself devoting a good deal of my time entertaining her children and being entertained by them. Of course, Rebekah and Sarah will be adding new members to our family too. I wonder if the offspring of my hyperactive twins will take after them. It would serve my daughters right!

Second, I am officially a follower of Jesus. Before Peter and Andrew returned to Jerusalem after Jesus rose, they marched our families to the nearby spring and baptized us. When Peter raised me, drenching wet, out of the warm water, he whispered in my ear, "Now you are closer to Jesus, but you are also closer to me." As a new person, living by the values Jesus taught, I definitely want to serve others more, to do more foot washing, as Peter calls it.

Already I'm a regular caretaker for Deborah, a destitute widow in town. Now that she is in her seventies, she is often in pain. Sarah and I take turns bringing her meals, laundering her clothes, and seeing that her house is clean and the oil in her lamps replenished. By ministering to Deborah, I'm imitating Jesus, who had a heart for widows.

Peter told me how Jesus once bestowed an enormous favor on a widow. Jesus and the apostles had left Capernaum and came to Naim, a town about twenty-five miles south of here. They met up with a large funeral procession. As usual, women walked at the head because Eve is the one who brought death into the world. The dead man turned out to be the only son of a widow and her sole means of support. The mother was probably sobbing loud enough to wake the dead. And in a way, that's what happened. Jesus felt sorry for the bereft woman, condemned to a lonely existence. He told her, "Don't cry," and then, remarkably, he brought her son back to life. In doing so, he gave the widow new life. How happy she will be when her son gives her a daughter-in-law and grandchildren.

And then there was the time Jesus watched a poor widow donate all she had to the Temple. How did he know that she had nothing left? Well, Jesus is God, who knows everything! Jesus praised the widow for being a generous person in stark contrast to the prideful religious leaders and stingy rich people. She trusted God to refill her empty purse. And I'm sure God did. After all, Scripture tells of another widow who, during a drought, had only enough bread and oil for one last meal with her son. Regardless, she shared it with the prophet Elijah. God repaid that widow by making sure that her jar of meal and jug of oil were never empty up to the time when the rains came and made the earth fruitful again.

What else can I do to serve? I bite my lip, adjust the water jar on my shoulder, and think hard. From nowhere, an idea floats into my mind. It must be the Holy Spirit within me at work! I will become a professional mourner for Capernaum. I've seen flutes for sale at the market. I'll purchase one. Then I'll ask Susanna, the oldest and most sought-after mourner, to teach me how to play it.

As early as I am, Sarah is already at the well. No one else is around. Sarah has to get a head start on her day's chores in order to complete them to Eli's satisfaction. Otherwise he yells at her. At the sound of my footsteps, Sarah looks up. Her solemn face breaks into a smile.

"Shalom, Sarah."

"Shalom, Miriam." My friend knows that Peter's departures leave me depressed. She gives me a keen look, as though she's inspecting me to see if I have a disease. I thought she might comment on Peter, but with typical sensitivity she says instead, "Your girls' weddings were wonderful celebrations. You must be totally drained after two weeklong parties in a row. I think everyone who came had a good time."

"Well, they certainly had a good appetite. There was hardly any food left at the end. Not that I need it with only three of us at home now."

Sarah nods. "Remember when Jesus stayed in Capernaum? You and Rebekah would provide for an army of men at a moment's notice."

"I enjoyed doing that. To be honest, I miss it. I feel like this empty jar," I say, tilting my water jar toward Sarah.

"Well, your house is full of people every Sunday when we have our prayer service."

"Yes, but that's different. It's more formal."

Sarah's water jar is already full. We're quiet for a while as I lower the leather bucket into the well and draw up the fresh water to fill my jar.

Suddenly Sarah's face lights up, and she snaps her fingers. "I've got it! Why don't you hold parties at your house just for us women?"

"Why, Sarah, what a wonderful idea! We would have a chance to chat other than at the well. I was just pondering what life changes I would make to fill my time."

"I'm sure the other gospel-widows would appreciate some adult companionship," Sarah comments. "And I would like a break from Eli. I might be able to persuade him to let me go. We could all bring something to add to the feast."

Just then Joanna and Dorcas arrive on the scene, carrying their water jars.

"Ladies," Sarah says, "how would you like to get together at Miriam's house for supper maybe every other week?"

"Just us women. Children if necessary," I clarify.

Our two friends look at each and burst out laughing.

"We were just saying that our lives lately are so boring," Joanna states.

"I for one would love to have a regular gathering besides our prayer services," Dorcas says firmly, as she lowers the bucket into the well.

"Of course, Mother and Aunt Leah would always be there. Should we invite anyone else?" I ask.

"What about Deborah, the widow you take care of? She might enjoy getting out of the house," Sarah suggests. "I'd be glad to bring her."

"Good idea, Sarah," I reply. "That would give her something to look forward to."

"Let's invite Esther. I'm sure that Tobiah wouldn't mind if she came," Joanna says. She takes her turn at the well.

"If Tobiah's wife comes, we should also invite Jairus's wife, Ruth," Sarah points out. "She's probably lonely since Jessica married and left home."

"Yes," says, Joanna. "And what about Salome? That would make ten of us."

"We might as well include her. She would be hurt if we didn't invite her," Dorcas says with a sigh.

"The children could eat with us. Then while they play, we would talk as freely as we wish," I explain, thinking out loud.

"Let's do it," Joanna says with uncharacteristic exuberance. The other two women nod.

Other women are approaching the well now from all sides, as in a morning ritual dance. The four of us move to the side to make room for the chattering, laughing group.

"Before we all head home," I say somberly, "I'd like your opinion. I'm considering learning to play the flute and becoming a professional mourner. What do you think?"

Everyone looks stunned for a few seconds, as though I proposed moving to Egypt. Then Sarah answers supportively, "Why not? I'm sure you will be a fast learner."

"We can always use another mourner," Dorcas remarks.

"Sometimes people end up dying on the same day. Besides Susanna isn't going to live forever. Someone will be needed to take her place."

Joanna adds, "A little extra spending money won't hurt either."

And just like that, the next few years of my life are mapped out. With a little ingenuity and the help of my friends, I will survive being left behind in Capernaum. I balance my water jar on my head. Then I walk home with a lighter heart and humming a little tune.

A week or so later, ignoring the threatening overcast skies, Aunt Leah and I go shopping. Ordinarily I'm happy to carry out this task. Lately, though, I've come to dread these trips to the market. It's all because of one man, Ahaz, who helps sell barley. We need barley for our daily bread, so I'm forced to encounter Ahaz often.

I like barley bread, especially with honey added. I like the feel of barley. Ever since I was a child, I couldn't resist running my hand through the smooth, slippery barley grain and letting it trickle through my fingers. To my dismay, I now associate barley with Ahaz. I'm afraid that it will always remind me of him, like a scar reminds us of an unfortunate event. Ahaz has ruined my positive feelings about barley!

A newcomer to town, Ahaz is somewhat of a mystery. We've never seen his wife. Evidently she lives in a nearby town, while he works in Capernaum to support her and any children they have. The man is quite handsome—tall and wiry, blessed with thick, curly black hair and a dazzling smile. If only his manners matched his looks.

Unfortunately, Ahaz seems to have become overly fond of me. No harm done at first. Ahaz would flash his smile at me and add an extra measure of barley to my bag. Even as he handed Aunt Leah's bag to her, he kept looking at me. I refused to meet his eyes. His inappropriate attention to me was obvious and a little embarrassing. Noticing his unwonted behavior, Aunt Leah commented on it. She asked, "Do you know that as we walk away from the booth, Ahaz keeps his eyes fixed on you?"

Sometimes as I toured the grain booth, Ahaz brushed up against me and I would smell his cloying sweet scent. In the beginning I assumed this physical contact was an accident in the tiny, crammed space and with the crush of customers. But then I realized that it was occurring too often to be by chance.

One day as I offered Ahaz the coins for the barley, he didn't just let them fall into his hand. He grabbed my hand and held it firmly. Alarmed, I turned to Aunt Leah, but she was not at my side. Ahaz leaned close and muttered, "You have the most beautiful eyes." Then he squeezed my hand and slid the coins out of it. I whipped around, located Aunt Leah at the adjoining stall, and made a beeline for her. When I told her what happened, she was upset as I was at the man's insolence.

"Husbands say such things, not sellers of barley!" I fumed.

"Don't look back, but Ahaz is staring after you with a foolish grin on his face," Aunt Leah informed me. "What chutzpah!"

"Maybe another woman would be charmed by Ahaz and flattered by his words, but I consider them an insult. Do I look like a slut that he felt he could take such liberties?"

"Not a slut, Miriam dear, but, face it, you have become a beautiful woman. And men will be men. Look how that poor girl, Esther's niece, was assaulted by two men in broad daylight last week as she was coming back from washing clothes. She had her two young children with her too." Frowning, Aunt Leah shakes her head. "Sadly, Ahaz's boldness is just one more sign that the moral fiber of our town is deteriorating."

If that episode weren't enough, when I told Mother about it, she revealed that she noticed Ahaz loitering around our house, as a thief does when planning a heist. The man's obsession with me scares me. So today when we are about to enter the hustle and bustle of the market, I ask Aunt Leah, "Would you please purchase the barley for both of us, while I stay out of sight by the jewelry?"

"I'd be happy to," Aunt Leah replies.

"I hope the romantic Ahaz doesn't harass you."

"No chance," says Aunt Leah, crinkling her nose. "He's totally smitten with you." With a laugh she departs for the place where Ahaz lurks. I head for the jewelry display, weaving through the customers who clog the path between the vendors.

Our ruse works well. Aunt Leah, carrying a bag of barley in her basket, soon rejoins me. "I had no trouble at all. Your boyfriend looked miffed that you weren't with me. He kept scanning the crowd, searching for you. He didn't even condescend to favor me with one of his toothy smiles."

"Too bad. Are you jealous?" I tease, relieved that I had avoided a meeting with Ahaz.

We begin browsing over the tempting assortment of jewelry on the black cloths draped over wooden stands. Aunt Leah spots a gold ring with a tiger's eye stone and tries it on. To my surprise, she says, "It fits. I'm going to buy this." She makes her way over to the vendor to pay for it. In the meantime a thin, silver bracelet etched with graceful floral designs catches my eye. I slip it over my hand and raise my arm to see how it looks on me.

"Miriam," a low voice at my side says, "let me come to you tonight. Please!" While I stand there shocked, my arm frozen in the air, Ahaz grabs my hand and plants a wet kiss on it. In an instant Aunt Leah is there, giving Ahaz such a good shove that I'm amazed he doesn't topple over. Taken by surprise, Ahaz blinks. "Leave her alone," my aunt growls and starts pulling me away by the arm. "Wait!" I say, removing the bracelet. As I toss it back on the cloth, I glimpse Ahaz slinking back into the crowd.

Horrified and trembling, I ask, "Aunt Leah, did you hear what he said? He wanted to come to me tonight."

"The cad!" she exclaims. "He should be ashamed of himself. What is this town coming to? It's common knowledge that Peter is away. You have only young Mark to protect you. Obviously Ahaz knows this too, or he wouldn't dare try to seduce you. Don't worry, honey. Your Uncle Joachim will take care of him."

My aunt gives me a quick hug with her one free arm. Her words are reassuring. Although we intended to buy a flute today, I say abruptly, "Let's go home." We walk a short distance in silence. My mind is in a turmoil. Then suddenly Aunt Leah states, "I bought that ring for a reason. I'm celebrating because I'm pregnant."

I stop in my tracks and stare at her in awe. "What?" I cry. "After all these years? Aunt Leah, if you're trying to distract me, you've succeeded! Uncle Joachim must be thrilled. I'm so happy for you both."

"I haven't told your mother yet, so keep it a secret. And pray for me and the baby. It isn't easy for an old lady like me to give birth. I'll be thirty-four years old."

"I promise. When is the baby due?"

"In six months. We decided not to share our news until I was further on in the pregnancy."

Given that Aunt Leah is roly-poly and swathed in cloth, it's likely that no one will guess that she is carrying a child for quite some time.

As Aunt Leah and I continue down the road, I feel a little tap on my head, and then another. Raindrops are painting black spots on the cobblestones around us. I tilt my head up so that the rain might cool my burning face. Finally the gray clouds let loose a shower, unusual at this time of year. We will be soaked to the skin, but I don't care. Although I did nothing wrong, I feel dirty. Maybe the rain will wash away this ugly feeling Ahaz left me with.

When I arrive home, although I am dripping wet, I go to the water jar straightaway. I pour water in the bowl and scrub my hand so vigorously that my skin might blister. Mother asks, "What on earth are you doing?" I tell her about Ahaz, his disgusting proposition and the kiss. I have to bite my tongue to refrain from telling her about Aunt Leah's pregnancy.

Mother is as angry as I expected. With vehemence she bellows, "If I could curse Ahaz, I would!" I'm relieved that Mark is not home. He is at Sarah's house, playing with Joel.

My problem at the market is soon resolved. Two days after the humiliating incident, Aunt Leah pops her head in our doorway and in a singsong voice says, "Miriam, I bring you good news about Ahaz." Coincidentally, I'm kneading dough and imagining that I am punching that man. Brushing the flour off my hands, I say, "Yes?"

Aunt Leah steps into the room and announces, "Ahaz won't be pestering you anymore, dear. Your uncle saw to that. Among other things, he informed Ahaz that your husband is a large, strong man with a hot temper. Peter would think nothing of breaking every bone in his body or the body of anyone else who dares to toy with his wife. Joachim reported that Ahaz gulped and turned as pale as a loincloth bleached by the sun."

"Oh, Aunt Leah! God bless Uncle Joachim!" I exclaim. Mother, coming in from the courtyard, has overheard the news and cheers.

Because of my experience with Ahaz, I can identify somewhat with Susanna, the harassed woman whose story is told in the Scriptures. Two lecherous old men tried to seduce her. When she refused to give in, they falsely accused her. But then the young prophet Daniel spoke up in her defense and revealed the treachery of the two old men. They were punished by death. I don't believe that anyone should be killed, no matter what crime they commit, but still, I find the fate of those evildoers very satisfying.

Uncle Joachim was my Daniel. Unlike the rogues who tormented Susanna, the depraved Ahaz is not killed. But he does leave Capernaum, making the market a safe place for me again. I sympathize with his wife and with any woman whose husband is a womanizer. For the thousandth time I praise and thank God that I'm married to Peter.

Chapter 26

A few weeks after Sarah proposed the woman's gathering, we are ready to enjoy our first meal together. I thought of inviting my daughters, but decided to limit the group to women my age and older. The girls can form their own group if they wish.

True to her word, Sarah brings the widow Deborah, carefully guiding her into the house and out to the courtyard. They are the first to arrive, along with Sarah's son, Joel, and her daughter, Barbara. Deborah's joy at being invited is written all over her. Her eyes sparkle, and she smiles widely, revealing her few remaining teeth. She moves more sprightly than I ever saw her move. Repeatedly Deborah thanks us. I'm glad that Sarah thought of including her.

Sarah hands me a basket of cheese and then settles the older woman next to Mother on the mat. Joel and Barbara politely greet my mother and me and then go straight to Mark, who is tossing seed to the chickens.

Shortly, Dorcas and Joanna arrive with their children, who join the other children. The women add a variety of fruit to the center of the mats. The wheat bread Mother and I made this morning is already there. Dorcas announces, "I'm wearing my new tunic for the occasion," and she twirls around so we can admire it. Stripes of wool dyed green, orange, and red brighten the natural tan color of the fabric. The rest of us are clothed in simple, solid-colored tunics of different hues, depending on the color of the sheep who donated their wool.

"It's lovely, Dorcas," Sarah says. "You could start your own business weaving clothes."

"Can you imagine what James would say about that?" Dorcas counters.

"I would think he'd be happy to have another breadwinner in the family," Joanna says.

"Knowing James, he would probably see it as a threat to him as head of the family," Dorcas explains.

Then Esther enters the courtyard, escorted by Tobiah, who is carrying a large bowl of lentil stew. She offered to provide the main dish, even seasoning it with pepper, which is an expensive spice. Ever since Jesus restored Esther's vision, she has been honing her culinary skills. She now prides herself on creating new recipes, to Tobiah's delight. He jokes that he no longer needs to fear being accidentally poisoned. Instead he has to worry about bursting the seams of his tunic.

We no sooner wave off Tobiah, than Salome and Ruth join us. Ruth explained that her sons stayed home with Jairus. The women seat themselves. Aunt Leah, who lives the closest, ironically is the last to arrive. She has brought the wine and begins to fill our cups. We call the children over, and, when everyone is in place, Mother says the blessing, praising God for the food we are about to enjoy. I glance around the table and think, This is good.

At first our conversation circles around mundane topics: the pleasant weather, the sewing projects we're working on, the rising cost of olive oil, the new family in the neighborhood, and the sick in town. After the children have had their fill of our feast, they scurry off to play with the others in the courtyard. Then, helping herself to a handful of raisins, Dorcas says, "Sarah, I'm surprised that Eli permitted you to come."

"Actually Eli thought it was a good idea that we women get together. He admitted that he feels sorry for you gospel-widows who have absentee husbands. Then he asked with a smirk, 'Aren't you glad you have a husband who stays home?' I just nodded. My nod was partially a lie because sometimes I wish Eli would disappear for a while." Our heads bob up and down in sympathy for our friend.

Esther says, "I admire you wives whose husbands are apostles. You remind me of something Tobiah told me. When he was studying Greek, he learned of a story about a Greek king, whose name I forgot. The king left his wife, Penelope, in order to fight in a war, which lasted for ten years. After the war was over, it took the king ten years to get home because he had one adventure after another."

"Penelope was alone for twenty years? I would die if Peter and I were separated that long. I'm grateful that he comes home periodically," I say.

Esther continues, "Well, Penelope wasn't exactly alone. Many men wanted to marry Penelope because she was a wealthy queen. Yet for all those years she stayed faithful to her husband. At one point Penelope told her suitors that she wanted to finish weaving a shroud for her father-in-law before she married again. She would work on the shroud during the day and then at night unravel what she wove. That way she managed to delay her decision for three years."

"Clever woman," Ruth remarks.

"Stupid men," snaps Mother. "Didn't they catch on that they were being duped?"

"So what happened after twenty years?" inquires Deborah in a thin, shaky voice.

"Penelope's husband returned home, killed all the greedy suitors, and made Penelope very happy. And someday you and your husbands will be reunited," Esther says, glancing at each of us gospel-widows.

"Miriam recently had a kind of suitor," Mother says, piquing everyone's curiosity. Then with Aunt Leah's help, she proceeds to tell our guests about Ahaz's unwelcome advances as well as their outcome. Uncomfortable, I keep still. Throughout the account Deborah tsks and shakes her head in disapproval.

Dorcas comments, "I wondered why I hadn't seen Ahaz lately." Turning to me, she says, "Undoubtedly you weren't his first victim, Miriam. Imagine what his wife has to put up with!"

"Miriam, I'm sorry you had that bad experience," Joanna declares soothingly. "To some men, women are only objects God created for their pleasure."

"Or possessions to run their household, satisfy their needs, and give them heirs. Look at the Jewish women in Jerusalem who are almost totally confined to their houses. We're fortunate to live in the country where rules in general aren't followed so strictly," Sarah adds.

"Sometimes I feel that we women don't count for anything," Aunt Leah says. "We are kept illiterate and aren't even obliged to pray. You'd think we had no brains, just bodies!"

"Don't forget, we aren't accepted as witnesses in court either," Salome says, scowling. "We might as well be children."

Esther holds up a finger and states, "Ah, but I know one man who respects and values women. Jesus. That Scripture verse about God creating men and women equal? He takes it literally."

"That's right," Joanna agrees. "Jesus allowed women to follow him as disciples. He regarded Martha and Mary, the sisters of Lazarus, as his good friends. Andrew told me that once when they visited that family in Bethany, Jesus let Mary sit as his feet and be instructed. No other Jewish teacher would treat a woman like a disciple that way. Even when Martha asked Jesus to send Mary to help with the food preparation, Jesus affirmed that Mary was at the right place."

I recall another example of Jesus' esteem for women. "Peter once recounted a beautiful interaction Jesus had with a woman. A Pharisee named Simon invited Jesus to dine at his house. While they reclined on the floor eating, a sinful woman entered the house through the open door. Her hair was unbound, and she carried an alabaster jar. She stood crying behind Jesus so that her tears fell on his feet. She knelt and dried his feet with her long hair. Then she kissed his feet and lavishly poured precious ointment on them. Its fragrance filled the room and wafted out to the street."

"An alabaster jar of expensive ointment? The lady must have carried on a thriving business," Mother comments wryly.

Looking baffled, Dorcas says, "No respectable woman goes out without a veil or with her long hair unbound. Jesus had to know she was a sinner. Wasn't he horrified and embarrassed? He should have scolded the party crasher and sent her away. In the first place, a Jewish man doesn't let a women touch him in public, let alone a sinner. How could Jesus be so bold as to break these taboos, and right in front of a Pharisee too?"

I explain, "That's exactly what the Pharisee wondered. He was aghast. But Jesus praised the woman for her great love and forgave her sins. He defended her. Here's my favorite part of the story. Simon had snubbed Jesus by failing to perform the honors due a guest. Jesus enumerated these missing courtesies and pointed out that the woman provided all of them!"

"Hah! The woman showed up the Pharisee!" Deborah says with glee.

Joanna eagerly adds to the discussion. "And think of the day Jesus rose from the dead. Any ordinary man would have visited the apostles straightaway. But who did Jesus choose to appear to first?"

In unison we all shout, "Women!" and dissolve into laughter.

After chatting for an hour or so longer, everyone helps clear the dinnerware and the leftovers. I make sure that Deborah takes home enough food for several meals. All agree that they had a lovely time and wish to continue our meetings. Because Mother and I host our Sunday prayer services, the women prefer to meet monthly rather than every other week. I protest, "Honestly, the more I have to do to take my mind off missing Peter, the better." But the others do not want to impose on us. They insist on monthly meetings. I give in. You can't always have your own way in this life.

Several weeks later, Mother is spinning, expertly drawing the wool from the distaff, twisting it, and winding it onto the spindle. Meanwhile I am absorbed in sewing a new white head cloth for Mark. The cloth will protect him somewhat from the sun's hot rays. Suddenly a booming "Shalom" bounces off the walls of our home, startling us. Aaron stands in our doorway, smiling from ear to ear. Mother and I spring to our feet and run to my brother. Each morning when you wake up, you never know what surprises the day will hold. It's said that fortunetellers can tell the future. I prefer not knowing.

Chuckling, first Aaron cheek kisses Mother and gently enfolds her. "It's about time you visited," she scolds. Her eyes, though, are swimming with unshed tears of joy.

Next I'm wrapped in Aaron's arms, my chin resting on his soft, purple garments. These clothes, Aaron's carefully trimmed beard, oiled hair, and the gems decorating his fingers all shout, "I am wealthy." I pull away and study his face, so familiar yet strange. His eyes are now heavy-lidded and his eyebrows are bushier than I remember. A jagged white scar streaks across one deeply tanned cheek like a miniature lightning bolt. I run my finger down it, and Aaron says, "A souvenir from a night bandits raided our camp. I was one of the lucky ones."

"That must be because Mother prays so hard for you."

"Well, come in and make yourself at home," Mother says, gesturing toward a mat.

Aaron removes his sandals, which are much sturdier than ours. He places his turban on a ledge and sits down cross-legged.

"Would you like some wine and cheese?" Mother asks.

"No, Mother. I ate not so long ago."

"How about some sweet carob pods to munch on?" Mother persists, ever solicitous for her children.

"All right."

"I'll get them," I offer. I locate the long, leathery, brown pods and set a few in a bowl.

"So much has happened since you were here last. You'll have to meet Leah's family and the twins' husbands," Mother is saying.

Handing Aaron the bowl of carobs, I add, "Mark will be so excited to see you. He's helping Tobiah repair his roof today. You'll hardly recognize your nephew. He has shot up like a reed."

"I have a lot to catch up on. I heard that Simon is called Peter now and that he is the head of the followers of Jesus in Jerusalem. Do you see him often?" Aaron asks me.

"Not as much as I'd like to. He was here for the twins' weddings a few months ago," I reply. "I look forward to the day when I'm free to join him."

A look of pity flickers across Aaron's face. I don't have to explain how hard it is to be without Peter.

I can't resist ribbing my brother. "You know, Aaron, my long-distance marriage is all your fault. If you hadn't come and told us about John the Baptist, Peter would probably still be here fishing for tilapia instead of away fishing for people."

"Sorry, Miriam. But I'm sure you are proud of your husband."

Just then Mark walks in the door, carrying a plate piled high with some kind of goodies. For a moment he's frozen in his tracks and speechless. Then he exclaims, "Uncle Aaron! How good to see you!"

Mark lopes over to us, sets the plate on the mat, and explains, "Esther gave me these date bars. She said they were my payment." Mark bends to hug Aaron and then sits with us.

Mother turns to Aaron and says, "Now tell us. What exotic countries have you visited selling your spices?"

"My most memorable trip was to the wealthy country of Ethiopia. I brought my spices and incense to the queen's palace there. The head of her treasury was delighted with these specialties from the East and purchased a large quantity. He is a tall, lean, dark-skinned man, very astute and more outgoing than I expected a treasurer to be. We quickly became friends. He told me that he is a Christian."

"A Christian? In Africa? How did that come about?" I ask.

"The man already was a believer in the one God. A while ago he was returning from worshiping in Jerusalem. He was reading a passage from the prophet Isaiah out loud. It just so happened that a deacon named Philip came along and asked if he understood the passage. The Ethiopian was perplexed by the reference to a suffering servant. Consequently, he invited Philip to join him in his chariot. There Philip explained that the puzzling passage referred to Jesus. That very day the Ethiopian was baptized. Now there is a thriving community of Christians in Ethiopia. I prolonged my stay there, and they introduced me to the fantastic story of Jesus, the true Messiah. Eventually I was baptized too."

"Praise God!" Mother exclaims, lifting her hands.

Aaron goes on. "I was told that Jesus spent a great deal of time here in Capernaum. Of course, I came home primarily to see you. But I'm also here because I want to visit the sites where Jesus taught and performed his astounding deeds. I'd like to speak to eyewitnesses."

"Well, you're sitting in one site right now," Mother says with a laugh. "Jesus lived with us when he ministered in town."

"You don't say!" Aaron's eyes widen in astonishment.

I suggest, "Tomorrow when you're rested from your journey, we can go to the place of seven springs. Several significant things occurred there, especially ones that involved Peter."

"I'd like that," Aaron says. "It'll be good to visit my old stomping ground. As young boys, James, John, and I used to hike there some days and watch their father and the other fishermen."

"Nowadays you'd be watching Mark. He is following in his father's footsteps." I give my son a quick hug.

"The fish we'll be eating tonight are from the catch I hauled in while I was with Zebedee last night," Mark boasts. "While the others manned the large trawler nets, I threw out a cast net. We caught a lot of fish, but not as many as when Jesus helped my father fish."

"Oh, Aaron, there's so much to tell you about Jesus," I say. "I was in Jerusalem when Jesus offered himself at his final supper with the apostles. I saw when he was killed, and I was there when he rose from the dead."

"Really?" Aaron says, looking duly impressed. "Did you actually see our risen Lord?"

"No, but Peter did. And Jesus appeared once to five hundred people here in Galilee. However, we three weren't privileged to be in the crowd."

"Salome was though," Mother says. "She and Zebedee were visiting relatives in a town near where Jesus appeared."

"Yes, I grit my teeth whenever she mentions it, which she does often," I admit. "I can't stand her gloating over it."

"I suppose we didn't see Jesus because we didn't have to," Mother says, patting my hand.

"Aaron, while Mother and I prepare supper, why don't you visit Zebedee and Salome? They will be tickled to see you again. They miss James and John. It will do them good to reminisce about the days their sons were young and at home."

"Fine. Maybe Salome will tell me about seeing Jesus in Galilee."

"She will. Trust me," Mother says, rolling her eyes.

Aaron, takes one more date bar, puts on his sandals, and walks out the door.

The following morning, after a light breakfast, the four of us head west for the place of the seven springs. There is no town there, but it is a prime fishing spot.

Providentially, the day for our excursion is warm, not hot— perfect for a hike and a picnic. Mark carries our provisions and leads the way. For Mother's sake, we walk leisurely. Aaron is quick to help her over ruts and stony spots in the path.

The olive trees are in blossom, their feathery white flowers lending a pleasant fragrance to the air. In several months men will be shaking the branches and whacking them with sticks to knock the fruit down for our oil lamps and our meals. After walking about a half mile, we reach a cove. On three sides a hill sloping down to the water forms a natural theater.

"We used to play a game here," Aaron recalls. "One of us would stand on the shore and speak in a normal voice. The other two would walk up the hill and see how far they had to go before they could no longer hear the words. Sometimes they'd be almost to the top of the hill, unless the wind was blowing. The acoustics here are amazing."

We pause at the cove and drink in the beauty of the tranquil scene. A few fishermen are in the shallow water washing their nets from the night's catch. The sea is sparkling in the early morning sun. Its waves are gently lapping the shore. Mother settles herself on a stony ledge.

I say, "Aaron, this is where Jesus spoke to people from Peter's boat one day. Your brother-in-law and James and John were washing their nets here on the shore, getting rid of the debris the nets had picked up along with the fish. Jesus started teaching. Before long, hordes of people congregated to listen to him. They were almost crushing him, so he climbed into Peter's boat and had him push off a little distance from the shore. As the boat bobbed in the water, Jesus sat and preached. Because his voice traveled over water, it was magnified."

Mother interjects, "People now call this the Cove of the Sower because it was here that Jesus first told the parable about the sower. That's the one about the seed that falls on different kinds of soil. All four kinds of soils Jesus referred to are found in this cove."

Nodding, Aaron states, "Yes, yes. I'm familiar with that story. Jesus used it to teach how God's word falls on different kinds of hearts."

I continue, "Well, when Jesus was finished teaching, he ordered Peter to go out to the deep water and fish. He didn't say, 'I see a shoal of fish out there.' He just said, 'Go.' Peter, being Peter, frankly told Jesus that they had fished all night without catching one fish. Common sense told Peter that it was ridiculous to obey a landlubber like Jesus. But, fortunately, faith compelled him to do what Jesus said. As a result, he caught heaps of fish. In fact, as Peter and Jesus were hauling them in, the nets were tearing. Peter had to call to James and John to come to their rescue. In the end, both boats were to the point of sinking."

"Imagine that!" Aaron says. "Peter must have been flabbergasted. I can just see the look on his face."

"Peter was so awed by the miraculous catch that he sank to his knees before Jesus, as though felled by an arrow. He called himself a sinner unworthy of being in Jesus' presence. But Jesus raised him up and told the three fishermen that they would be catching people."

Mark chimes in, "Father tells that story over and over. He says that the terrific catch was a good joke Jesus played on him."

I shade my eyes and gesture toward Mount Eremos, which is wreathed in fushia bougainvillea and patches of pink cyclamen. "That is where Jesus gave us the Beatitudes. I was here that day with my friends," I inform Aaron.

"Ah, the Beatitudes, the guidelines for becoming blessed and happy," Aaron says. I'm pleased to see that he knows about those teachings of Jesus.

Mother gets up off the rock with a grunt and says, "Well, let's forge ahead before the day becomes too hot."

As we stroll on, following the seashore that skirts the hill, the grass becomes even lusher. We pass Abraham's balm bushes. Their hand-shaped leaves are reminiscent of the raised hand of the angel who stopped Abraham from sacrificing his son. Then among some rocks we spot three brown coneys. The rabbit-like animals with short ears are lounging in the warm sun and making chirping sounds.

Mark says, "Remember, Mother, when I wanted Father to catch one of those for a pet?"

"Yes, thankfully he was not about to scramble over the rocks after one. He asked if you would settle for a fish instead!"

We come to the place of seven springs, which is a natural harbor. The shore is crammed with boats pulled up on the beach. Green algae float eerily in the sea. The warm spring water that feeds into the sea here encourages its growth. The algae attracts the fish that attract the fishermen. Two breakwaters stretch across the blue water like protective arms. This shore is where Jesus first called Peter and the others to follow him. If I could write, I would create a memorial and chisel in rock the words "Here is where Peter's life changed—and his wife's."

If we climbed Mount Eremos, we would be treated to a magnificent view of the Sea of Galilee. But the trek would be too taxing for Mother. Even here on the shore the sweeping vista is breathtaking. Directly across the glistening sea stands the mountainous Golan Heights. In the hills surrounding the sea, villages are set. To the west extends the fertile Plain of Gennesareth, a name that aptly means garden of riches. And the majestic steep cliff of Mt. Arbel near the town of Magdala looms above the western shore.

A flock of fat-tailed sheep grazes by a stream near us. Their shepherd in his knee-length tunic leans against one of the many date palms, playing a dual-pipe flute. His haunting minor melody pierces the air. The scene is idyllic. I think Eden with its four-branched river must have looked like this.

"What a lovely, serene picture," Aaron says, echoing my thoughts. "It feeds my soul."

"Speaking of eating, this is the place where Jesus multiplied the bread and fish to feed thousands. You've heard about that, Aaron, haven't you?" I ask as I carefully step over two snails crossing the path.

"Of course," Aaron replies. "It's one of the stories told most often when we celebrate the breaking of the bread."

Mark comments, "This is also where the risen Lord cooked breakfast for my father and his friends after he helped them catch a whole boatload of fish."

"And here is where Jesus gave Peter the triple command to feed his flock," I add.

"And that is what Peter has been doing ever since—feeding the flock and adding to its number," Aaron says. "Your fisherman has become quite an accomplished shepherd."

"Well, I'm ready for a snack. Let's go sit in the shade," Mother suggests. All the talk about eating, as well as the fresh air and hike, must have made her hungry.

We move to where a carob tree grows and sit under its spreading canopy. I say, "I like how Jesus compared himself to a good shepherd. That image is right for him in so many ways. Jesus is with us, guiding us on right paths. He feeds us at the breaking of the bread. And he laid down his life to save us from evil."

"And if we stray from God's laws like lost sheep, Jesus does his utmost to bring us back to safety," Aaron says.

"That all may be true," Mother responds. "But I don't particularly like being compared to a dirty, smelly sheep."

"Mother, why don't you think of being a cuddly lamb instead?" Aaron teases.

Mother shoots him a withering look, while Mark and I laugh.

Munching on some pistachios from the basket, Aaron says, "As I recall, that spring cascading into the sea as a waterfall here is known as Job's spring. Supposedly Job used its water to treat his sores. And the cave in the rocks above that spring is Job's cave. It's thought that he lived there for a while."

After we've eaten, Aaron stretches out on his back on the ground and links his hands under his head. "What a far cry this is from the stress and busyness of my daily life. This is heavenly."

I remark, "The world is so exquisitely beautiful sometimes. Just imagine what heaven must be like."

For a good hour we bask in the sun like the conies we saw in the rocks. We fill in for one another the missing pieces of our lives during the years we've been apart. We get to know one another again. Then, our hearts sated with peace and the quiet joy of being together again, we pack up and return home.

A week later, Aaron departs, promising not to stay away so long again. After waving him off, we come back into the house to resume our normal life. Mother notices a brown, woolen bag with a drawstring propped up in a corner. She picks it up, pulls it open, and gasps, her hand flying to her mouth. I take the bag from her and peer inside. There are enough silver drachmas to feed us for many months.

Chapter 27

~~~~~~

It's very late at night, and I'm so tired that I could sleep standing up like horses do. Mother and I worked together to deliver Rebekah's baby. I was hoping for a boy, a companion for Aunt Leah's infant son, but it was not to be. After an unusually long labor, a little girl came slithering into the world, screaming at the top of her lungs and flailing her arms, as though in protest at being evicted from the comfort of her mother's womb.

I am touched that Rebekah and her husband, David, chose to name their baby Miriam after me as well as after David's deceased grandmother. I look forward to spending a lot of time with my namesake. David is a hardworking farmer. Since families help bring in the harvest, soon Rebekah will be in the fields reaping wheat. I don't exactly care for the idea of my daughter swinging a sharp sickle for hours under the hot sun. But that is the lot of a farmer's wife. The hard manual labor doesn't really matter to Rebekah because she loves David and he is good to her. Now that my household chores are diminished, on occasion I might lend a hand in the fields. For certain I'll gladly volunteer to care for tiny Miriam while Rebekah works.

During the delivery David was outside pacing and praying. Our mission accomplished, I open the door and softly call, "David, come meet your daughter." The young man hurries in, tripping over his own feet. At the sight of his wife and child, he is so overcome with emotion that he is speechless for quite some time.

Mother and I begin to take our leave. I can't resist casting one last look at the sleeping little girl nestled against her mother's side. I also glance at my daughter. Rebekah's face, framed by tendrils of damp hair, is a vision of peace and joy. It's hard to believe that not long ago while I was urging her to push, she was screaming, "I can't do this. I can't do this!"

David says that he will escort us two women home, but we politely refuse his offer. No one is on the street at this hour, and we live close by. So Mother and I return home in the dark, our path illumined only by the small oil lamp that I carry with care. The moon and stars are hiding tonight under a cover of clouds.

Mother stumbles slightly on the cobblestones, and I tighten my grasp on her arm. Although she sometimes complains of pain in her knees and hips and has trouble walking, she is quite healthy for a great grandmother. I thank God for that. Sometimes I wonder what I will be like when I am as old as Mother is. By then surely I'll be with Peter!

I break our companionable silence and lament, "If only Peter were here to see his grandchild."

"If only Jacob were here to see his great grandchild," Mother adds wistfully.

Mother has mellowed in her old age. We have become good friends. One common bond is that we both miss our husbands.

We turn the corner and step onto our street. Usually as we near our house, the beautiful Sea of Galilee is in sight. Now it is invisible, cloaked in darkness. Still, I know it is there. Points of light from the torches of a few fishermen out at sea look suspended in the air like fallen stars arrested in their course.

It occurs to me that tonight the Sea of Galilee is a symbol of God. Our sea's mighty waves can break rocks during storms, and its fish are food that keeps us alive. Likewise our God is all-powerful, and he is our source of life. Just as I am not able to discern the sea tonight, my eyes can't behold God. But God is there, as surely as Mother is next to me. As the psalm says, God is like a constant shepherd, leading me to good things and walking with me in bad times.

I say, "Mother, the sea tonight is like God, isn't it? We can't see God but we know he is there."

"Miriam, you and I have seen God, she says emphatically. "He lived in our house with us. Remember? Every time we looked at Jesus, we saw the face of God. Isn't that strange? God told Moses that no one can see his face and live. Yet day after day we saw Jesus, and here we are, still breathing."

"You're right, Mother. We now know firsthand what God is like."

"Yes: kind, concerned about the poor and unloved people, compassionate to sick people like me, and merciful to bunglers like your husband."

"And patient with slow learners like me."

"Best of all, we now realize the depths of God's love for us. He could have annihilated our race and begun another one. Instead, he did the unthinkable and died to save us."

"Mother, I still have nightmares about the last time I saw Jesus. Then he was a bloodied corpse hanging on a cross. I wish I could have seen him alive again like some disciples did. Peter told me that before the risen Jesus appeared to other apostles, he came to him privately."

"Really? What did Jesus say to him?"

"That I don't know. I think it was very personal, something meant to be kept just between Jesus and Peter."

"Well, according to Jesus, we will all see him again someday when he returns to earth."

"When do you think that will be? Next month? Next year? I hope Jesus doesn't come back before the new babies in our family have a chance to grow up and experience all that life has to offer."

When we arrive at our house, we rap gently on the door. There's no response. We knock again, harder. This time we hear the wooden bar scraping. The door opens a crack and reveals Mark with rumpled hair, peering at us through half-closed eyes. He must have fallen asleep while waiting for our return. We report to Mark that he is the uncle of a little girl named Miriam. My tall, lanky son cracks a smile and says, "Congratulations to all of us." Then we go straight to bed.

At the well the next morning, after I happily shared the news of Miriam's birth with the other women, Sarah suggested going for a walk after breakfast. Because the weather today is pleasant, breezy and not too hot, I agreed.

So now, a few hours later, Sarah and I are leisurely walking to the shore of the Sea of Galilee. There are only a few boats out. The fishermen have worked during the night, and most of them are home sleeping. Several men are mending nets in their docked boats or on the beach. Sarah and I walk to a deserted area of the shore where a small group of boys is noisily tossing a rather large, leather ball back and forth. We pick our way over the large and small stones carpeting the beach.

"We haven't heard from Peter. Have you heard anything from Matthew?" I inquire.

"Odd you should ask. I was going to tell you this morning, but your news about your granddaughter distracted me. Yesterday a merchant passing through town brought us greetings from Matthew and Abigail. Eli stopped work and invited the man in for a little refreshment. The merchant told us that Matthew was busy spreading the word about Jesus among other Jewish people. Remember how on the day Jesus returned to heaven, he told the apostles to preach and baptize people of all nations? My brother and your husband have taken this command to heart. Now Matthew is talking about going to Ethiopia of all places!"

"Ethiopia? I wonder how Abigail feels about that, "I say.

"No too pleased, I imagine," Sarah says. "She's already sacrificed her home and her family here to be with Matthew in Jerusalem. She gave birth twice there without the help of her mother and aunts. Moving to a foreign country with two young children in tow won't be easy."

"Yes, but she's fortunate that she is with her husband. I'm jealous."

"Be patient, Miriam. The day will come when you will be with Peter. Oh, how I will miss you!" Sarah says and gives me a little hug.

"We'll just have to enjoy our time together while it lasts. Wait a minute." Balancing with the help of Sarah's arm, I untie my sandal, take it off, and shake out a white pebble.

As I wiggle my foot back into my sandal, Sarah says, "This is interesting. The merchant who came yesterday showed us cups and vases made of material that you can see through. He said that it's mainly melted sand and has been used to make perfume bottles for years. He handed me a small cup. Just as I was holding it up to the light streaming through our window, a bee flew in and startled me. The cup fell from my hand and crashed on the cobblestone floor. Eli scowled at me. When I stooped to pick up the pieces, the merchant cried out, 'Stop. The edges are very sharp. You'll cut yourself.'

"I told Joel to bring the broom and sweep the pieces into the corner. I took care of them later. The merchant was kind enough not to charge us for the cup. Good thing. Otherwise I'd never hear the end of it.

"Apparently the Romans are producing more and more of these transparent items. The merchant predicted that in the future, vessels made of this new material will replace most of our clay and metal ones. Personally I don't see how they will become popular when they are so fragile and dangerous."

As I listen to Sarah, I'm mindlessly watching the boys play with the ball. One kicks the ball into the sea, where it floats out farther and farther, riding the waves. The boys stare at it awhile, and then one of them runs into the sea on his scrawny legs. Oh, no! He is going to try to recover the ball. I'm surprised because as a rule we don't swim.

"Sarah, look! There's a boy in the water, and he probably can't swim."

Squinting, she gazes across the water. "That's Simon," she says. "His family moved onto our street two weeks ago."

Soon Simon is up to his neck in the water. Aware of the danger he's in, the other boys wade into the water a little way and start shouting for help.

The ball is still floating, but the boy's head has disappeared. My mother's instinct kicks in. I make a mad dash to the sea. Heedless of my clothes and any onlookers, I stride into the cool waters as fast as I can and, when it's deep enough, dive in.

"God, help me," I pray over and over. Swimming with a few strong strokes in the direction of the ball, I spot Simon submerged a few feet from it. I take a deep breath, dunk my head under the water, and grab the boy under the arms from behind. As though he doesn't know that I'm trying to save him, he fights me off. Somehow I manage to lift him up and flip him on his back. Then with one arm I drag him to shore, desperately trying to keep both of us afloat.

Weighed down by my waterlogged clothes, I stagger onto the shore with my load. I deposit Simon gently on the ground. He lies there inert, like a big beached fish. I drop to my knees beside him and pray that he is alive. In a few seconds, Simon's eyes fly open. He spits up some water, coughs, and sits up. I give a deep, shaky sigh. Simon's friends, who are huddled around us, laugh and clap. "Foolish boy," I scold, shaking Simon by the shoulders. "Your life is more important than a ball."

Simon scrambles to his feet and runs away like a scared rabbit—and without a word to acknowledge what I did for him. Only when I start wringing out my soggy tunic am I aware that several men have gathered. They are staring at me with as much astonishment as though I were a sea monster from the watery depths. The men probably witnessed the rescue and, no doubt, are astonished that a woman swam.

Remarkably, my veil has survived the ordeal and still clings to my head, but it is askew. Instantly Sarah is at my side, adjusting the veil and tucking my sodden tresses back under it. "Miriam, you scared me to death when you jumped into the water. I thought you would drown." Tilting her head and wrinkling her brow, she asks, "How were you ever able to save Simon like that? You certainly didn't learn to swim in the mikvah. I've heard that in times of crisis God sometimes gives people superhuman powers. Your swimming today must have been a miracle!"

Thinking fast, I say, "Well, if my husband can walk on water, I guess I can swim through it." I leave it at that.

The truth is that Peter taught me how to swim long ago. I haven't had much practice, though, since he left. One very hot night shortly after Peter and I were married, we were on the roof, trying to sleep. Finally, exasperated, Peter said, "Sleep is impossible in this stifling heat. Let's go for a walk. Maybe we can catch a breeze by the sea."

We stealthily climbed down the steps, like two youngsters about to play a prank, and let ourselves out of the house. We spoke only in whispers until we came to the sea. There were some fishing boats far in the distance, but no one was around. It was a beautiful, serene night graced with a full moon embellished by a thin, wispy cloud. Hand in hand we walked along the shore for a while. Now and then Peter flung a stone into the sea and we watched it skip across the surface. Suddenly Peter turned to me, cupped his hands around my face, and murmured, "You are so lovely in the moonlight." Then with a devilish gleam in his eye he said, "Let's go swimming."

"Don't be silly, Peter. You know I can't swim," I remonstrated. "You just as well might suggest flying to the moon."

"I'll teach you how to swim. Come on. Trust me. I won't let you drown." Peter wiggled his dark eyebrows and looked at me with pleading eyes. He looked like a little boy begging his mother to let him keep a pet snake.

"All right," I said with a nervous giggle. At that point I was so much in love with my husband that I would cut off my right arm if he asked me to. Yes, I would even do something as intimidating as swimming.

Peter rapidly pulled his tunic up over his head and tossed it on the beach. I kept mine on, just in case someone happened along. Then Peter took me by the hand, and we splashed into the warm water together. That night he taught me to float and to swim. The sensations of being buoyed up by the sea and of propelling myself through it were exhilarating. I managed not to swallow too much seawater.

"You're a fast learner," Peter said, when we sat on the beach afterwards.

"I had a good teacher," I replied.

"Maybe you're part fish, a mermaid in disguise," Peter suggested.

"Well, I'm lucky you caught me then."

Gesturing to the moon hanging low and large in the sky, Peter said, "Some people see a man's face in the moon. Others see a rabbit."

"I always see the man's face. I imagine that he is smiling on all of us."

"Just think. Right now people everywhere—in Jerusalem, in Cairo, and in Rome—all see the same moon looking down on them.

Miriam-bird, if we are ever separated, look at the moon and think of me. I will look at the moon and think of you."

"Peter, why are you saying that? Are you leaving me?"

"Not in a million years, if I can help it," and he leaned over and kissed me a long kiss.

I've always believed that little Leah was conceived that night.

A few years later Peter left me to search for John the Baptist and began to follow Jesus. Whenever I saw the moon I would think of him thinking of me. I still do now that Peter is in Jerusalem—or wherever he is. It seems to me that on the night Peter taught me to swim, he had a premonition that we would be apart.

Of course, I never told anyone what happened on that magic night, not even Sarah. Some things between a married couple are too special and intimate to be shared with others.

On the day after Simon's miraculous rescue, a thin little woman comes to our door, carrying a basket of fruit and nuts under one arm. Her face is drawn and solemn. Dark shadows under her eyes are a sign that she doesn't get much sleep. A baby rides in a sling on her back, and on each side of her a toddler clutches her tunic, which has two neatly sewn patches. The woman is gripping the hand of the boy I recognize as the daring ballplayer.

The frazzled mother speaks quickly, as though she's eager to get the visit over with. "Shalom, I'm Naomi. I believe you saved my boy's life yesterday. My husband came home with the news of Simon's latest caper. Seems you are the town heroine." She releases the boy's hand and gives him a little push toward me. "Simon, what do you say to this woman who risked her life for you?"

With downcast eyes and jabbing the street with the toes of one foot, Simon mutters, "Thank you for pulling me out of the water. We brought you a gift." Then he raises his head and, looking at me with narrowed, resentful eyes, mumbles, "I wasn't going to drown, you know." His mother cuffs him on the side of the head.

"I apologize for my son's behavior. Simon thinks he is invincible," she says, shaking her head. "I don't know what I'm going to do with him. The other day on a dare he shinnied up a tall palm tree. Last week Antonius, the Roman centurion, brought him to our door and reported that Simon was caught trying to ride one of their horses." Tears well up in Naomi's eyes. Simon folds his arms and pouts on hearing the catalog of his misdeeds.

"Take heart, Naomi. I know another Simon who was very much like your Simon as a boy. He got into one scrape after another. You'll be happy to know that he grew up to be a wonderful person. In fact, today he's my husband and an apostle of Jesus."

"Jesus? I've heard of him," Naomi said. "Wasn't he a healer who lived in Capernaum at one time?"

"Yes, he lived with us right here in this house. But he was more than a healer. He is the Messiah."

"Don't you mean *was* the Messiah. Didn't the Romans crucify him?"

"They did. I actually witnessed his horrendous death. But Jesus came back from the dead. He's alive. My husband and his friends have seen him and talked with him."

"I've never heard of anyone surviving crucifixion. This Jesus must be extraordinary."

"He definitely is, Naomi. We believe that he is God come to earth as a man." I notice that Simon has stopped sulking and is listening. But by this time one of the little ones, the younger boy with the smudged cheek and runny nose, is tugging on Naomi and whining, "Mother, let's go home."

"The followers of Jesus meet here each Sunday to pray and talk about him. We recall his marvelous feats and his teachings."

"So God lived in your house? This must be a holy place now."

"Well, actually our whole world is holy because God breathed our air and walked our roads. Naomi, why don't you and your family come to our house this Sunday? You will learn about Jesus and also meet your neighbors."

"I'll see what my husband thinks about your invitation. As for me, I'd love to come."

"I want to come too," Simon says. The story of Jesus seems to intrigue him. Who knows? Our Lord might captivate this little scamp's heart and reform him.

"If you aren't able to attend our meetings, I'd be happy to tell you more about Jesus anytime. Believe me, he can give your life meaning and fill it with hope and peace."

Naomi hands me the basket and says with a slight smile, "I'd like that. Perhaps you will turn out to be not only Simon's savior but mine too."

This morning is my first flute lesson with Susanna, our chief mourner who is near death herself. I approach her house with mixed emotions: excitement with a tinge of apprehension. This must be how Mark felt on the first day he went to Tobiah's house to learn the Law. I'm carrying my precious flute, a key to free me from ennui and uselessness until I'm reunited with Peter. The reed flute is swathed in a soft wool bag. I sewed it last week as carefully as I used to sew clothes for my babies.

Last week when Aunt Leah and I were at the market, I finally went in search of a flute. I picked out a medium-sized one. When the vendor, a corpulent fellow with the sly look of a cat ready to pounce, quoted the price, I was amazed. After all, the flute wasn't encrusted with jewels. It required quite a bit of haggling, but eventually the original cost was reduced by half, which was still more than I planned to pay.

Aunt Leah urged, "Go on. Get it. When you are good at playing it, the flute will pay for itself."

"You mean if I'm good at playing it."

"Of course you will be good. You're my niece!"

"Well, I can always sell the flute to someone later," I rationalized.

So now I'm the proud owner of a flute made of reed. When the stems of these towering plants are dry, they are hollow and as hard as wood. I wonder who conceived the idea of turning reeds into instruments. It was probably some illiterate shepherd with a sharp knife who was bored watching sheep all day long.

I arrive at Susanna's door to find it open and welcoming. Susanna stands right within it, like a child who can hardly wait for her father to come home. Her brown face, wrinkled like a prune, is alight with a smile, and she claps her hands for joy. "Shalom, dear Miriam. I've been expecting you. I'm only too happy to prepare someone to replace me when I can no longer serve the bereaved."

Susanna waves me into her house, a dim room with few appointments. A pot of flowers, stalks of blue iris mixed with white daisies, is its one spot of glory. We seat ourselves on a thin mat on the floor. Unlike Mother, Susanna is limber. She reminds me of a little wren.

Pushing her veil back off her shoulders, Susanna shifts into a serious mode. Looking me in the eye, she says, "Being a professional mourner is a privilege and an honor. I always find it gratifying to be able to do something for people who are coping with the mystery of death." Eyes twinkling, she says, "Let me see if your instrument is worthy of this great mission."

I offer my flute, and Susanna takes it reverently into her hands that are crisscrossed by blue veins. She rubs my flute lovingly, weighs it with her hands, and peers into its holes. "This looks like a fine flute. It ought to serve you well," my teacher decides and returns the flute to me. I'm pleased with her judgment, for it justifies the flute's expense. "Now let's hear how your flute plays," Susanna says, and she lifts her own flute from a shelf on the wall.

For the next hour Susanna shows me how to hold the flute, blow into it from my stomach and not my chest, and how to place my fingers over the holes to coax different sounds out of the instrument. At first I am awkward, and instead of gentle wailings I produce explosions of sounds alternating with screeches. But by the time my session is over, I am rather proud of myself. Susanna agrees to meet me again next week.

I'm eager to practice before I forget what Susanna taught me. So I don't go straight home but amble over to my olive tree. In that isolated spot I will be less likely to offend others' ears. On the way I pass a clump of mushrooms that sprang up in the moist, rather cool weather of the past several days. Their cute little caps decorate the field, but not for long. These mushrooms are the edible kind. I'll be picking them for supper on the way home. Settled on a low branch with my back propped against the tree trunk, I begin to serenade whatever creatures are within hearing distance.

Before long, I decide I've practiced enough. With the flute lying in my lap, I gaze at the Sea of Galilee, and naturally my thoughts turn to Peter, who practically lived on that sea. I wonder if he misses fishing. His gear and boat are not idle. Mark has become a good fisherman in his father's footsteps. Zebedee has taken our son under his wing and hired him part time. Mark's pay supplements our dwindling funds.

The play of the sunshine on the water, the humming of insects, and the warmer weather today are mesmerizing, and I begin to reminisce. I recall when Jesus climbed into Peter's boat to preach and then helped catch a huge number of fish. That was the day Peter acknowledged that Jesus was his Lord. It took me a little longer. The memory of how rude I was to Jesus when he first came to our house is like a sore that never heals. Knowing now that Jesus is the Son of God makes me ashamed of myself.

I glance down and spy a delicate spider's web rippling in the breeze. It adorns the green grass like a piece of superfine needlework.

Father once told me that some spiders ingest their webs every day and recycle the silky thread the next night, producing another exquisite web. Wouldn't it be lovely if we could take the stuff of a day that we didn't like and spin the day all over again? What a lot of time and energy spiders devote to catching a meal. It strikes me that in a way the fishermen mending their nets on the shore to catch our food resemble the spiders, and I laugh to myself.

My thoughts return to Peter. I picture him telling us how Jesus had him walk on the water. Then I mentally relive the night Peter taught me how to swim, relishing one recovered moment after another. A wave of sorrow washes over me. How I miss my man! Sometimes in the market the tenor of a man's voice resembles Peter's. My heart skips a beat, and I look for my husband. But, of course, he isn't there. Often Mark will have a quizzical expression on his face just like his father's, or he'll shrug his shoulders like Peter does, and a fresh grief will strike me like a flash of lightning.

What is Peter doing right now? Preaching? Meeting with the other apostles? Walking to another town? Is my husband tired? Safe? Worried? Happy? Jesus charged Peter with strengthening his brothers, the other apostles. He always was their leader, their spokesman. What is his role asking of him now? It can't be easy to guide a brand new religious movement. If I were with Peter, I could help him bear the burdens of his office.

Then I ponder our relationship. Does Peter think of me as often as I think of him? Will he still love me when my skin is wrinkled and my hair gray? Does he remember what I look like? One morning when Peter was home and I woke up before he did, I studied his face, trying to memorize every facet of it. As I gazed on him in repose, his eyes flickered open and he asked what I was doing. Slightly abashed, I admitted that I was memorizing his face. Leaning on his elbow with his head propped up on his hand, Peter smiled lovingly. He pulled down the neck of his tunic, revealing the forest of black hair on his chest. Pointing to his heart, he said, "I've got your image right in here, permanently. I carry it wherever I go."

O God, bless Peter. Be with him to guide and protect him. Give him the gifts he needs to carry out his ministry. And please, speed up the days until we are together again.

Chapter 28

~~~~~~~~~~~~~~~~~~~~~~~~~~~~~~~~~~~

I have to wait four more years until Mark marries and I'm free to join Peter in Jerusalem. To my delight, Sarah's daughter, Barbara, became Mark's wife, which makes Sarah and me co-mothers-in-law. Peter told Mark that because I will be moving to Jerusalem, he needn't build a house. The young couple could move into ours as long as they let the believers continue to gather in it. As I expected, Peter returned to Jerusalem immediately after the wedding.

Mother is gone now. She contracted a fever again, and this time Jesus wasn't around to cure her. Considering her life of hard work and bearing three children, I'm grateful that we had her with us as long as we did. She wasn't sure when she was born, but I guess she must have been about fifty years old when she died. Sometimes I can still hear her somewhat strident voice inside my head instructing or reproving me!

During the course of these four years, the maniac Herod Antipas was exiled, due to the finagling of his nephew Herod Agrippa, who subsequently was made ruler of his uncle's territory including Galilee. Then after Emperor Caligula was assassinated, the conniving

Agrippa helped Claudius become emperor and was rewarded with Samaria and Judea. That made Agrippa king over all of Israel. But we can't complain. Agrippa's reign has proved to be a welcome respite from the oppression of our other rulers. He not only supports and defends Jewish law but lives by it himself.

More and more Gentiles are being brought into our fold, mainly because of Paul's efforts. In fact, in Antioch a new name for us was coined to distinguish us from the Jewish religion. We are now known as Christians. The word *Christ* is Greek for our Hebrew word *Messiah.* I rather like the name Christian. Whenever I hear or say it, I'm reminded of Jesus.

After weeks of dithering about what to take with me to Jerusalem, I'm ready to go. The gray donkey is loaded down with my extra clothing, jewelry, and keepsakes as well as my favorite cookware and provisions for the journey. I feel sorry for the gentle beast. He looks at me, brays so loudly that I jump, and swishes his tail so that the tassel on the end rubs across my arm. It's as though he is acknowledging my silent sympathy. Under all his burdens, his back is marked with a dark cross, a trait all donkeys share. Was it just a coincidence that Jesus came into Jerusalem riding a donkey the week before he died on a cross?

Uncle Joachim volunteered to go with me to the Holy City as a protection, for which I am grateful. My children with their spouses and my five grandchildren, Aunt Leah, Sarah, and other friends in town come out to the caravan to see us off. Amid embraces, tears, and blessings, I depart from the town where I was born and grew up, maybe never to see it again. Ah, I remind myself, your beloved is anxiously awaiting your arrival.

In five days we are within the gates of Jerusalem, and the caravan breaks up. It is Passover again, so the streets are jammed with people. Peter stays at John Mark's house, which has become a center for the

Jerusalem community. I remember where it is. Before long, Uncle Joachim and I are rapping at the door in the gate. At first no one answers, and I wonder if we are at the wrong house. But then the door swings open, and I see Rhoda's familiar face, but her eyes are red and swollen as if she's been weeping. "Miriam," she says in a raspy voice, "we've been expecting you." I introduce my uncle, and Rhoda directs us to the enclosure where we can tie up the donkey. We will unload it later. I take the bag with my jewelry and return to the door with Uncle Joachim.

Rhoda escorts us into the room where John Mark's mother and other disciples are seated. Casting a quick glance over the group, I don't see Peter. Something is definitely wrong. Everyone's face is pale and drawn. However, they welcome us, and John Mark's mother, Mary, tells Rhoda to bring us something to eat. I'm grateful. In our eagerness to get to our destination, we put off having a respectable meal. We just nibbled on dried fruit.

"Where is Peter?" I ask tentatively. Mary asks in a soft voice, "Are you aware that Herod arrested several Christians a few days ago?" Uncle Joachim and I shake our heads. She presses on, "Do you know that Herod had James killed?" "No!" I exclaim in horror." Dully Mary says, "He was slain with a sword." One of the disciples sitting with the group says mournfully, "I'm afraid his hot temper attracted unwanted attention."

My first thought is that Zebedee, Salome, and John, particularly John, will be grief stricken when they find out. My second thought is that Peter too is killed. I always tend to think the worst. Mary reads my mind and quickly reassures me, "Your husband is still alive as far as we know."

"How could Herod be persecuting us?" Uncle Joachim asks, bewildered. "I thought he was a friend to Jews."

"He is," another disciple says bitterly. "That is why he is against us. We're no longer Jews, remember? We're Christians. To the Jews we are heretics, a breakaway group who follow a blasphemer."

Mary explains, "When Herod saw how pleased the Jews were after he had James killed, he had Peter arrested. Peter is in prison now under heavy guard. I heard four soldiers for each of the four watches of night are assigned to him so he can't escape or be rescued."

John Mark adds, "Herod is planning to bring Peter out to the public after Passover as a spectacle. The fool thinks this will increase his popularity."

Rashly I cry, "I must go to Peter!"

"Absolutely not," Joachim says sharply. "Your life is in danger too, especially as Peter's wife. Besides the guards would block you from reaching Peter."

"But you can join us in prayer, both of you," John Mark suggests. "We haven't stopped praying since we heard of Peter's arrest."

In a low voice his mother says to me, "My son is very upset. He and Peter have become very close. Peter confides in him. I think Peter has told John Mark just about everything that occurred between him and Jesus. I encourage my son to write things down so nothing is forgotten."

"Where is Mary, the mother of Jesus?" I ask, hoping that she is near so that I can see her again. Her presence would be a comfort to me. But John Mark's mother replies, "John took her to a little house in a rural area of Ephesus. She will be safe there."

Rhoda brings us a tray of bread and assorted cheeses and fruit, but my stomach is churning now. I feel I can scarcely breathe, much less eat. When I decline Rhoda's offering, I think she and Mary understand. I'm glad to see that Uncle Joachim helps himself to some of the food. Some people eat more under stress.

That night people take turns praying while the others sleep. Of course, what with sobbing and asking God to save Peter, I can't sleep a wink. Close to morning I do doze off out of sheer exhaustion, only to be assailed by terrifying dreams of darkness and blood. Most of the following day when we are not eating, we are praying aloud together for Peter. I envision him beaten, whipped, starved, and languishing in prison. Having a vivid imagination is not always a blessing.

Night falls again with no news, good or bad. Mary, her eyes soft with pity, serves me wine with spices to calm me and help me sleep. I curl up at my place on the floor and fall into a deep sleep. The sound of loud knocking jars me awake.

Shortly I hear Rhoda yelling jubilantly, "Peter is here. Peter is here. He's at the gate." I sit up and see the shadowy figures of people hurrying to the door. "You're crazy," someone says gruffly. "It's Peter's angel," another one says. "If it's Peter, where is he?" Mary asks calmly.

"Oh," Rhoda says. Her eyes open wide, and she claps her hand over her mouth. "I was so happy to see him that I ran to tell you and left him there."

All the while the knocking persists. We all pour out of the house and dash to the gate. My heart is in my throat. John Mark opens the door and there is Peter, looking frustrated, his arms akimbo. I call out, "Peter," and, heedlessly pushing the others aside, I run to him and leap into his arms, tears streaming down my face, happy tears now. How quickly my melancholy has changed to euphoria. Peter hugs me tightly, rocking me from side to side, and says, "Miriam-bird. I'm fine. I'm fine." Everyone is overjoyed and walks Peter into the house, hugging him and clapping him on the back. He never lets go of my hand.

In the house Peter is peppered with questions:

"Did Herod have a change of heart and decide to let you go?"

"What did they do to you?"

"How did you get here?"

Peter holds up his hand, and the group falls silent. Then he gives an account of his release. "There I was, sound asleep in prison, bound not with one but with two chains around my wrists and a soldier on either side of me. Guards were also at the door."

"How could you sleep Peter? Weren't you petrified?" I ask.

"I knew that either our Lord would save me somehow, or else I would be killed and be with him again. It was a win-win situation. Anyhow, all of a sudden I was awakened by someone tapping my side. A bright light lit up the cell as if the sun got in, and an angel was there saying, 'Get up quickly.' The heavy chains simply fell off. The angel instructed me to put on my belt, sandals, and cloak, and follow him. Groggy from sleep, I did as he said. At first I thought I was dreaming or having a vision. I followed the angel past a first guard and then a second guard without being detected. It was as though we were invisible or the guards were blind. When we came to a locked gate, it swung open all by itself, and we went outside into the moonlit night and walked along a lane. Then the angel disappeared, and I realized with astonishment that God had rescued me. I came straight here."

"And then Rhoda wouldn't let you in!" a disciple teases. Everyone laughs giddily while Rhoda turns as red as an anemone. Another disciple quips, "You walk through prison gates, but you can't walk through Rhoda's gate!"

Peter somberly directs, "Let James and the other believers know what happened." James, an apostle and a relative of Jesus, is the leader of the church in Jerusalem. A man of integrity, he has earned the nickname James the Just.

Rhoda appears with a tray of food and offers it to Peter. "Wonderful! I'm famished," he says, helping himself to a cluster of plump, purple grapes. I'm glad to see that his harrowing experience hasn't hurt his appetite.

When Peter has polished off his midnight meal, he says gravely, "When Herod discovers I'm missing, he will start looking for me with a vengeance. I must go into hiding." Turning to me, he says, "Miriam, come with me." I'm relieved that Peter risks taking me with him. I'd rather be his companion in danger than his gospel-widow safe, but worried sick. I gather up some clothes and other essential items that I unpacked the previous day. The rest I will leave here for Mary. What she doesn't want can be distributed to the poor.

At the door as we are departing, Peter cheek kisses Joachim and says heartily, "God bless you for accompanying my wife. You better return quickly to Capernaum. Give everyone there my love. Assure them that Miriam and I are fine, but ask them to keep us in their prayers."

After hugging Joachim and Mary farewell, I disappear with my husband into the night and far away. We are fleeing from Herod Agrippa just as the infant Jesus and his parents fled from Herod Antipas.

Later we learn that when Herod found that his prize prisoner was missing, he took out his anger on the prison guards and had them executed. This Herod turned out to be as ruthless as his Uncle Herod had been. Not long afterwards, Herod Agrippa, who sought to kill my husband and who murdered my friend James, is dead himself. To be honest, I am glad to hear that Herod died from a horrible, painful disease. I'm afraid that isn't very Christian of me.

Chapter 29

The spread of the church is phenomenal and in a large part was brought about unexpectedly and in a way that demonstrates how God draws good from evil. For after Stephen's death by stoning, believers fleeing the persecution that followed carried the good news of Jesus beyond Israel to other lands, just like a stone flung into the sea sends out ripples across the face of the water.

Another crisis for the church occurs in 50 A.D., when Peter and I are living in Jerusalem. Paul and Barnabas were doing fantastic work among the Gentiles in Antioch. But then some overly zealous Jewish Christians from Judea traveled there and interfered. They taught that the Gentile Christians were obliged to follow Jewish customs, including circumcision. This caused an uproar and split the Antioch community that had been so carefully and joyfully nurtured by the more open-minded missionaries.

To settle the conflict, Paul and Barnabas travel to Jerusalem to meet with the apostles and other church leaders. Peter invites me to attend the council as an observer. I have a hunch that the council will result in a landmark decision.

At the council meeting, I see Paul for the first time. Because of his reputation as an unflagging, fearless missionary, I imagined him to be a towering figure, a handsome giant. Instead, a rather short, stocky, balding man with thick eyebrows tramps into the council room. Fascinated, I watch him interact with the other men. Despite his unprepossessing appearance, Paul exudes energy and commands your attention. He has a certain charisma.

At the council the Christians who are Pharisees insist that the Gentiles must abide by the law of Moses. A long and heated debate ensues. Just when I think I can bear the arguing no longer, Peter rises and reminds everyone that God made it known through the conversion of Cornelius that Gentiles can become Christians. Peter is a lion of a man now. His hair is all gray and his beard is full. The room is hushed while he speaks. He asks the assembly why they are placing a yoke on the necks of the Gentile Christians. Masterfully Peter concludes by pointing out that we will all be saved, Jew and Gentile alike, through the grace of the Lord Jesus.

Now subdued, everyone quietly listens to Barnabas and Paul take turns telling about the wonders God worked with the Gentiles. In the end, James decides that the Gentiles should only be bound to refrain from sexual immorality. Any God-fearing person would do that. But James also says Gentiles should abstain from food offered to idols and from meat tainted with blood or from strangled animals. I don't see the reason for that. James probably mandated it to pacify the Pharisees. At least the Gentiles won't be forced to undergo circumcision. I deduce from the strained look on Paul's face that he is not totally happy with the decision.

Peter and I visit the Christian churches in several countries. Peter takes care of making all the arrangement. Traveling is difficult. I especially dislike sailing, not because of the monsters that purportedly dwell in the depths of the sea but because the motion of the ship makes me nauseous. How ironic, being that I'm the wife of a fisherman! We always manage to find shelter in inns and in people's houses, but I miss not having my own home. And I keenly miss my children, grandchildren, relatives, and friends back in Capernaum. Everyday in my prayers I ask God to bless them and keep them happy and healthy. I include Nathan, who is no longer a scribe but a disciple in Jerusalem, and my merchant-brother, Aaron, wherever he may be.

In each town we visit, Peter addresses the communities of believers at the breaking of the bread and speaks about the life and teachings of Jesus. In informal groups, usually with the women, I share my recollections of the Messiah with joy. The listeners are in awe that Jesus actually lived at our house. I can scarcely believe it myself, now that I know that Jesus is the Messiah and the Son of God.

Peter and I spend quite some time in Antioch, the glorious city in Syria where many Christians fled after Stephen was martyred. Peter founded the church there years ago, and he enjoys reconnecting with his former converts. We become accustomed to eating with the Gentile Christians in Antioch—that is, until Jewish Christians from Jerusalem arrive for a visit. Stuck in their old ways, like chariot wheels sunk in mud, they are still promoting circumcision for Gentiles. In deference to them, we stop dining with Gentiles. Even Barnabas, Paul's partner who worked so very hard to incorporate Gentiles into our church, caves in to the conservative group. It is a pity because a number of the Gentiles are our good friends, and eating together both celebrates and builds up friendship.

Then one day Paul, the champion of the Gentiles, shows up and confronts Peter in front of the other Jewish Christians. Paul accuses him and us of hypocrisy and goes on at length about our unfairness to the Gentiles. "We believe in Christ Jesus so that we might be justified by faith in Christ and not by the works of the law," he bellows, pounding his fist into his hand. No one can put a word in edgewise.

Mortified, Peter and all of us stare at the floor and shift uneasily from foot to foot. That little former persecutor made us ashamed of our unchristian behavior. Paul's lambasting forced us to open our eyes to see that we were not acting like Jesus.

Afterwards, when Peter and I are alone, while massaging his neck I ask, "How are you?" He gives a long sigh and says humbly, "Paul was just doing what he had to do. I remember that Jesus once taught that if someone in the church was at fault, we are obliged to go to that person and set him straight. I was wrong, and the Holy Spirit sent Paul to let me know." My husband has his flaws, but in my opinion that just makes him more compassionate toward the rest of us. "I love you," I say with feeling.

Peter and I travel to wild, wealthy Corinth, a busy city with two seaports, one on each side of its isthmus. Corinth is known for corruption. For one thing, a "Corinthian girl" is a synonym for prostitute. But Paul had spent eighteen months there, and against all odds had founded a flourishing church. While in Corinth, we stay at the house of Simon and Rachel, Jewish Christians who had migrated there from Jerusalem.

Rachel is one of the most beautiful women I've ever seen. She could easily be the statue of a Roman goddess come to life. Rachel needs no makeup. Her eyes are large and luminous with long lashes. I would say they are like a camel's eyes, but that doesn't sound too flattering! Perfectly formed eyebrows set off Rachel's eyes. And her smooth skin, the color of shelled almonds, is flawless. If her namesake in Scripture was anything like her, I can understand why Jacob was willing to work fourteen years to marry her. Rachel and I quickly become good friends. Some people you immediately feel at ease with as though your hearts are attuned.

On our second day in Corinth, I am rested from our journey and anxious to see more of this famed town. While the men are talking business, Rachel flashes me a gorgeous smile and asks politely,

"Would you like a tour of the city? I'm sure my friend Sarah would come along so we would be safer."

"I was just wishing I could see more of Corinth," I reply. "Coincidentally, my best friend back in Capernaum, my hometown, is named Sarah too. And I also have a daughter Sarah."

We stroll down the street to Sarah's house, which isn't far. She is happy for the opportunity to leave her housework behind and go out to enjoy the beautiful day. Sarah looks like she is a few years older than Rachel. Ordinarily Sarah would be considered attractive with her wide-spaced eyes, high cheekbones, and full, shapely lips. However, standing beside Rachel, Sarah pales in comparison.

The city is eye-hurting bright and spacious in contrast to Jerusalem. Most of Corinth is spread on a plateau over which looms a massive rock crowned by a temple. Gazing up at this unique landmark steeply jutting into the sky, I comment, "My, that's a gigantic hill!"

"Oh, that's our acropolis. It's almost two thousand feet high and serves as a wonderful protection for us," Rachel says proudly.

"It wasn't much help against the Romans though," Sarah recalls. "They completely destroyed the town about two hundred years ago. But Julius Caesar rebuilt it, and now Corinth is a major city in Greece."

As we walk over the vast forum, our sandals slapping on the marble slabs that cover it, I remark, "I can tell that Corinth is a Roman colony. Your city is glutted with Roman statues and basilicas."

Pointing to a large, stately building, Rachel informs me, "That's the temple of Apollo. It was built over the original one, which was constructed about seven hundred years ago. Originally it had thirty-eight limestone columns, but some were removed to use in the forum."

"And there on the very top of the acropolis you see the temple of Aphrodite," Sarah adds. "It appears on some of the coins. There are at least twenty-six places of worship in Corinth."

"It must be difficult to be a Christian here," I say.

"Very difficult," Rachel says tersely, rolling her eyes. "We are surrounded by temptations. When Paul was here, he inspired us and goaded us to be true to the teachings of Jesus. Many Christians now are backsliding."

"You know, Paul even sent us letters. In them he continued to guide and admonish us like a father. I really do miss him," Sarah admits.

"On the other hand, we never dreamed that Peter would come here. We have heard so much about him," Rachel says.

"We're thrilled that he's visiting. You too, of course," Sarah says as an afterthought.

"Yes," Rachel agrees as we climb some marble stairs onto a higher terrace. "What a treat to hear from people who experienced firsthand what Jesus did and said."

"Look," Sarah commands. "This is one of the best views of the Gulf of Corinth."

"Ah, it's splendid," I say. But with a twinge of homesickness, I think to myself that it can't compare to our beautiful Sea of Galilee.

"When Paul was here, he earned his living by making tents. He stayed with Aquila and Priscilla, who ran a tent-making business. When Paul left, they accompanied him to Ephesus. What does your husband do?" Rachel asks.

"Back home Peter was a fisherman and a very successful one at that. We have some savings, but Christians are always ready to supply our needs. For instance, look at the hospitality you and Simon are showing us, Rachel."

We're walking past a row of shops now, and Rachel stops at one stall that sells pottery. Shelves are lined with colorful vases, jugs, and cups of all sizes. Large storage vessels stand on the ground, waiting to be purchased and put to use. Rachel says, "Corinth was known for its pottery until Athens took over the business. Look at these pretty cups." She walks over to the row of cups and eyes each one. I notice that the young vendor is eyeing Rachel!

"I want to give you a cup as a souvenir of Corinth, Miriam. Which one would you like?"

The last thing I need is something else to tote from town to town, but I'm touched by Rachel's generosity and choose a small cup decorated with painted almond blossoms and palm fronds. Carefully holding the cup, I say, "This will remind me of Corinth, but it will also remind me of you."

When Rachel and I return to her house, Peter and Simon are still talking. Peter looks up and asks, "How was your tour?"

"Great," I reply. "It's like being in Rome. Maybe Simon will show you the sights tomorrow."

"By all means," Simon says. "I was planning to do that."

"See the lovely cup Rachel bought for me." I hold out the delicate cup and gently place it in Peter's large hand. "If you behave, I'll let you drink from it sometime," I tease.

Chapter 30

~~~~~~~~~~~~~~~~~~~~~~~~~~~~~~~~

*A*fter many years, Peter and I move to Rome, the seat of the Roman Empire. Here it is difficult for our church to flourish. To say that we aren't popular in that pagan city would be an understatement. The Romans expect everyone to worship their gods in order to bring blessings on the empire. Because we refuse to do so, they view us as unpatriotic rebels. They are also suspicious of our night gatherings and accuse us of cannibalism. This stems from our suppers in which we celebrate with the body and blood of Christ. Also, because we call these suppers "love feasts" and are known to emphasize love, the Romans jump to the conclusion that we are guilty of sexual immorality. Even our referring to one another as brothers and sisters they misinterpret as evidence of incest. Yet, we staunch Christians refuse to be intimidated and do our best to live our faith in Jesus and spread it to others.

One day we learn that Paul is in Rome under house arrest. As soon as possible we go to visit him. After identifying ourselves to the Roman soldier at the door, we enter the little house. Paul is absorbed in writing something on parchment at a small table. When he looks up and sees us, his black eyes light up with amazement and delight. He carefully places his reed pen across the clay inkpot and comes to greet us. Peter and Paul embrace. I'm happy to see that there are no hard feelings between them after the debacle in Antioch. Paul looks tired and has aged significantly. Of course I have too, as my wrinkled hands dotted with brown spots remind me. How privileged I am to be in the presence of these two pillars of the church.

Paul has made missionary journeys throughout the Roman Empire, covering thousands of miles and at great personal cost. Word sometimes filtered through to us about the beatings, whippings, and stonings he suffered for the sake of the Gospel.

We sit on a bench, and Peter gets right to the point. "Paul, how do you come to be in prison in Rome? The last we heard, you were imprisoned in the capital, Caesarea."

"Ha!" Paul says vehemently. "Yes, I was there for two years, thanks to the repeated accusations of the Jewish leaders who loathe me. But because I was born a Roman citizen, I had the right to appeal to the emperor and finally had the sense to do so. I was sent to Rome with other prisoners on a ship."

"I do not enjoy traveling on the sea," I comment.

"You certainly wouldn't have enjoyed our voyage," Paul says darkly. "Our ship was caught in a dreadful storm, and strong winds blew us off course. For two weeks we drifted in the dark, like a frail leaf floating aimlessly on a stream. Then our beleaguered ship went aground on the island of Malta. We stayed there for three months. And then finally made it to Rome."

"Praise God that you are still alive!" Peter says. "What does your imprisonment entail?"

"It's not too bad," Paul says, smiling. "I'm free to meet with people, anyone who comes here. That way I continue to teach about our Lord. And, as you see, I convey the good news in written form too," he says, gesturing to the table where his scroll lies. "Now tell me about Jesus, all that you remember. I've only met him twice. Once, as you know, on the way to Damascus and then again when I was a captive in Jerusalem. There one day I was made to stand before the Jewish council, a horrendous ordeal that ended in mayhem. That night the Lord appeared near me and urged me to keep up my courage. He said, 'Just as you testified for me in Jerusalem, you must bear witness in Rome.' So here I am, just as he said. Now what do you recall about Jesus?"

For the remainder of our visit, we tell Paul stories about Jesus, miracles that we witnessed, and some parables that he told. Paul mostly listens with his eyes closed as though he is trying to picture scenes. Sometimes he rocks back and forth, his chin cupped in his hand, lost in thought or prayer. I'm sure our accounts are fueling Paul's love for our Lord and his zeal to proclaim the kingdom of God. After several hours, when it is growing dark and time to go, Peter and I promise to come back often. And we do.

One evening Peter and I attend a gathering of Christians at the house of Petronella, a holy woman who has been a disciple for years. The meeting begins on a sour note. Linda, a Gentile woman with ravishing good looks, who had recently become a believer, is the topic of conversation. It had come to light that although she was married, this vivacious redhead was involved with a young Roman soldier. When we arrive, people are discussing what to do about Linda, who is not present that night. Some are in favor of excluding her from the church, period. Others more sympathetic propose that Petronella speak to Linda privately and try to dissuade her from her grave sin. Then Peter takes the floor.

"There was a time," he says, "when Jesus was confronted with a similar problem. While he was teaching a crowd in the Temple, scribes and Pharisees dragged before him a woman who was caught in adultery. Before everyone's staring eyes, she stood there limp, red-faced, and miserable. The religious leaders stated that according to the law of Moses she should be stoned. They asked Jesus his opinion."

A Christian who used to be a scribe interrupts Peter. "What the law actually says is that the man and the woman are to be stoned. Where was the man? And the two who are accused are supposed to have a fair trial first."

"Of course," Peter agrees. "It was all a ruse. The religious leaders merely wanted to trap Jesus into contradicting Moses so they could accuse him of flouting the Law. They were using the women as a tool to do their underhanded work."

"How nasty!" a woman blurts out.

"But Jesus outsmarted them. He bent down and with his finger wrote something on the ground. Then with a ghost of a smile, he suggested that the person without sin should throw the first stone at the woman. One by one the accusers silently slunk away. When they were all gone, Jesus, feigning surprise, asked the woman, 'Where are they? Has no one condemned you?' She muttered, 'No one, sir.' Then Jesus said he didn't condemn her either and simply sent her on her way with a warning not to sin again."

This is not the first time I heard about that event. I always wonder what Jesus wrote. I like to think it was the names of the mistresses of the scribes and Pharisees. And what about the poor woman? After her brush with death and encounter with Jesus, did she change her life, or was she sucked into her old ways again, like being trapped in quicksand?

Peter's story sways everyone to adopt the second course of action. Petronella agrees to confront Linda, and we promise to support her with our prayers. With the tense atmosphere dispelled, we celebrate the breaking of the bread and thank the Father for his overwhelming love that sent Jesus to us.

Afterwards, as Peter and I walk home in a comfortable silence, the night around us is soft and warm. Our love is almost palpable. I'm full of peace and quiet joy, the frame of mind that our assemblies usually leave me in. We are almost home when suddenly Peter says, "Look! The sky in the east is a vivid orange. There must be another fire burning."

"I hope it doesn't come in our direction," I remark and begin thinking what items to rescue from our house if the flames do reach us.

For six days the fire rages, its tall flames licking the sky and polluting our air with an acrid smell and falling ashes. We thank God that our house is spared. Everyone assumes that the fire was an accident like most of the other fires. But then, after a grand palace is built over the blocks that were destroyed, the rumor circulates that Emperor Nero himself deliberately caused the catastrophe.

Not long after that, Benjamin, our neighbor, comes to our house, clearly distraught, his eyes wide with terror. Without even greeting us, he says in a shrill voice, "Something terrible is happening."

"What's wrong?" Peter asks with concern.

"It's Nero," Benjamin says. "Because people are blaming him for the fire, he's redirecting the blame to Christians. He's making us scapegoats and threatens to rid Rome of us. Paul has already been beheaded."

"No!" I cry, shaking my head in disbelief. Not Paul, our friend who underwent so many sufferings and lived to tell of them. His marvelous ministry is over, cut short to preserve the reputation of a petty, pagan emperor. How revolting! A sob escapes me, and I burst into tears. Peter puts his arm around me, and I burrow my head into his shoulder.

"I've got to warn the others," Benjamin says and disappears out the door.

Patting me on the back and resting his chin on my head, Peter says, "I know. I know. Look at it this way. Paul is now face to face with Jesus, the one he served so valiantly all these years. And his death was quick. Isn't he fortunate?" Those are consoling words, but when I raise my head to look at my husband, his eyes are filled with tears.

Persecution of Christians begins in earnest. One after another our friends disappear—Petronella, Sylvester, Cecilia and her husband, Ezra, a number of people whom Peter baptized. We hear ghastly news about their martyrdom. They are tortured and killed in a number of cruel ways. Some of our brothers and sisters in Christ are dressed in the hides of wild animals and thrown to dogs. Others are put in waxed shirts and set fire to as human torches that light the city at night. And some Christians are crucified. In Nero's Circus on Vatican Hill, our sufferings and deaths provide amusement for the public. I cannot comprehend how human beings can do this to other human beings. Evil is loose in Rome like a roaring lion.

Once Peter realizes the extreme danger we are in, he says, "We better leave Rome while we can." We hurriedly pack our clothes and some food and start on our way early in the morning, hoping no one will apprehend us. As we walk in haste down Appian Way, a large Roman road, Peter suddenly halts. I hear him say, "Lord, where are you going?" Then he turns to me, his face white as a ghost's, and says, "I must go back."

"What happened, Peter?"

"Didn't you see Jesus?"

"No. I just saw you stop and heard you say something."

"Our Lord was walking toward us. When I asked where he was going, he said, 'I'm going into the city to be crucified again.' He means that I should return. I've disappointed him before. I'm not going to this time. His church in Rome needs me. I'll see if I can locate someone who can take you to safety."

"No, Peter," I protest, clinging to his arm. "If you're going back, so am I. "

"No, I don't want any harm to befall you. I love you, Miriam, dear, and if you love me, you will do as I wish."

"Peter, these last twenty years that we've been together were like heaven for me. I'm not going to be separated from you ever again."

"Save yourself for the sake of our children and grandchildren then," he cajoles.

"They have their own lives to live, and I have mine. I choose to spend the rest of my life with you, whether it's long or short."

Peter eventually accepts the fact that he will never win this argument. We turn around and slowly retrace our steps back to our house. It isn't long before we are arrested.

Locked in a dank prison, Peter and I sing and pray together with other Christians. We also while away the hours and mentally remove ourselves from the stench and filth of our cell by sharing our memories of Jesus. Many of our fellow prisoners have not personally experienced him and are strengthened and encouraged by our stories. Recalling the life, death, and resurrection of Jesus confirms for Peter and me that no suffering, not even death, can make us regret that we devoted our lives to him.

Facing certain death, I reflect back on my bittersweet life. What a gift it has been. I had a happy childhood and grew up surrounded by beauty in Capernaum. Jonah and Rebekah were good parents, and Aunt Leah and Uncle Joachim were like second parents to me. I was blessed with a precious friend in Sarah. Then there is Peter. Who could ask for a better husband, even though for years he was just part-time as I shared him with Jesus? I praise and thank God for the day the cat and spilled olives brought Peter and me together. I brought four healthy children into the world, who weren't too much trouble. Now they are good spouses and good Christians busy raising their own children. At last count Peter and I have seventeen grandchildren. I only regret that I am not there to share in their lives and enjoy their antics. Some of my grandchildren do not even know me and now never will. That is the price I pay for being a disciple at Peter's side. Instead of helping to bring up my children's children, I'm nurturing the church of Jesus in its infancy.

My life has been specially blessed in that I personally knew the Savior of the world. I witnessed his works and heard his teachings firsthand. No one in the generations to come will be able to say that. And the Messiah whom past generations longed to see actually lived in our home for a time. I've lived longer than both of my parents, and I am ready to leave this world if God so wills it. He has always taken care of me, and I trust that my future is in his loving hands.

Roman soldiers, their armor clanking, approach our cell. Fear instantly floods the room. We are all holding our breath. One of the soldiers unlocks the door and thunders out my name. Everyone looks at me with sympathy and dread. They know their turn is coming. So I am summoned to meet my fate before Peter is. The incongruous thought crosses my mind that although I was a gospel-widow, I will be spared being an actual widow.

Peter and I get awkwardly to our feet, and Peter hugs me fiercely. Then he holds my hands until a squat Roman soldier with bad breath roughly separates us and binds my hands together with rope. The soldier shoves me toward the door, making me stumble. Regaining my balance, I square my shoulders, determined to face my destiny with dignity. As I leave the cell, Peter calls after me in a strained voice, "Miriam-bird, remember the Lord."

All the way to my place of execution in the Circus I visualize the face of Jesus as I knew him in Capernaum. I am shaking like a fig leaf in the wind, but in my heart I know that my death will be just a door. Soon I will be on the other side of that door and behold my Lord Jesus face to face once more. I trust in his promise of eternal life for those who believe. In time, Peter will join us, and we will share an everlasting love. We will never be parted again.

Epilogue

~~~~~~

According to tradition, Peter was martyred on a cross sometime between 64 A.D. and 67 A.D. during the persecution under Emperor Nero. The second-century apocryphal book Acts of Peter gave rise to the belief that because Peter didn't consider himself worthy to die as his Lord had, he asked to be crucified upside-down, and the soldiers complied. He was buried on Vatican Hill a short distance from the Circus of Nero.

Today Peter is acknowledged by most Christians as the primary leader of the early Church. They celebrate June 29 in his honor, a feast day he shares with St. Paul. Catholics regard Peter as the first pope. The Basilica of St. Peter in Rome, originally founded by Emperor Constantine in 324 over St. Peter s grave, is one of the largest churches in the world. In front of it on either side stand colossal statues of Peter and Paul. Statues of eleven other apostles, the Redeemer, and John the Baptist crown the façade of the basilica. St. Peter s Square, the magnificent piazza in front of the basilica, is enclosed by a colonnade that contains two hundred and eight-four columns, eighty-eight pillars, and statues of one hundred and forty saints.

Inside St. Peter's Basilica there is a large, bronze statue of Peter seated, the right hand raised in blessing and the left hand holding the keys of the kingdom. Toes on the right foot are worn away from the touches and kisses of pilgrims down through the centuries. Every June 29, this statue is clothed in the vestments of a pope. Excavations under the main altar of the basilica unearthed ancient bones, which some believe to be those of St. Peter. Near them were the bones of an old woman, possibly his wife. It is thought that in the ninth century the skull of St. Peter was removed and placed with St. Paul's skull above the high altar of the Basilica of St. John Lateran in Rome.

Two letters in the Bible are named for Peter. Scholars debate whether he is the actual author or if an unknown author gave his own writing credibility by attributing the letters to Peter, as was sometimes the custom. Another theory is that a secretary or a disciple recorded Peter's ideas.

Peter is immortalized in other, less grandiose ways. Restaurants in Israel offer St. Peter's fish, supposedly the kind of fish from which Peter extracted the coin for the temple tax. In addition, the expression "for Pete's sake" is a minced oath, a euphemism for profanity, derived from "St. Peter's sake."

Capernaum, as Jesus predicted, is mostly ruins and a tourist site. A thirteenth-century pilgrim named Burchardus noted that "the once famous city of Capernaum is now a sad sight to behold: it consists only of seven wretched fishermen's huts." The Church of the Seven Apostles, a lovely Greek Orthodox church, brightens the stark former fishing village. In Capernaum archaeologists discovered a fourth-century Byzantine synagogue built over the thick, black basalt walls of a first-century synagogue, probably the one where Peter prayed and Jesus taught. They also excavated a block of first-century houses between this synagogue and the Sea of Galilee. One large house in the block contained many lamps, suggesting that it was a place where early Christians worshiped. This house is traditionally thought to be Peter's. In the fifth century A.D., an octagonal church was built over it. Today a large, modern church stands over this older church. Through a window in the floor, visitors can view the first-century house.

In Tabgha, a town about two miles from Capernaum, the Church of the Primacy of Peter was built on the edge of the Sea of Galilee. It commemorates Peter's threefold avowal of love for Jesus and his commission to care for the flock of Jesus. Inside the church is a large stone called "the table of Christ" where it is believed that Jesus served breakfast to the apostles. In the garden outside stands a bronze statue of Peter kneeling at the feet of Jesus and holding onto a staff that Jesus extends.

As for Peter's wife, the proverbial woman behind the throne, she has faded into oblivion. There is no trace of her. We don't even know her name.